A PROMISE
KEPT

MARIANNE DELAFORCE

Published by Marianne Delaforce

A Promise Kept

The Promises Series

Delaforce, Marianne (1964–)

ISBNs: 978-0-6486334-6-4 (ebook)

978-0-6486334-7-1 (paperback)

Cover design by Marianne Delaforce

Cover layout by Ally Mosher

Cover Images Copyright © Marianne Delaforce except image of woman licensed from Shutterstock.

CHAPTER 1

COONABARABRAN

JUNE 1980

Lilly stood at the gate watching her mother and father drive away. Her heart was aching, she wanted to run after them, but she had to stay strong. She knew how hard this was for her mother to leave her here, she was only fifteen and a half, her brother Fred had just turned seventeen, and now they were being left behind on a three thousand acre farm thirty-five kilometres from town. Two teenagers alone for the next five months. Their father had decided he'd had enough of the farming life, and he was returning to

Kempsey to start up an earthmoving business and find a place to live, which meant their mother had to go with him. He would not go alone. When her father decided he wanted to do something, that was it, there were no negotiations. Lilly was in the middle of year ten and would be sitting her exams for her high school certificate in four months, and they did not want to disrupt her schooling. Also the fact that the lease on the farm still had six months to go and they had to stay there until the contract was up. Fred would be sorting out the farm and finish selling the rest of the stock and equipment, while Lilly would go to school on weekdays and when she arrived home would do all the household chores.

As she watched the dust from the car take her mother further away she could not contain herself any longer and burst into tears, how could she possibly do this without her mother there? Who would protect her mother from her fathers' temper and abuse?

"It's alright Lilly, we will be fine, I'll take care of you." Fred wrapped his arms around his little sister trying to comfort her. He hated seeing her upset, she sobbed in his arms, Fred also felt trepidation of the task that was set for them, but he knew he had no choice, they had five months here before being able to return back to the coast and join their parents. He also felt relief that his father would not be there and at least for the next few months they could be free from his tyranny and abuse, but it did worry him that his mother now had to suffer alone with him. "Come on, let's go for a bike ride out the back to our track."

Lilly looked up at her big brother, the tears streaming down her face, she idolised Fred he was always there for her, she wiped the tears from her face with her t-shirt, she would have to be strong, there was no other choice. "Okay, maybe for a little while, I have to feed the chickens and tidy up a bit before I cook dinner."

"Well, let's go then we can go for an hour, and when we get back I'll help you clean up."

It was just what Lilly needed, she straddled the bike, pulled the clutch in, lifted her body off the seat, placing her foot on the kick starter and using her body weight, kicked all the way through, the bike coughed and sputtered to life. It was an old bike, a hand me down from Fred, a four-stroke red Honda CT125 farm bike. Lilly rolled back the throttle, released the clutch and moved forward slowly then with a quick twist of throttle she accelerated, chasing after Fred across the paddock. Weaving along the rough dirt track, it seemed like the air was filled with insects, zooming past her helmet and clouds of dust billowing out from behind her tyres. Lilly loved bike riding and she found it exhilarating. On a bike, she felt free and charged with energy. The feel of the wind rushing past her body, the sound of the bike as the gears shifted, her senses heightened as she rode along. The smells frequently changed from the open dusty paddocks to the cool shady cover of the trees, she felt the temperature drop as they came under the trees and could smell aromas of the bark and loam. They arrived at the dirt track at the back of the farm, Fred had constructed a motocross track in the gully. The trail wove up and down the small hills, they had made a mound so they could jump over it high into the air. Lilly didn't go very fast over this mound, it scared her a little, whereas Fred would go full speed and fly high up into the air, twisting the handlebars to a full lock in mid-air then straightening them before landing and flying with the throttle flat out around the track. Lilly was sure Fred thought he was "Evil Knievel.' They stayed out and rode around on the bikes for an hour before heading back to the house.

The days were all the same, Lilly would get up early each morning and get ready for school, riding her motorbike the eight hundred metres down to the front gate to catch the school bus to town at seven-thirty each morning. On returning home, she would put on her running shoes and go for a two- kilometre run with her kelpie dog Rusty following close behind. She had to keep up her training for her athletic events at school, she would then feed the chickens or 'chooks' as they called them, collect the eggs, help Fred if he needed her and then cook their dinner. On the weekends Lilly would do the washing and clean the house. Fred's day consisted of checking the stock and cleaning up around the farm, preparing the last of the farm equipment for sale. Once a week Fred would pick Lilly up from school, and they would do their weekly shop in town at the local supermarket.

Lilly was really missing her mother. They had been down to Kempsey a few times in the last four months to see them for the weekend. Lilly hated leaving her mother, but she had actually enjoyed not having to put up with her father's constant criticism. Lilly had completed her exams and had also won the sixteen-year girl champion at the athletics carnival; she wished her mother could have been there to see her. Today was her sixteenth birthday. Her mother had called her this morning to wish her happy birthday and to check if she needed anything. Lilly could hear the sadness in her voice and disappointment that she wasn't there to share this day with her youngest child, but she knew she had no choice in the matter. Tonight they were going into town to the local Chinese restaurant for dinner, then to the picture theatre to watch the movie Private Benjamin with their friends Robert and Lisa from the farm ten kilometres down the road. Robert was the same age as Fred and also loved motocross riding, Lisa was a year younger than Lilly. While the boys would go bike riding the girls would sit and look over the latest Dolly magazine, do each other's hair, put makeup on and dance to loud music in the now sizable empty lounge room as the furniture had gone to Kempsey with their parents.

Lilly had won a magnum bottle of champagne in a local raffle, and even though they were too young to drink alcohol, they had decided to have a few glasses each to celebrate. Fred did not drink as he was the sensible one and also the driver for the night. After their meal and more than a few glasses of bubbly each, they headed for the picture theatre. Lilly began to feel unwell, her stomach was churning, she was not sure if she wanted to vomit or curl up in a ball on the ground, she was clammy and perspiring, and the room was spinning. Robert gave her a cup of black coffee trying to help sober her up. Lisa had disappeared twenty minutes ago to go to the toilet and had not returned when her friend Lalicia came up to tell them that Lisa had stumbled outside and had been sick in the gutter just as the police car came around the corner. They had stopped and picked her up and taken her back to the station where she was now waiting for someone to go and get her.

Lilly stood outside the police station trying to muster up the courage to go in to get her friend, this was her fault, she felt so bad and not only that, what would her father do to her when he found out? She walked up the front steps trying to appear as sober as possible, once inside she could see Lisa sitting in the dock with her head and hands over the rail, just at that moment Lisa was sick all over the floor.

"Um hello, I'm Lilly, Lisa's friend. I've come to get her." Lilly's voice was shaking, and her legs felt like jelly and her head was pounding.

The police officer looked up from his papers. "Is that so, so you're her friend?" Lilly nodded. "Well Miss it's not that simple, she is underage and has clearly been drinking so her parents will have to be informed and they will have to come and get her. Have you been drinking as well?"

Lilly lowered her head and nodded, shuffling from one foot to the other, "Yes Sir, it's my sixteenth birthday today, and we had a few glasses of champagne to celebrate. I'm very sorry we have never had alcohol before."

"Well it better be the last time until you turn eighteen young lady! I've phoned her mother, and she is on the way in to collect her. I think you better sit in there with her until she arrives and you can clean up that mess she has just left on the floor." His tone and words were bracing and felt like a slap in her face. The Sergeant stood up and handed Lilly a mop and bucket. "Go on then clean it up."

Lilly cleaned up the vomit from the floor, a mix of bile and half-digested food, the pungent smell wafted up her nose making her half gag, she had almost finished when Lisa spewed out the last of her Chinese dinner, looking up at Lilly the tears spilled from her eyes, and she whimpered. Lilly thought to herself, I am never eating Chinese food again or drinking alcohol. Lisa's mother arrived glancing briefly at her daughter and Lilly sitting in the dock, shaking her head. Lilly could not look at her. She felt so ashamed, this was all her fault, Lisa was only drinking because she wanted to help cheer her up because her mother wasn't there with her. Mrs Walsh spoke to the Sergeant for a few minutes, Lilly could not hear what they were saying, the officer glanced over at her, his cold look softened just for a moment. Lilly dropped her gaze to the floor. She was embarrassed and ashamed, after a few more minutes of discussion, Mrs Walsh thanked the Sergeant, shook his hand and walked over to the two girls.

"Come on you two let's get you home, Fred and Robert are outside waiting for us." She put her arm under her daughters and helped her to stand. Lisa stumbled out to the car as Lilly followed silently, walking with her shoulders hunched and her eyes cast down at the footpath beneath her.

After placing her daughter into the car Mrs Walsh turned to Lilly, "Honey I don't condone drinking and what you have done is wrong and I'm sure you are feeling very sorry for that at the moment. I have asked the officer not to contact your parents, I told him I would deal with it." She pulled Lilly into her chest and gave her a hug. "I know you're missing your mother darling and I know what your father is like, so I think it's best we don't tell them about this, as long as you promise it will never happen again."

Lilly burst into tears, "I'm so sorry Mrs Walsh it was silly of me I know it's wrong I promise I won't do it again, please don't punish Lisa she was only trying to cheer me up. I miss Mum so much, and I'm worried about her."

"I know honey, it's okay, I'm sure you have learnt your lesson. How about you come over tomorrow afternoon for some cake and a cup of tea." She bent and kissed Lilly's head; she felt so sad for this young girl, only just sixteen living so far away from her parents helping to run a property with her brother while attending high school. Mrs Walsh waved as she drove away, Fred took Lilly's arm and led her back to the car, he didn't have to say anything, he knew Lilly was feeling bad enough as it was without him giving her a lecture. Lilly's head had started to throb, and no doubt she would have a massive hangover in the morning like she had seen her father after a big night on the drink.

The next six weeks passed quickly, Lilly sang at the local school assembly and received her school certificate as well as her medal for her athletics. They packed up their belongings, and their father came out to pick up the last of the furniture to take back to Kempsey. Lilly was pleased to be going back to her mother, but she was also sad to be leaving. She had made such good friends in the two years they had spent here and she would miss them, especially her best friend Lalicia. Now it was back to the coast to start another part of her life's adventure.

CHAPTER 2

SOUTH KEMPSEY 1981

Fred and Lilly had been back living with their parents now for six months. They were living on five acres of land that their father had purchased in South Kempsey in a caravan with a shed built off the side, part of the tin shed had a lounge room which also served as a dining room, they ate their meals here at the small table at one end. The floor was concrete with mats thrown on top of the hard floor, the cooking was done inside the caravan or outside on the BBQ. Lilly and Fred had bedrooms partitioned off with curtains in the shed while their parents slept in the caravan.

The bathroom was out in a tin shed with a toilet and shower. Lilly had wanted to stay at school and do her higher school certificate, but her father had refused and told her to get out and get a job and stop bludging off him. So she found a job working at the local supermarket in West Kempsey five days a week, packing shelves and working on the cash registers. Lilly enjoyed being at the cash register and helping the people as they came in, hearing their stories and what they had been up to for the day, she would pack their groceries into the brown paper bags and if needed, someone would help them out to the car with the shopping.

She had made new friends and for the last four months had been dating a young boy named Patrick, he was two years older than Lilly and worked at a local glass and window factory making windows and screens. Patrick had his own car, an EH Holden station wagon, he played guitar, banjo and mandolin, he was a talented musician, and they would sit for hours on the weekend playing and singing. He tried to teach Lilly guitar but she struggled with the neck of the guitar, her fingers were too short to get around it.

Patrick was tall and thin with short dark wavy hair, he was no stunner in the looks department, but he had such a beautiful soul and was gentle and caring, and he adored Lilly, they spent as much time together as possible.

Lilly spent as little time as she could at home, her father was drinking more than usual, and his verbal abuse was getting worse every day. Lilly found it hard to keep her mouth shut at times, but she knew to hold her tongue; otherwise, he would become violent and hit her or lash out at her mother. It was the weekend, and Lilly was helping her mother move the large concrete blocks that had been dropped off at the front of the house around to the back, where the retaining wall would be built. It was heavy hot work, and they had stopped to have a rest and cold drink in the shade.

"Mum, why don't you leave? It breaks my heart to see the way he humiliates you all the time," Lilly begged her mother to leave her father but once again she refused, she did not have the courage to, and she was afraid he would make good on his threat to hunt her down and kill her.

Rose shrugged her shoulders and frowned "Maybe when you and Fred have married and have lives of your own. Then I'll leave." Rose took Lilly's hand in hers. "I made myself a promise to take care of you kids, no matter what." Lilly could see the flicker of sadness in her mother's eyes.

"But Mum, why should it be at your expense? We are all old enough to take care of ourselves, Ruby is settled in Port Macquarie, happily married and has a child, Fred has Victoria and I have Patrick. You don't need to worry about us, we're adults now. We will manage."

Rose was about to answer when Jimmy came through the door. "What are you two lazy bitches doing? I thought I told you I wanted all those concrete blocks moved from the front of the yard around to the back today." His hands were balled in fists, his body stiff and anger blazed in his eyes.

"Sorry Jimmy, it was just so hot we needed a cold drink, we just stopped for a moment to have a break." Rose stood up and started for the door. "Come on Lilly, let's get this done."

"For Christ sakes Dad, you work us like slaves and treat us like slaves too."

"Don't back-chat me girl." His voice was a snarl and had become dangerously threatening.

"Lilly come on, it won't take us long." Rose pleaded with her daughter, she knew this would not end well, Lilly could be as stubborn as her father.

"Yes hurry up Lilly do as you're told, you're bloody useless and lazy and..."

"Yes I know Dad I was supposed to be a boy and I was a mistake. I've heard it all before. I'm not lazy. I do everything you ask, and then some and I'm sick of being treated like shit, you taught me not to take shit from anyone, so I'm not taking your shit anymore. Treat me with respect and Mum too." Lilly stood defiantly in front of her father, she'd had enough of his constant put-downs.

Jimmy strode up to Lilly and shoved her "You ungrateful little bitch, how dare you speak to me like that. You can pack your bags and get out of my house and don't come back." He pushed past her and headed out the door. "You can help her Rose, pack her shit up and drop her anywhere you like as long as she's not here when I get back."

"Oh Lilly, why did you have to do that? You know from experience to just be quiet and let him rant."

"No Mum I'm sick of shutting up, he treats us like shit, and I'm sick of it." Their eyes locked in a shared understanding. Rose sighed, "Ok, well I'll ring Mum and see if you can go stay with her."

Lilly loved living with her Nana and Grandfather, she could catch the bus to work, and Patrick lived only two hundred metres down the road. Her grandparents were so cool. Nana Loretta would watch "Countdown" the music show with her and sing along, sometimes dancing with her in the lounge room. She taught Lilly to crochet and make pickles and cakes. Lilly loved to sit and watch the cricket with her Grandfather, and he showed her some handy tips, how to pinch someone with your big toes and that a cup of tea poured from the pot always tasted better when the milk went in first. For the next few months, she worked hard and saved as much money as she could. Lilly had passed her driving test and wanted a car of her own, so she didn't need to rely on anyone, she wanted to be independent and in charge of her own life. It was only two weeks until Christmas, and the town was busy, which meant she had picked up extra shifts at work. Lilly was just about to finish her shift when she received the news her mother was in the hospital.

The nurse showed her into the room where her mother lay in the bed with wires and patches hooked up to her chest, and the steady beat of the ECG machine monitoring her heart. Lilly stood inside the door looking at her mother sleeping, she looked so pale and vulnerable, she felt a lump in her throat, and her stomach felt like it was in knots, the tears were welling in her eyes. She loved her mother so much she could not bear the thought of losing her. Rose opened her eyes and smiled. Lilly went to her mother and placed her head on her chest and cried.

"Oh Mum I love you so much, are you okay? What happened? Did Dad do this to you?"

"No honey, it's my heart. It was just beating too fast, the doctors had to slow it down. I'm going to be fine. I just need to change a few things in my lifestyle, that's all. Don't worry, I will be okay." Rose tried to comfort Lilly.

"I'm sorry Mum I'll make peace with Dad, and I'll move home, so I'm there for you, I couldn't bear it if anything happened to you." Lilly hugged her mother tightly and promised herself she would watch her tongue with her father, she needed to be there to make her mother's life easier.

Her father had accepted her apology and allowed her to move back to the caravan, the new house her parents had been building for over a year was almost finished, and they would be moving in soon. They celebrated the new year quietly, her father was in a good mood most of the time and the next few months went by without incident. Jimmy would still not allow Patrick to stay overnight, even though they had been together over a year now, he didn't think Patrick was good enough for Lilly and constantly told her so. Lilly had saved her money and had bought her first car for five hundred dollars, it was as old as she was, a 1964 EH Holden Premier sedan it was gold with a white vinyl roof. It had a three-speed automatic column shift gear stick. The seats and leather interior were tan and brown, a centre console with heater controls and a radio, there were carpet mats on the floor and flash wheel trims, it was in good condition. Lilly loved her new found freedom, being able to go wherever she wanted but it also came with the responsibility of paying the car registration and fuel, she really felt like an adult now even though she was not quite eighteen. Lilly was still unsure of what she wanted to do for a career, she didn't want to work in a supermarket all her life, she loved cooking and wanted to get an apprenticeship to become a chef. Patrick had been in the Army Reserves for two years now, and often Lilly would go along on Tuesday nights and watch him on parade, listen to his stories of the camps and training exercises. It interested her, maybe the Army would be a way of getting the career she wanted. She felt lost and unsatisfied, not sure of what her future held, Lilly loved Patrick very much, but she wanted more for herself, it was time to make a decision.

CHAPTER 3

MOSMAN, SYDNEY

7th April 1983

Lilly stood outside of the WRAAC school at Mosman Georges Heights in Sydney, her stomach churning, she felt like she would be sick, the uncertainty of what she was about to embark on frightened her. Had she made the right decision? She had passed all the entry tests and had been accepted into the Army, Patrick had driven her down to Sydney to drop her off for the three months of training. They had spent the weekend together at Manly, and now it was time for him to leave. While she was excited to take her first steps towards a new life, she was sad to be saying good-bye to Patrick, they hugged and kissed for the last time and she waved as he walked away. There were about forty other girls lined up awaiting direction, they were shown to the rooms and met their new roommates. Lilly was allocated a room with three other girls, Linda was tall and slim with long dark curly hair, and Lilly liked her instantly, she had such a warm, caring air about her. Tracey was the same height and build as Lilly and had short light brown hair with a bubbly laugh. Amanda had blonde hair and was also tall and slim, but was very reserved and a bit "up herself", and it was apparent she did not want to be here.

They were given time to unpack their few possessions before being taken on a tour of the compound, then it was time for the fitting of their uniforms, they were all given the same trousers, shirts, army boots and black dress shoes. Green t- shirts and tracksuit pants with ARMY embroidered on the back in gold. The dress was very much WWII issue, it was light khaki cotton which was called a giggle dress, tan stockings were to be worn at all times while wearing the dress with black lace- up shoes, which were better known as beetle crushers. They were also assigned additional duties, they were to set the tables in the mess hall for meals, clear away afterwards and then back to their rooms for study or to clean their boots. Rooms had to be neat and tidy at all times plus the floor was to be polished with the big heavy polisher which seemed to have a mind of its own and would spin off in all directions. The rooms were sparse with a single bed, a small bedside table, which was also used as a desk and a locker for their clothes.

Lilly had decided before entering the Army to cut her thick shoulder-length curls to a short, neat crop to make it easier and less time consuming to look after. Every day was the same up at six am to be on parade by seven thirty, beds had to be made a specific way so that you could bounce a coin on them, if it wasn't done to perfection on room check each morning, the bed would be stripped, and you would have to make it again. Shoes had to be spit polished every night and trousers and shirts ironed to perfection. On parade, they were inspected for personal cleanliness and the condition of their weapons, equipment and clothing. A clean, smart appearance was demanded at all times.

Every day they were taught the techniques of marching and saluting. The drill was used as an exercise in self-discipline, alertness and obedience; these qualities are essential to endure the hardship of operations. Drill work formed a common bond and a unity of spirit and purpose within the team, and Lilly enjoyed the marching and drill work. At attention keeping her heels together and in line, feet turned out at the precise angle, knees braced but not locked, body erect and her weight evenly distributed on both feet, shoulders back, level and square to the front, arms straight, elbows close to her side, hands closed thumbs straight, eyes straight ahead. They learnt to stand at ease, stand easy, right dress, to march and mark time, how to turn while marching and how to wheel around in a straight line pivoting on the soldier at the end of the line. Lilly had trouble at first mastering the front salute with the right arm to be kept straight and raised sideways until it was horizontal with the palm of the hand to the front, with the fingers extended and the thumb close to the forefinger. The upper arm kept stationary and the hand and wrist straight, the elbow bent until the tip of the forefinger was two centimetres over the right eye, or touching the brim of the hat in front of the right eye. The forearm, wrist and fingers are kept together in a straight line and the palm of the hand is in a vertical plane then down the right arm is cut to the attention position by the shortest route. During the downward movement, the fingers of the right hand are curled. Linda helped her practice at night until she got it right.

Lilly, Linda and Tracey formed a close bond, but Amanda kept to herself not joining in on their chats or their walks they would take around the compound. Sometimes they would go up to the parade ground and practise their slow march, the foot is forced forward forty centimetres with the toe turned out very slightly and pointed towards the ground but just clear of it. Keeping the head and eyes looking directly to the front, arms steady by the side, elbows tucked in against the body and shoulders steady and square to the front and the weight of the body on the rear foot. The pace was completed by gliding the leading foot forward a further thirty-five centimetres, the ball of the foot had to make contact with the ground first. The weight of the body is transferred onto the leading foot, and the rear foot is forced forward in a natural line before beginning the next pace. They would stumble and laugh but kept practising until they had finally mastered it. They repeated pulling their rifles apart, cleaning and reassembling them as fast as they could. They had the best view in Sydney when they were on the Parade ground overlooking the harbour, it was easy to get distracted, but you were quickly brought back to reality when the Drill Instructor would catch you daydreaming and would yell further commands.

The WRAAC School was located on the Georges Heights headland with majestic views over Sydney Harbour with its sheer sandstone cliffs and steep wooded slopes. Their sleeping quarters were single story sitting on brick piers with metal roofs and clad in timber weatherboards and had seen better days. Georges Heights was recognised as an essential site for the defence of Sydney Harbour. In 1871, construction began on the Georges Head Battery, there were six circular gun pits and zig-zag passages and tunnels which lead to underground shot magazines that had been used to defend the city in case of enemy ships entering the harbour in the war times. It was a bit scary at night heading back to your room. If you walked alone between the officers' mess and the hole in the wall which was an opening to the tunnels, you always wondered if someone would jump out and grab you.

Lilly was missing home, her mother and Patrick, she would phone them every few days and Patrick had been down one weekend when she'd had a day pass, they had spent the day together at the beach enjoying the sunshine and lunch at one of the many cafes. She loved her new life and the new friends she had made, the discipline was very tough and strict and took some getting used to but that was Army life, and it was going to be her life for the next three years. Lilly and Linda would often walk up to the headland at night to sit on the rock which overlooked the harbour with its twinkling lights of the houses dotted around the shores and watch the ships come in and out, the Manly ferries taking their passengers to and from work and home again. They would talk about their dreams and hopes for the future. The rock was a meeting place, a safe place where the girls would come and sit and talk or just sit and look at the beauty around them,

there were many birds and native animals in the bush-
land surrounding them, and even though they were
close to the city it felt like they were in the middle of
nowhere. They had also explored the tunnels a little
but it was dark and gloomy inside and a bit scary, and
besides they weren't supposed to go in there. Amanda
had not settled at all and hated the Army life and the
strictness of it all, she had come from a well-off family
and had been forced into the armed forces by her
father. They had day leave last Saturday, and they had
gone into Mosman to look at the shops, on returning
for roll call that evening Amanda was nowhere to be
seen. She had gone AWOL, and they never saw her
again.

They were only three weeks from their graduation
parade and had perfected their marches, salutes and
completed all assignments and tests, they had been fitted for their uniforms to wear after they marched out,
and were sent on to their next assignments. Lilly had
been having trouble walking for a few days, her feet
were in constant pain with all the excessive training,
marching and slamming feet into the ground. It had
taken its toll, there was no support in the heavy black

army boots. Now she sat in the doctor's office and could not believe what he had just told her, the arches in her feet had collapsed, the muscles were bulging out the side of her feet, they were very sore to touch let alone walk. She was now flat-footed and unable to continue in the Army, she would have to be medically discharged.

"I can't believe they are discharging you, it doesn't seem fair." Linda sat on the edge of Lilly's bed as she packed up her belongings.

"I know and so close to finishing too. But I'm not the only one it's happened to, there is another girl in Block C also being medically discharged for the same thing. I don't know what I'll do now, I thought my life was mapped out for the next three years. I promise that we will always be friends and I will come back and watch you on your march out parade." She hugged Linda tightly. She had nicknamed her "Slim" as she was so tall and thin the total opposite of Lilly who was short and curvy, they had become very close, and she knew they would remain friends for life.

Three weeks later Lilly kept her promise and watched her friends at their graduation parade. She felt pride and a sense of sadness that she would not be going with them on their next adventure.

CHAPTER 4

KEMPSEY

After returning home Lilly decided she would move into a flat of her own and managed to get a job at the new Mexican restaurant in the main street of town, she worked five nights a week waitressing, and one night a week she would sing there with Patrick playing the guitar, entertaining the diners. Patrick and Lilly had been dating for two years now, and his boss had opened up a workshop in Sawtell, an hour's drive away and had asked Patrick to run it, which meant he was going to be away all week only coming home on some weekends. They sat at Lilly's unit now on the balcony having drinks watching the sunset over the hazy blue mountains of the Great Dividing Range, the Macleay river carved its way from the mountains of the New England Plateau to the sea at South West Rocks.

"Um, Lilly, I have something I want to ask you." Patrick reached out for her hand, holding it in his, his hands were trembling. Lilly turned to face him and their eyes locked. The reflection from the setting sun danced in her eyes. Patrick swallowed nervously and his mouth felt so dry. "Lilly, will you marry me?"

Lilly sat in silence for a moment unsure if she had heard him correctly. "Marry you?"

"Yes, I'm going to be away a fair bit now with work, and I want you to know that I'm seriously in love with you, I want to marry you. We could be engaged for a couple of years while we save for a place of our own, we don't have to rush. I just want you to know I'm committed to you." He reached into his pocket and pulled out a small black box opening it to show a small single solitaire diamond on a gold band.

Lilly looked at the ring and then at Patrick, she did love him, he was her first serious boyfriend, and they had lost their virginity to each other. She wasn't sure if she was ready for marriage, but they could be engaged for a few years anyway. "Yes Patrick, I will marry you."

Patrick placed the ring on her finger, pulled her close and kissed her passionately, they sat cradled in each other's arms and watched the last slither of the sun drop down behind the mountains. They knew it would not be easy Patrick's mother was a very dominant, stern woman and as far as she was concerned no one was good enough for her son.

The following day they went to see her parents to tell them their good news. Her mother seemed happy for her, but her father was not impressed.

"You're only eighteen Lilly, too young to be getting married." Jimmy's cold gaze fixed on Patrick.

"Mum was sixteen when she married you Dad, besides we aren't getting married straight away we want to wait a few years." Lilly was disappointed, she had hoped her father would have been happy for them.

"Things were different then, I would prefer you wait a few years, for both of you it's your first real relationship."

Patrick was usually quiet spoken but not this time "I promise you Sir, I will take care of her, I know we are young but we love each other, and that's why we will wait until we have enough money to support ourselves, buy a home and start a family. Do we have your blessing?" Patrick put his hand out hoping that Jimmy would take it and give his approval.

Jimmy stood for a moment, staring directly into Patrick's eyes, then took his hand and slapped him on the shoulder. "Okay as long as you wait."

Their next stop was to Patrick's parents. "Over my dead body, you will not be getting married." Patrick's mother was not impressed, her face hardened as she looked Lilly up and down her eyes were a mixture of shock and disgust, she could barely contain her anger. "She's not good enough for you."

"Mum she is standing right here beside me, please don't be so nasty." Patrick tightened his grip on Lilly's waist, he could feel her trembling.

"I don't want to hear this. Get out both of you. I need to be alone." She leant forward in her chair, her hands clenched on the armrests and her knuckles white. "Get out!"

"But Mum." Patrick pleaded.

"Best you go now son come back later." His father ushered them towards the door. "You know how she gets Patrick, she is overprotective of you, just give her time." He smiled warmly at Lilly. "Don't take it personally Lilly, no one will ever be good enough for her boy. Congratulations." He kissed her cheek and went back inside.

"Well, that went well." Lilly looked at Patrick and they laughed, they didn't care what anyone said they were in love and that was all that mattered. It was hard with Patrick being away all week and only having the weekends together, Lilly missed him. They would talk on the phone just about every night until he came home for the weekends, then they would talk about what they wanted to do for their future. They would save and buy a block of land, it didn't have to be too big, maybe with a house on it and enough area to grow their own vegetables, have chickens and possibly a dog.

Lilly had started a new job, she was working on the forestry commission as an "axeman" on a twelve-month contract. Duties included ring-barking trees, blowing stumps and clearing the forest tracks, planting new trees and conducting control burns. There were ten new employees altogether, their first job was to clean up in the blackbutt plantation where a fire had burned through a year before destroying the trees, they had then been cut off at the base so new saplings would grow. Blackbutt trees were a high quality of timber, natural regeneration and quick growth. Used for making poles, railway sleepers, flooring, building framework, cladding, joinery, lining boards, furniture, wood chipping and decking. With dark fibrous grey-brown spongy bark covering the lower part of the trunk, which came away in long strips. The bark and branches higher up were a glossy cream, occasionally with scribbles from insect larvae, the leaves bright green to dark green, they flowered in September to March leaving cute little gum nuts. They would be working in pairs, and Lilly was teamed up with Mick, she would first clear around the tree with a brush hook and cut the smaller saplings, then Mick would come along and pick the best sapling to leave and cut the rest with his axe. They had been working here for almost a week now.

"Hey Mick, it's almost smoko how about we head for the truck and grab a cup of tea?"

"Yep sounds good, I'm bloody hungry, let's cut through here." Lilly followed Mick as he pushed aside the shrubs, they came out into a fairly clear area with hundreds of plants in black pots. "Oh shit." Mick stopped dead in his tracks.

Lilly had never seen plants like this before, and she wondered why they were in the middle of the state forest amongst all the trees, they were set out in neat lines and stood almost two metres high. "What sort of plants are these?" She went to put her hand out to touch one but Mick grabbed her hand.

"Don't touch them, Lilly, they're marijuana, come on let's go see the boss and tell him, I think it's best to leave them alone. They must belong to those guys we have seen riding around on motorbikes, the ones that keep stopping near us and just sitting and watching." They made their way back to the boss and told him of their find.

"Best to leave them alone and not tell anyone what you have found. We've had too many trucks, graders and equipment destroyed by these guys after we have informed the police. If we leave them alone they leave us alone. Understand?" They both nodded. "Now back to work, we only have to finish that run and we are moving to the next location to plant some seedlings."

Patrick had become preoccupied in the last month, and Lilly could feel he was keeping something from her, just what she wasn't sure, his mother was making it very difficult for them, Lilly could not understand why, she had never done anything to upset her. She stood on the balcony watching the cars and trucks cross the Macleay bridge, watching for Patrick's car, he was due home today and should be arriving very soon. The phone rang "hello."

"Hi Lilly it's me, I've been held up at work here at Sawtell, I won't be back until tomorrow now, sorry honey."

"Oh Patrick really, I was looking forward to seeing you, it's been two weeks since you were home last." Lilly was disappointed she wanted to talk with him and find out what was going on.

"Sorry I gotta go, I'll see you in the morning" that was it the call ended abruptly, no miss you, or I love you.

Lilly sat down on the bench seat and continued to stare at the bridge lost in thought, what was going on with him? It's like he's avoiding me. Suddenly she saw his car moving across the bridge coming up the hill. She waited for him to turn into her street, but he went straight past. That's odd, he had just called and said he wouldn't be back until tomorrow. So, he had lied to her, or maybe he was going to surprise her later. Lilly waited for two hours. She called his sister and asked if he was at home. His sister seemed uncomfortable and told her that he would not be back until tomorrow. Something was definitely not right, and she intended to get to the bottom of it.

Patrick arrived just after ten the next morning. "Hi honey, sorry I got held up at Sawtell yesterday." He kissed her forehead "I really wanted to come home but it's work you know?" He looked at her and looked away, unable to keep eye contact.

"Really, so you didn't come home yesterday afternoon?" Patrick could tell by the look on her face that she already knew, it was no good lying he was not a good liar.

"Um well yes I did actually come home yesterday, I went straight home to Mum's and stayed there. I just needed to think." He could feel his face going red, sweat had started to form on his brow.

"Don't lie to me Patrick. I called your mother's house and spoke to your sister. What's going on?" Lilly could feel that she was not going to like the answer to her question, but she did not want to be with someone who lied to her either.

"I'm sorry Lilly" he lowered his gaze, he could not look her in the eye. "I was with Janelle last night, she needed someone to talk to, her and Brian broke up, and she needed a shoulder to cry on."

"What do you mean with Janelle? Did you stay there the night?" Lilly could feel her heart start pounding harder and faster. Patrick stood there in front of her staring at his feet, there was silence for what seemed forever. "Answer me Patrick!"

"I'm so sorry Lilly, we slept together last night, it just happened, I'm so sorry it won't happen again it was a mistake, it was wrong. I love you."

Lilly stood frozen to the spot, Janelle their friend, the one she had confided in, her close friend, Janelle had just broken up with her boyfriend and had come crying on Lilly's shoulder for support, this can't be happening. It felt like the room was swaying and she had an aching hollowness inside.

"Please Lilly say something" Patrick's eyes pleaded with her for forgiveness, glossy tears filled his eyes and spilled down his cheeks, he shuffled from one foot to the other. "Please Lilly, forgive me it was a huge mistake."

"Mistake! You knew it was wrong and you did it anyway. Get out!" Patrick went to step forward to hold her, Lilly pulled back. "Don't touch me, just get out and don't ever come back. I will never trust you again, and you tell Janelle if I ever see her she had better run. I mean it Patrick we are over, I never want to see you again."

Patrick knew better than to argue, he would leave and give her time to calm down, maybe then she would let him back in, he turned and walked slowly away. Lilly sat on the couch and the tears flowed, it felt like something in her heart had broken, how could he do this to her? She had given him her virginity, her heart, and he repays her by sleeping with some-one else. Patrick kept calling and showing up on her doorstep, but she refused to see him, when she told her father his response was 'well I told you he wasn't good enough.' Finally, after a few stern words and possibly a threat from her father, Patrick finally left her alone, his friends kept telling her how sorry he was and it was a mistake, he still loved her and wanted her back. For Lilly there was no going back, how could she ever trust him again?

CHAPTER 5

KEMPSEY 1984

Lilly enjoyed her job on the forestry commission, they were long days, but fun. She had also joined a women's twilight cricket team and they played once a week, she found she could bowl quite fast and at the odd times put a spin on the ball. Lilly had a crush on their coach Trevor, he was tall, well built and muscular with short dark brown wavy hair, brown eyes under luscious thick eyelashes. Lilly thought he was very good looking, she knew he was divorced and had been told by one of the other girls that he had a young daughter aged six.

Lilly had become close to one of her teammates Wendy, she had asked Lilly to come with her and her husband Dave to Port Macquarie on Friday night for dinner and a show. Lilly had kept to herself since breaking up with Patrick and Wendy thought it would do her good to go out and let her hair down. Lilly had just finished getting ready when she heard the horn beep outside, they were here, she grabbed her bag looked in the mirror to make sure she looked okay before locking the door behind her, on reaching the car she could see someone in the back seat, Wendy had not told her someone else would be going with them. The car door opened and Trevor hopped out, she felt her heart start pounding, he looked so handsome in his denim jeans, loose blue cotton collared shirt with the top two buttons undone. Lilly could see small tufts of his chest hair poking out.

"Hi Lilly, I didn't know you were coming with us" Trevor smiled and looked slightly embarrassed.

"Hello Trevor, that makes two of us. I thought it was just the three of us." Lilly glared at Wendy, who gave her a wink and a smile, she had confided in Wendy that she had a crush on Trevor and now

Wendy was setting her up. They chatted about cricket during the half hour drive and had dinner at the Indian restaurant before going to the club to see the band. Trevor was a good dancer and easy to talk to, Lilly soon realised he was eight years older than her, not that he looked it, his daughter was now living with him and his ex-wife had moved to Sydney. On the way home, they whispered in the back seat so as not to be overheard.

"I'm sorry Trevor, I think Wendy is playing Match-maker."

"I figured that when we pulled up outside your place, she said she had a friend coming with us. It's okay, I don't mind." He reached out and took her hand. "Maybe next time we could go out with just the two of us if you'd like."

"I would like that." Lilly was happy; it had been a wonderful evening.

Trevor bent towards her and kissed her gently on the lips. "Good, it's settled then."

Lilly worked on the road clearing crew for three weeks, clearing stumps and widening some of the forest tracks. The hot summer months would be upon them soon, so today they were going out into the forest to do a controlled burn-off. They were set a designated area and were to keep the fire contained within it, by back burning and using roads as buffers, the burn offs helped reduce fuel build-up and decreased the likelihood of dangerous hotter fires. They bumped along the dirt forestry track in the old work truck towing a trailer with all their equipment heading for the Ballengarra forest near Cooperabung, with its rolling hills to steep slopes with ridge crest elevations of lithic sandstones and mudstones. It was a dry open forest of hardwoods and rainforest occupying the moist, shaded gullies at lower elevations. Lilly adored working in the bush, the freedom of being outside, working with the sun on her face and the breeze blowing softly, carrying the smell of the trees and flora, it was euphoric. Their boss Tony had worked on the forestry commission for nearly thirty years and had so much knowledge of the area, Lilly was a willing student and was learning a lot from him.

Lilly stared out the window thinking of her date with Trevor last night, they had been seeing each other for a month now, he was so dreamily handsome, she knew she was starting to fall in love with him, but she was unsure about his daughter, was she ready to take on someone else's child? After all, she was only twenty herself. Lilly watched the passing bush trying to recognise each tree, the Casuarina she-oaks with long pine needle leaves and little woody oval structures resembling a conifer cone. The big old ironbark with its rough, hard furrowed bark that was almost corky in appearance. Spotted gums with their tall, straight trunks with smooth powdery bark of white, grey or pink in patches and small white flowers. Lilly's favourite tree was the scribbly gum with its distinctive features of 'scribbles' made by moth larva as it tunnels between the layers of bark. The scrub where they stopped was thick with lantana and a lot of undergrowth. They had selected the area on the side of a hill. Tony dropped Lilly and Mick off with their fire torches and gave strict instructions. Lilly would walk along the top of the road while Mick went a hundred metres to the bottom of the hill, they were to keep an eye on each other and keep a steady pace, staying together. Tony and the rest of the crew would go a kilometre further up the road and wait for them there.

"Okay I'm ready Lilly." Mick called out from the base of the hill.

"Okay I'm ready too, start now, and Mick, call out if we lose sight of each other."

"Righto" echoed up from the bushes below.

Lilly strolled along the edge of the road lighting the brush. If all went to plan the two fires would meet in the middle and burn each other out, creating a fire break. There was a light breeze blowing, and the smoke was drifting across the road. She couldn't see Mick anymore; the forest was too dense at the bottom. The crackling sound of the fire starting to take hold was becoming louder, she called out to Mick but there was no answer. Suddenly in front of her a strong gust of wind blew through the trees and bush catching it on fire, and now there was a massive wall of flames across the road in front of her, jumping the road and making its way up the hill. Lilly called out to Mick but she could not hear anything over the roar of the fire, it sounded like a freight train was heading straight for her, the winds started gusting around the fire, sucking in all available oxygen, the smoke was becoming thicker it was hard to see more than a few feet in front of her. The smoke plumes were so dense they turned day into night, the soot grabbed at her throat and made her cough, she pulled her shirt up over her mouth and nose trying to breath, there was no way she could go through the fire, turning back she found she had another firewall behind her. Giant balls of flame seemed to roll across the trees, branches crackled and snapped and burning embers floated on the air falling around her. The heat was becoming unbearable; it felt like her face was on fire. For a brief moment she caught a glimpse of the sun through the smoke, it was a hellish red. Panic set in, her heart was pounding so hard in her chest she thought it would explode, her eyes were stinging and watering from the smoke. What could she do? She couldn't go forward or back, and they had been taught at their safety briefing never try to outrun a fire as the fire moves more quickly uphill than down, when going uphill the flames were much closer to new fuel and would spread quickly, she needed to find somewhere to wait it out and hope she would survive. It was only a small forest road and not very wide, there was an embankment just a few metres in front of her about two metres high with a drain that ran alongside the dirt embankment, it was her only hope to lay down in the drain, and hope that the flames would not reach her.

"Tony!!! Tony!!! Help me, please help me, I'm stuck in the fire." Lilly screamed she had no idea whether she could be heard above the wind, it had increased and the sound of the fire was deafening, her throat was parched, and breathing was becoming more difficult. "Tony, Mick can someone hear me, HELP!!!"

Lilly laid down in the dirt drain; it was not very deep and she hoped and prayed it would be enough. She began to cry, she had only just started her life, was this where it was going to end in a ditch on the side of the road, burnt to death? She thought of her mother, brother and sister, her grandparents, her short life really did flash before her eyes as she thought about what could have been. She pulled her shirt further up trying to breathe, lowered her head into her hands and prayed.

Mick emerged from the bush and swaggered towards the truck, looking around for Lilly. "Where's Lilly?"

Tony turned "She's not here yet" he turned back towards the road in the direction she should have been coming from, the smoke was thick and the flames were coming up the hill from where Mick had just lit. "You were supposed to keep an eye on each other Mick!"

"Oh. I know, I lost sight of her then the wind came up and I couldn't hear anything."

"Shhh listen. What's that?" They stood quietly and there it was again, a scream and a cry for help. Tony went white, oh god she was trapped in there, in the fire, he didn't hesitate. "Let's go, we need to drive through and find her." They bundled back into the truck, turned around and started through the smoke; they could only see a few metres in front of them as they drove slowly with the lights on. "Keep your eyes peeled, she's in here somewhere." The fire was licking at the side of the old truck, and the heat inside was rising. Tony prayed that they would not catch on fire, but he was not going to leave Lilly out there.

Lilly lifted herself up and crouched in the ditch, she knew she had been told not to try and outrun the fire but what choice did she have? She could hardly breathe, and the smoke was making her cough. It was so hot, the flames were getting closer, she had no idea where her crew were, or if they had even realised she was missing. Lilly scrambled up the side of the rocky embankment, she had scraped her knees earlier, blood was now trickling down the side of her leg from the cuts. The fire was about to cross where she was crouching. She had to make a decision. The ditch was not deep enough to save her, as she looked up the hill she could see that the fire had crossed onto both sides it was more than likely it had gone over and joined at the top, she could be running into her inevitable death. What was that noise? Lilly stayed still, she strained to hear the sound again, it was so hard with the crackling and roaring of the fire around her, could it be? There it was again, the horn of the truck, she could just see the dull white lights coming through the smoke, it was her crew they had come for her, she jumped out onto the road as they reached her, Mick swung open the back door and dragged her in.

"Got her!" yelled Mick, "Tony get us out of here!" Tony floored the truck and drove as fast as he could through the smoke and the flames.

Lilly clung to Mick and lost all control, tears running down her face, she was sobbing uncontrollably and shaking, they handed her a drink of water, but she was shaking so much she couldn't hold it steady and it splashed all over her, Mick held her in his arms.

"I'm so sorry Lilly, I'm so sorry this is my fault, are you okay? Are you burnt or hurt?" She looked up at him all he could see was the white of her eyes, she was covered in black soot from head to toe. Lilly could not speak, the shock had set in and her throat was so sore and dry, she just shook her head and cried.

CHAPTER 6

KEMPSEY 1985

The contract had ended at the forestry commission at the end of last year, and Lilly had managed to get a new job, starting the Monday after she finished with the forestry. Her new job was at the Woolworths store that had just opened in town, she was working in the variety section, restocking the shelves, tidying and working on the checkout when needed.

Lilly and Trevor had been seeing each other for a few months now, going out to dinner or a movie, to the beach to swim or fish or catching up with friends. When Lilly met his mother and siblings, they had been warm and welcoming. Trevor was committed to raising his daughter, and they were living with his mother for the moment while he saved money to find them a place of their own. Trevor would stay over at Lilly's three nights a week in her little two-bedroom unit, they had a lot in common and he was very affectionate and caring, he was also very family orientated which Lilly liked. She had met his daughter Nancy, who was finding it hard having another woman in her father's life, she was reserved when Lilly was around, it was to be expected, and Lilly knew that she would have to win her over, she didn't want to be her mother, she just wanted to be her friend. Their relationship was getting serious and they had talked about the future and moving in together, so Lilly needed Nancy to accept her as part of her father's life.

They found a little old farmhouse at Euroka, it would be their first house together. The house was small and run down with only three main rooms and two smaller rooms that had been enclosed on the verandah, the rent was cheap and it wasn't too far out of town, Lilly liked the fact it was only a few minutes to her mother's home. They didn't have much furniture to start with, but with the help of friends and family, they managed. Lilly had her glory box, with things she had been saving for when she had her first home. Her grandmother Loretta had helped her with linen, her mother had given her some of the kitchen things that she no longer needed, now she had moved into her new house and had bought new plates, saucepans and cutlery.

Lilly was turning twenty one today, her mother had organised a party for her friends and family at her house later that afternoon. Trevor had just arrived home from work, she could hear him whistling as he came up the front steps. Then the thud as he took his boots off and dropped them beside the screen door, he pushed the door open holding a bunch of flowers, looking as handsome as ever, he smiled that big cheeky grin, his eyes sparkling with happiness, he grabbed her around the waist and kissed her.

"I need to ask you something." Trevor held her at arm's length.

"Yes, what is it Trevor?" Lilly saw something playful in his expression, and there was a twinkle in his eyes.

"How about it?" he grinned at her sheepishly.

"How about what?" Lilly did not understand his question.

"How about we get married?" he chuckled.

Lilly wasn't sure she had heard him right, was that a proposal? "What?"

"Let's get married, I love you and I want to have a family with you, so how about it?"

Lilly laughed, "well it's not the most romantic proposal, but yes." She flung her arms around his neck and kissed him strong and hard on the mouth to seal the deal. They announced their engagement at her party, her mother was delighted and Lilly hoped now that she had found someone, that her mother would finally leave her father, there was no reason for her to stay now.

Trevor and Lilly decided that they would like to marry in May the next year, they booked the church and started making their plans, Trevor worked on the railway and Lilly still worked at Woolworths and had been promoted to service supervisor, running the checkouts and training new staff. Nancy had warmed up to Lilly but was always reserved, she did not like the fact that she had to share her father with someone else.

Sometimes Nancy would ignore Lilly and refuse to do as she was asked, once when Lilly had asked her to clean her room, Nancy turned to her and said: "I don't have to do what you say, you're not my mother." Lilly had put her foot down and made it quite clear she had no intention of trying to be her mother, but she was going to take care of her and that they would be married soon so Nancy would just have to accept her because she was here for the long run. Trevor let Lilly have whatever she desired for the wedding; his only request was that it be a red and white wedding after his favourite football team the St George Dragons. Lilly was so happy that she had met her prince charming and would be married next year and maybe a family soon after if they could afford it.

It was the first week of March and the wedding plans were well underway, the church had been booked, the RSL club was organised for the reception, material bought for the dresses, flowers ordered, a photographer booked and the church and table decorations were being made by Lilly and her mother. Lilly had just returned from the doctor's office. She could not believe it, she was pregnant, they had decided to try for a family, Lilly had been on the pill for four years and thought it would take six months or more for her to fall pregnant, to their delight she had fallen straight away. This meant she would be five months pregnant when they married, luckily they had not started making her wedding dress yet, so now she would have to modify it to cover the growing belly she would have. Trevor had been waiting impatiently for her to arrive home.

"How did you go at the doctor's?" she could see by the expression on his face he was excited and hopeful.

"I'm pregnant, due at the end of September, I still can't believe that I fell so quickly, it means it will make it harder for us to save if I'm not working."

Trevor pulled her onto his lap and kissed her forehead. "It will be fine, don't worry about it, we will manage. Nancy will be excited she is going to have a little brother or sister to boss around."

"I hope so, I don't want her to feel put out in any way. I'm going to be fat for my wedding, so much for that slim fitting dress I was going to have. I have to go see Mum and tell her the news, her baby is having a baby."

Lilly stood on the church steps, her father by her side. They were waiting for the music to start so she could enter and walk down the aisle to say her vows. She wanted this more than anything, a marriage to the man she loved, the desire to give her children a stable, happy family life that she had missed out on growing up. Her dress was made of white satin, embossed with orchids, the neckline was scalloped with lace up to her neck and long fitted lace sleeves. The dress was made to fall from the waist, with a satin belt tied loosely around her waist, and a hoop skirt underneath to hold out the dress and cover her expanding belly. Her mother had made her bouquet from silk flowers. Lilly had made her own headpiece it was a halo of small white flowers and had long clear strings of flowers and pearls down her back. The three bridesmaids consisted of her sister Ruby and Trevor's two sisters. They were dressed in knee-length red satin dresses, the same material as her dress with a small teardrop-shaped red hat with red lace. The flower girls were Nancy and

Ruby's daughter Liana, they were dressed in cute little dresses made similar to hers and from the same material, with a halo of white flowers in their hair and carrying small baskets full of red and white flowers.

The organ started playing the traditional wedding march, she could feel herself trembling with excitement, tears began to form in the corner of her eyes, this was it, she was getting married today. She glided down the aisle on her father's arm, Trevor was standing there waiting for her at the altar with the biggest grin on his face. Trevor had decided he wanted white suits with a red cummerbund, red handkerchief in the pocket and red bow ties, he looked so smart, Lilly could not believe that she was about to have what she had always dreamed of, a loving caring husband and soon a family of her own.

Josie and Lilly would catch up twice a week for a cuppa and chat, Josie had a nine-month-old baby girl as well as two boys. She lived only a few minutes away and was an amazing mother, Lilly valued her advice about raising children.

"Oh god, I feel so uncomfortable and fat, at least it's only two weeks until my due date, the baby has stopped kicking like a footballer and seems to have settled a bit, now it's just the occasional feet under my ribs pushing out. I find it hard to get out of bed my belly is so big, I have to roll over to the edge, then get down on the floor on my hands and knees to push myself up." Lilly rubbed her belly, she was starting to get a bit nervous and excited about the impending birth of her first child. Josie was breastfeeding her beautiful little girl who already had a mass of blonde curls.

"Not long now, you know it's going to hurt a lot, it's much more fun putting it in than getting it out" Josie laughed "but they can give you something for the pain if it gets too bad." She looked down at the baby in her arms "but it's all worth it when you hold them in your arms, they are so precious."

"Yes, I've been told that you forget the pain. I am nervous though, I know how to make a baby and how to have one, but I'm not so sure what to do once I have them home. What if I'm no good at it?"

Josie chuckled "It will come naturally to you, don't worry, it's true what they say about motherly instinct, and I'm not far away if you need help." She patted Lilly's hand "you'll be fine. I was only sixteen when I had my first baby, I had no idea what to do but it does come naturally."

"I hope so, or you might find me camped up here on your lounge for the first few months." Lilly adored Josie, she was such a good friend and so easy to talk to, Josie was six years older than her, she felt blessed to have met such a beautiful woman.

Lilly awoke at quarter to two in the morning on the twenty-fifth of September with a sharp jabbing pain gripping her stomach. "Trevor, wake up. Trevor!" She pushed him again "I think I'm in labour."

"Mmm, what?" Trevor rolled over and rubbed his eyes, he had been doing the late shifts and hadn't been in bed very long.

"I think I'm in labour." Lilly grabbed her stomach as the pain shot through her again.

"Are you sure it's not those Braxton hicks things you have been having the last few months?" Trevor mumbled at her half asleep.

"No this really hurts, and my stomach went so hard, ohhh crap there it is again." Lilly bent over trying to ease the pain that was gripping her belly.

"Oh shit, well we better get you up and dressed and to the hospital." Trevor bounded out of bed now wide awake. He helped Lilly up and to get dressed, grabbed the bag that they had ready for the hospital.

"I need to call Mum."

"It's two thirty in the morning Lilly."

"I know, but Mum said she didn't care what time it was she wants to be there with me." Lilly dialled her mother's number, and to her surprise, she answered it in two rings.

"Lilly."

"Yes, Mum I'm in labour, were you awake?"

"Yes, I woke up about half an hour ago. I just had a feeling, I'll meet you at the hospital."

"Mum." Lilly's voice was shaky.

"It's okay baby, it will be fine. I'll get there as quickly as I can."

The nurse ushered them into an examination room and checked to see how far along she was. "Your only three centimetres dilated it will be many hours yet before you give birth especially with your first one, they usually take their time." She smiled reassuringly at Lilly, the bell rang for the front door.

"That will be my Mum, I called her to come, when will the doctor be here?"

"It's no good her being here this early. You have at least eight to ten hours maybe longer before you're ready to push. I'll tell her to come back later, we will call her when it gets closer. I'll call your doctor when it's closer to delivery, no good waking him yet." She went to answer the door and tell Lilly's mother what was happening.

Fifteen minutes went by, and Lilly's contractions had started coming close together, Lilly felt like she wanted to push, Trevor called for the nurse to come and check. "I think you are panicking because it's your first baby, you just need to relax. I'll have a look and see how you're progressing." She lifted the sheet and let out a surprised gasp. "Oh dear, you're almost fully dilated. I need to call the doctor and your mother, just pant when you have a contraction we'll move you into the birthing room."

Lilly's labour only lasted three hours and twenty minutes, she was unable to have anything to help with the pain, it was like this child was trying to rip her apart from the inside out, she felt like she wouldn't be able to do this but it was too late now, there was no other way. At five minutes past five that morning she gave birth to a healthy boy weighing seven pounds six ounces. When they placed the screaming baby in her arms everything else faded away as she gazed down into his little wrinkled red face, she felt a love so deep and intense, a love that she had never felt in her whole life. This was her child a part of her, she had made this tiny human being, it had grown inside her for nine months, Lilly knew she would be a good Mum all she had to do was love him and take care of him. She looked up at Trevor who had tears in his eyes, he bent and kissed her forehead.

"Well done honey, well done, I love you so much." Lilly handed him the baby, she could see he was so pleased to have a boy. He gazed lovingly at his son and whispered "Hello Mark."

CHAPTER 7

KEMPSEY 1987

Three months had passed, and Lilly had settled comfortably into motherhood, it was just like Josie had said, it came naturally. Lilly had been to see her mother this morning, she had been so happy for the last few months, her father had finally agreed to a divorce, and he'd been living in Queensland for three months now, apparently with another woman. Her mother had started seeing Tom, a lovely man who lived at Hat Head. She had just finished feeding Mark and had put him back in the cot when the phone rang.

"Hi Lilly, it's Mum."

"Hi Mum, what's wrong?" Lilly could hear the fear in her mother's voice.

"Your father just phoned, I told him about Tom, and now he says I'm not to see anyone he said he's coming back to talk to me." Her mother sounded anxious and was close to tears.

"Mum you can't go back to him, he will never change."

"I know love, I have no intention of that, Tom is coming to get me so I won't be at the house for a few days. I don't trust your father; he still scares me, and I'm not sure what he will do. If you need me I'll be at Tom's, you can call me there. I'll be fine, Tom will take care of me."

"Ok Mum, but be careful."

"I will honey don't worry, it will be okay. I'll call you tomorrow morning, love you, bye."

"Love you too Mum." Lilly hung up the phone. Why couldn't her father just leave them alone and stay out of their lives, he didn't want her mother, he just didn't want her to have anyone else.

Lilly was hanging the nappies on the line when she heard the phone ringing, she ran inside to answer it.

"Lilly, you'd better get over here." It was her father on the phone, her heart dropped.

"Why Dad? What's wrong?"

"It's your mother, get over here now!" The phone clicked dead and there was a frightening silence.

Oh no! Had he done something to her mother? She was supposed to call her today to let her know she was okay and Lilly hadn't heard from her, she must have gone back to the house for something and her father had her there now, god knows what he would do. Lilly was all too aware of how violent he could be. Lilly picked up her three-month-old sleeping baby and placed him gently in his capsule, carrying him as she ran to the car. It was only a five- minute drive to her parents' house, but it felt like an eternity. Why hadn't she called her brother Fred before she left home to ask him to meet her there, too late now, her only concern was to get to her mother before anything happened. She could tell by her father's voice that he had been drinking and she dreaded what she would find when she arrived.

Lilly carried the capsule inside her parents' house and placed the sleeping baby in the hallway where she could hear her father in the study scratching around and mumbling to himself.

"Mum!" Lilly called out for her mother, fearing the worst.

"The fucking bitch isn't here. Where is she?" Jimmy was standing at the door holding a rifle he stumbled against the door frame.

"I don't know Dad. I thought she was here."

"Well she's fucking not, the slut, she's been whoring around with some bloke. I suppose you know all about it too you little bitch."

"Dad, there's no need to swear at me and call me names. Besides you and Mum called it quits months ago and you're getting divorced, so why does it matter to you if she is seeing someone else?"

"Of course you would take her side, you're a fucking slut just like your mother." He spat the words at her. "You get that bitch on the phone right now or I'll shoot you and that bastard child of yours!"

"I'm married, he is not a bastard, and I am not a slut, how can you speak to me like that? I'm your daughter."

"Are you?" Jimmy levelled the rifle at her head. "Call your fucking mother now."

"Okay I will, but only if you promise to speak to her rationally and not yell and swear at her." Lilly dialled Tom's home number her mother had given it to her in case of an emergency, and this was an emergency.

"Hello, Tom speaking."

"Hi it's Lilly, can I speak to Mum please." Lilly tried to keep her voice calm even though her insides were doing somersaults.

"Hi Lilly, are you alright?" Rose tried to steady her shaking voice.

"Mum, I'm at the house. Dad is here, and he wants to speak to you."

Jimmy wrenched the phone from her hand. "Where are you? You get back here now you fat cow, I'm your husband and you will come home right now."

Rose felt her heart go into her throat, Jimmy had Lilly at the house, and she probably had the baby with her, she had to try and talk sense into him, she could tell by his slurred words he had been drinking and she knew Jimmy well enough that he would have the rifle with him.

"Jimmy I am not coming home, we are over, you agreed last year that we would get a divorce, you have moved on and so have I, now let Lilly leave."

"She's not going anywhere until you get back here, if you don't come back now, I'll shoot her and that fucking bastard kid of hers, and it will be your fault." Jimmy slammed the phone down and sneered at Lilly. "You better call her back and tell her not to call the police either cause if she does I'll guarantee no one will leave this house alive, there will be a shoot out and you'll get the first bullet."

Lilly never doubted a word her father said, she had seen him in fits of rage before. It was apparent he had been drinking heavily, empty beer cans were laying all around the floor, and he had two rifles on the desk fully loaded and the one in his hand.

"Mum, it's me again, Dad said don't call the police or he will shoot it out with them." Lilly's voice was shaking, and Rose could hear the fear in her daughter's voice.

"I won't, I've called your brother Fred he is on his way. Try not to antagonise him Lilly, I won't forgive myself if anything happens to you and the baby."

Jimmy grabbed the phone from Lilly again "Hurry up ya fucking bitch, I'm losing my patience and tell that bastard who's fucking you to show his face if he's got any balls, I know you're with him."

Rose put the phone down, she could not listen anymore, she broke down in sobs unable to control the fear that was gripping her. Jimmy had told her many times that if she left, he would hunt her down like a pig and kill her, and now her baby daughter and grandson were in his firing line.

"Rose let me go, maybe I can talk some sense into him." Tom's heart was breaking watching Rose go through this, he would gladly put his life on the line for her.

"No Tom, he would shoot you as soon as you walked in the door. Fred will be there soon, and Lilly has been around her father long enough to know what to do and say. I just hope" she couldn't bring herself to finish the sentence, the thought of what Jimmy might do was unbearable.

Lilly watched her father fill the chamber on the rifle and lock and load it, he had made her sit down on the chair in the office, she could see her sleeping son in the capsule in the hallway. Even with all this commotion, he was still fast asleep. She prayed he would not wake and cry, god knows what her father would do. She had to stay calm and try to reason with him.

"Dad, you know that it's no good talking when you've been drinking, Mum is too scared of you, she won't come while you're threatening her or me."

Jimmy looked up from polishing the barrel and grunted.

"Dad, you and Mum have been unhappy for years, why drag it out any longer? Move on and find some-one else. Just let me leave with your grandson, and I'll come back tomorrow and bring Mum and Fred, and we can all sit down and talk about it reasonably." Lilly stood up and started to walk towards the door.

"You're not going fucking anywhere you fucking little slut, get back here and sit down." Her father was screaming at her now.

Lilly turned to find the rifle only inches from her head, her father was looking down the barrel at her, an evil glint in his eye and his finger hovering on the trigger. Lilly knew the rifle was loaded and that if he wanted to, he could end her life right there and then.

So many things ran through her mind, her baby, her husband, how would her mother cope with her death, she would blame herself. At that moment Lilly fully understood why her mother had stayed and put up with the physical and verbal abuse for all those years, what she feared Jimmy would do was exactly what was unfolding right now.

Lilly had a choice to make, stay or try to leave, her protective motherly instincts kicked in and at that moment she remembered something her father had told her. She bent down and picked up the baby capsule stared back at her father defiantly and with as much strength and commitment as she could muster.

"Well Dad, you taught me a lot of things in my life, and one of them was to stand my ground and not to take shit from anyone. I am not a slut, I am not stupid, I am not useless, I can be whatever I want to be, and one thing is for sure, I am never going to be anything like you. I'm not taking any more of your shit, so if you're gonna shoot your grandson and me in the back like a coward then do it, because I'm leaving." Lilly's legs were like jelly, she walked out to the car placed the capsule in its holder and got in the car and drove away.

It wasn't until she was further up the road and out of sight of the house, that Lilly pulled over and broke down, her body shaking, she had called his bluff and had lived to walk away, she needed to get to a phone and call her mother and let her know she was ok and call Fred to stop him from going to the house.

Lilly and Trevor had returned to her parents house the next day to speak to her father, he denied the fact he had pulled the rifle on Lilly telling her she had made it all up. She knew it was no good arguing with him, it's what her father always did, he talked himself into believing whatever he wanted to believe. Jimmy agreed to let Rose go, but he would not allow her to return to the house, she would get nothing, she could leave with just the clothes on her back. What boxes he did pack up and let Lilly take to her mother he had poured oil and chucked dirt in, destroying whatever was in there. Rose didn't care she wanted no reminders of him or what she had left behind, her family had rallied around her, supporting her and Tom gave her whatever she needed to start anew. Rose had a new happy life now, she didn't need material things, she had Tom, her children and her grandchildren, but most of all she was loved, cherished and she was finally safe.

Lilly refused to speak to her father after that, having a rifle pointed at her baby boy was the last straw for her, she wiped her father from her life. How could he have done the unspeakable and then deny it? She didn't need that sort of aggression or the negative vibes in her life, she had her own life to get on with and a new baby of her own to care for. Now she had a child of her own she could not fathom how any parent could treat their children the way their father had treated and hurt them and their mother over the years. Lilly was not sure if she could ever forgive him. Maybe in time, but not right now.

CHAPTER 8

EUROKA

Lilly had returned to work at Woolworths when Mark was nine months old, she had weaned him to just one breastfeed at night, Josie was still at home caring for Tammy, her eighteen-month-old baby girl and had offered to look after Mark for her when she had to work. Lilly was grateful, she felt terrible going back to work and leaving her son, but at least he would be well cared for and have someone to play with. It was upsetting to leave her baby boy behind, but she had to work. They were saving to buy a home of their own, a place for their children to grow up in. The small farmhouse they lived in was cramped. It really was only three rooms, with two smaller rooms that had been enclosed on the existing verandah, the kitchen also served as the dining room. The lounge room could just fit a three seater couch and a TV in it, there was a small room off this which was Nancy's bedroom then a bedroom for them which had the smaller room off it which they used as a nursery and ironing room.

The house was old, and the windows were hard to open and the roof leaked in a few places. A draught could be felt most of the time through the whole house coming through the gaps in the boards, but it was the only thing they could afford at the moment. The house sat up on a small hill looking back to the river across paddocks with cows grazing contently on the lush green grass. There was an old double shed outside which consisted of three walls and a rusty tin roof. They parked the car on one side, and Trevor, who was really good at woodwork, had converted the other side into a work area for him to potter around in and make things.

Trevor had the day off today, so he was taking care of Mark and doing some housework. He was in the nursery which also served as an ironing room. It was a tiny room with Mark's cot on one wall and the ironing board and a small cupboard. Trevor had given Mark his bottle and put him down to sleep in his cot, so he could fold and iron the clothes. Mark had already started crawling and pulling himself up on the furniture and was an inquisitive little boy. Trevor had finished ironing all his work shirts and turned to hang them on the rack. Mark had pulled himself up on the edge of the cot and reached out and grabbed the cord of the iron, he pulled it towards him. Trevor turned around just as the hot iron tumbled from the board and fell hitting the side of the cot spewing boiling hot water all over Mark who fell back in the cot screaming.

"Oh shit." Trevor grabbed his son and pulled off his wet top and pants, the boiling water from the iron had hit him on the left side of his face, leaving an angry red streak. Blisters formed immediately on his left hand and arm, and the top of his leg. Trevor ran cold water over him then added fresh Aloe Vera plant to the burns, he rang Lilly at work to meet him at the hospital then bundled Mark into the car and headed for the hospital. Lilly arrived not long after, the nurses had already taken Mark into emergency and were treating his burns. "I'm so sorry Lilly I was ironing, and I only turned for a minute when he grabbed the cord on the iron and yanked it, the hot water went all over him, I'm so sorry." Trevor was beside himself with how he could have let this happen to his son.

"It's okay, it was an accident, don't blame yourself, it could have easily been me." She knew it would be no good yelling or blaming her husband, she could see he felt bad enough as it was. "What's happening now? Can I see him?"

"They're treating him now, they have given him a sedative to calm him down and something for the pain, I came out here to wait for you while they are bandaging him up." Lilly put her arm around Trevor as he sat with his head in his hands crying, tears streamed down her face, her poor baby boy.

Mark lay in the vast hospital bed sleeping from the medication, the doctor informed them he would be fine, and hopefully, there would be no scarring, but they wouldn't know for a few months until the skin had time to grow back and heal. He had first degree burns to his face and hand, they were superficial and should heal with no scarring, but the one on his leg was a second-degree burn. His cloth pants had held in the heat and caused it to blister, the area surrounding it was red and would be painful for some time, Mark would have to be brought to the burns clinic at the hospital each day to have his bandages changed, and they would show Lilly how to reapply them.

CHAPTER 9

EUROKA 1988

It had been six months since the accident and Mark's burns had healed well, luckily there was no scarring on his face or hand, but he had been left with an oval scar on the top of his left leg about the size of a large egg. Mark's burns had not slowed him down in any way he was now walking, and into everything he could get his hands on, he was so curious and learned very quickly. Trevor had gone through the whole house making sure that there were no other dangers that his son could get into. Lilly had had a health scare as well finding two separate lumps one in each breast, they had operated and removed the lumps and had them tested, luckily both were benign, and she now needed to do regular checks on her breasts and have a mammogram every two years.

Trevor was digging a vegetable patch out the back of the house so they could grow their own food and hopefully save a bit more money towards buying their own home. He had borrowed a rotary hoe from a friend to make the job a little easier. Nancy was staying over at her cousin's house for the night for a birthday party, Lilly loved her, but she pushed her to her limits at times refusing to do the things she asked and playing Lilly and her father off against each other, it caused many fights between her and Trevor. On a blanket in the shade of the house, Mark was keeping himself amused playing with his toys, and with their new puppy dog, a German shepherd they had called Sara. Lilly kept a watchful eye on him while Trevor used the rotary hoe, once he had loosened all the earth Trevor turned the machine off and asked Lilly to help him pull the grass out of the upturned soil. With Mark settled on the blanket Lilly bent down to pull out the grass, she turned to check Mark just as he walked up to the trench digger.

"NO!! Don't!!" she yelled but it was too late Mark had grabbed hold of the hot muffler and was now screaming with pain, he had burnt both hands. "Quick Trevor, get the car, we need to get him to the hospital." Lilly rubbed fresh Aloe Vera on Mark's little hands as Trevor drove flat out to the hospital. Once again they were waiting in emergency for the doctor to treat his burns. "My god Trevor they are going to think we are bad parents; it was only eight months ago we were here last time with him with burns." Lilly started to doubt her parenting skills; surely it had not been this hard for her mother.

The doctor smiled at them sympathetically "Well it looks like this child is going to be a handful and one you will have to watch constantly, he's too curious for his own good. Well Lilly, you know how this works we'll see you tomorrow at the burns clinic." He patted her hand, smiled and left to finish his rounds.

CHAPTER 10

SOUTH KEMPSEY 1990

They had been in their own home now for five months, they had managed to save enough money for a deposit and had borrowed the rest from the bank. The house sat on a corner block in South Kempsey opposite the Commandant Hill church. The same church her mother had been married in and Mark had been christened in, it was a three bedroom home on a sloped block, the front of the house was level with the yard, but the back dropped away and had a large garage built underneath it. There was a lot of potential to improve the home later on, but that would have to wait. They had set an area up at the very back of the yard and had planted vegetables and fruit trees. Lilly was pregnant again with their second child due in July, just like her first pregnancy her blood pressure was low and she had dizzy spells each morning but luckily not much morning sickness. Nancy was now thirteen, she had started to blossom into a young woman and had become a bit more accepting of Lilly once she realised she was not trying to take her mothers place, Nancy's mother lived in Sydney, so she only saw her in school holidays as it was a six-hour drive to Sydney. There had been tough times, and Nancy liked to see how far she could push the limits. The most frustrating thing for Lilly was that whenever anything happened, Trevor always took Nancy's side even when she was apparently in the wrong. This really got on Lilly's nerve as she had taken his child on and treated her no differently to her own, as far as she was concerned there was one rule for everyone, it didn't matter whose child you were, they would all get treated the same.

Even though she was five months pregnant Lilly had joined the local Marching Girls team and would go to marching practice twice a week learning new drills, she enjoyed it so much and she enjoyed the new group of women she had found, they ranged in age from sixteen to sixty. Through discipline and practise the team aimed to move as one, either when they were performing complex patterns or straight marching. You needed skill and focus rather than sweat and muscle, proving it was challenging at times, more tedious rather than strenuous. They designed their own uniforms and frequently added a touch of glitz and glamour with fringing, amulets and lanyards, gauntlets or gloves and of course the long white boots. With their fingers cupped to extend their knuckles parallel to the ground, arms extended fully and swung waist- high, front and back, they would heel-march 120 beats to the minute, following a plan based on military precision marching. They were training for competition, and Lilly hoped that after the birth she would be able to go away and compete as well. It was an excellent exercise for her and the bigger she got, the harder it was getting to do the turns with swinging arms and a big belly.

Lilly had just been to her Doctor for her checkup, she only had four weeks to go, Dr Bull had told her that he would be away this weekend leaving on Friday evening and joked with her not to go into labour until he got back. Dr Bull had delivered Lilly twenty-five years ago and was now going to deliver her child, it was going to be an extraordinary moment for both of them. Lilly started to have contractions on Friday morning at regular intervals, she was unsure if she was in labour or not, there was no pain with each contraction, so she thought it best to go straight to the hospital where Dr Bull was in surgery all day, she did not want to risk him not delivering this child. On the twenty-second of June and only two hours of labour, Lilly gave birth to her second baby boy, they called him Jake he was six pounds six ounces. Luckily he had arrived three weeks early, the umbilical cord had been wrapped around his neck and if she had gone full term, she could have quite possibly lost him.

He looked just like his brother Mark, they were the spitting image of each other, Lilly stared down at the small child in her arms, he had spent the first few days under constant supervision, he had some jaundice and was being tube fed as he would not suck, now finally Lilly had him on the breast and he had settled down well. Jake was only five weeks old when Lilly travelled away with the team for their first marching competition. Sixteen excited women all bundled onto the bus early in the morning heading for Port Stephens to compete in the State titles. They all took turns looking after Jake. They loved having a baby on board the bus with them, he had become their mascot. Because Lilly had gone straight back to marching practice after the birth, she had slimmed down quickly and was feeling great.

CHAPTER 11

1991

Lilly had entered into the New South Wales Sports Girl Awards run by the Royal Blind Society. The awards were held to recognise the valuable role women play in promoting sport in their local area. Lilly was excited to be representing her sport of Marching, and with the help of her teammates, friends and family set about raising awareness and much-needed money for the Royal Blind Society. Lilly had approached local businesses to donate goods so that they could raffle them to raise money, she also held meat raffles at the Kempsey Bowling Club, as well as a barefoot bowls day and a disco.

After many months of fundraising, she was on her way to Armidale for the regional judging, Trevor was driving as she sat nervously looking out the window. Trevor could sense her distress, as much as she loved being on stage in front of people performing it still made her nervous. "You're going to be great honey," he reached over and took her hand. "They will love you, just do your best, that's all you need to do" he squeezed her hand and smiled.

"Thanks babe, if I could only stop my stomach from doing cartwheels I'll be okay."

She smiled nervously, she just had to control her nerves and she would be fine. Seven other contestants were waiting when she arrived at the club where they would be judged. First, they had a fifteen-minute interview with three judges asking questions about their role in their chosen sport and what they knew about the work that the Royal Blind Society did in the community. Lilly was feeling pleased with herself after her interview, she thought she had done exceptionally well. Next, the contestants would all speak for five minutes in front of an audience and the judges, then Lilly would perform a short display of her marching routine. Once everyone had finished the judges took a half hour break to decide who would be selected as the finalist from the region to compete at the final in Sydney. Lilly was speechless as her name was read out as the winner, she could not believe it, she had won and would now be going to Sydney for a week.

Lilly spent a week on the northern beaches at the Narrabeen Sports Academy with nine other finalists and twenty blind and vision impaired people, they participated in numerous activities, they went abseiling, tandem cycling, water skiing, tai chi, yoga, surfing and hot air ballooning. The finalists also had a chance to experience what it would be like to be blind or visually impaired when they were blindfolded and led around by someone or what it would be like to have a cataract or lose some of your vision by trying on glasses to replicate the disability. Lilly had a whole new appreciation for people with a sight disability now, they showed such strength and ability to take on tasks that she as a sighted person found daunting.

At the end of the week the judging took place at Kirribilli Ex-Services Club, once again they had a fifteen-minute interview with the judges and also a public interview in their sporting attire. Lilly looked smart in her yellow pleated sports skirt, long sleeve royal blue jacket with white cording and epaulettes, white gloves, long white boots laced up tight and topped off with her bright yellow Akubra hat that was specially made for the Kempsey Marching Girls team at the local factory in Kempsey. The judges only took fifteen minutes to decide the winner, Lilly was disappointed that she didn't win but was grateful for the chance to meet such lovely people and to have an experience that she would never forget.

CHAPTER 12

1993

For the past six months Lilly had been working for the local radio station selling advertising on the radio. She had just returned from the Tamworth Country Music Festival where she had conducted interviews with Keith Urban, a new upcoming star, John Williamson, Graeme Connors, Jean Stafford, Lee Kernighan and of course, her sister Ruby who was doing very well with her music. They had live feeds via phone back to the studio in Port Macquarie, and Lilly loved every minute of it. It had been a busy time over the last few months, working as a co-compare for a karaoke show two nights a week, and she was about to start co-hosting a game show with one of the local radio announcers at the Bowling Club in Port Macquarie. The game was called Go Racing. It was a lot of fun, Lilly enjoyed all her hosting jobs, she wished she had enough courage to do her own show but she doubted her ability. She was fine when she had someone beside her but found it hard to be on her own on stage.

Lilly had shoulder length curly hair and had decided to cut it all off short again, as her co-host was always playing tricks on her she decided to get him back, she rang the club saying she would not be able to host tonight, but her identical twin sister would be taking her place. She had them fooled for hours. Every week she would dress up in different fun outfits for each show, one week when it had rained for two weeks and some of the roads were being cut off by the rising water. Lilly turned up wearing a wetsuit with a big yellow inflatable duck around her belly, goggles, snorkel and flippers, another time she dressed up as Dolly Parton, even wearing her wedding dress one night.

Trevor and Lilly had set up their own karaoke show and were doing really well, they had a show two or three nights a week, sometimes four. Lilly liked doing the show but craved to do something on her own, Trevor was a good singer, but she wanted a solo show.

"Don't you think I'm good enough to sing with you?"

"That's not what I think at all Trevor, for once in my life I want something that I can do on my own." Lilly was getting frustrated trying to make Trevor see that it had nothing to do with him and was all to do with her. She had always had someone beside her on stage and she felt ready now, she wanted to do it by herself.

"So you want me to stay home and watch the kids I suppose, while you go out and enjoy yourself." Trevor was now sulking and feeling left out.

"Only if you want to, I would like you to come with me for support, it'll be fun." Lilly wrapped her arms around him "Babe it has nothing to do with you, I just want to try and do this on my own."

Trevor bent and kissed her head, he was being silly, he knew that. "Okay I understand, I'll support you if this is what you want. But I'm happy to stay with the kids, you will be amazing, you don't need me there to help you."

As well as doing her solo shows, Lilly and her friend Marcus had started a six-piece country rock band they rehearsed in the garage under Lilly's house once a week, the group was sounding great, the fiddle really set off the band. They had a few gigs booked in a couple of months but needed to learn more songs, so they had decided to start practising twice a week. Trevor was not happy, he could not understand why Lilly needed more music in her life, she was already doing two solo shows a week. How do you explain to someone who doesn't have the same passion, how much it means? Lilly knew Trevor didn't understand.

It was the bands first live performance and Lilly was feeling sick in her stomach, they had been practising for months, she had learnt all the songs, both she and Marcus would be doing some of the lead singing. Lilly was the only one in the band who didn't play an instrument so she chose a tambourine, at least she would have something in her hand. Being on stage with a band was something else. Lilly loved being up front singing, communicating with the audience, introducing the members of the group, the songs and building a rapport with the audience. It was the last song of the night, the band was buzzing with energy they'd had a great show. Lilly was finishing the show with her favourite song, as the music started and the fiddle played the long intro, Lilly lost herself in the music and the moment, her voice was full of energy, warmth and honesty, she swayed with the music, pouring out her heart and soul capturing the audience's attention. As the song came to an end, she raised her arm indicating to the band to watch for the ending as she held the last note, dropping her arm sharply as they finished together. The crowd loved it and clapped and cheered loudly, Marcus smiled at Lilly and grinned, they had done it, all the hard work had paid off.

The next day Lilly couldn't wait to see Josie to tell her about the show, she made her way up the side of the house onto the back verandah, she could hear shouting and then glass shattering as something hit the wall. Lilly froze at the back door, Josie and Bruce were having another argument, it was too late to retreat they had seen her, Bruce screamed at Josie then stormed out the front door leaving Josie in tears.

"I'm sorry Josie, are you all right?" Lilly held her friend in her arms while she sobbed, looking at the smashed wedding photo now laying on the floor with shattered glass everywhere.

"I'm sick of it Lilly, I can't do this anymore, he's having another affair, he wants me and her and who-ever else he can have. It's not the first time, he was sleeping with that other little slut from up the road, while I was in the hospital having Tammy." Josie wiped her eyes and made her way to the kitchen. "I'll make us a cuppa, how was the gig last night?"

"It was good, I wish you could have been there." Lilly knew that Bruce wouldn't let Josie go out unless he was with her. "We don't need to talk about that right now. What are you going to do?"

"I'm leaving, I'm going to go up to Grafton and stay for a while, I need to get away from him, if I stay here he will hound me." Lilly nodded, she knew what Josie meant, she had tried to end it before when she had found out about the last affair, but Bruce's constant barrage of apologies and promises to change lead her to give in and take him back, plus she had nowhere else to go and no money, Bruce controlled all the finances. Josie did leave and stayed away for two months until Bruce stopped giving her money to support her and the three children and he promised to change if she would just come home.

CHAPTER 13

SOUTH KEMPSEY 1994

Lilly had just returned from Tamworth where she had competed in the final of the Outback Club Vocal Talent Search at the West Tamworth Leagues Club. She had won her heat the week before beating nine other contestants. Ruby had encouraged her to go, she knew her little sister loved to sing, and this would be an excellent experience for her to gain some confidence. There were ten finalists and when the winner was announced they were told that it was a tough decision for the six judges as the talent was of such a high standard and that only one point separated first and second place. Lilly placed second behind a local entrant from Tamworth. It made her more determined to follow her heart and to continue to do what she was passionate about, and that was singing and entertaining.

Lilly wanted more in life for herself and her children but Trevor refused to look at any compromise. She wanted to move closer to Sydney or maybe up the coast towards Brisbane while the children were still young, to give them more opportunities as they grew up, but Trevor refused to leave Kempsey, he wanted to stay close to his family. Trevor became distant and detached and was jealous of her singing, she knew that he would never admit it, but he was. They would sometimes fight when she came home after a show.

"So who hit on you tonight?" Trevor had drunk a few beers and was not in the best mood.

"No one hit on me Trevor, I did my gig and came home. Even if someone did, I would tell them to piss off because I'm a married woman." Lilly was becoming increasingly sick of these accusations. Trevor just grunted and went back to staring at the TV. "You could come with me, you know I've never stopped you. It would be nice to have some support."

"Huh support really, that's what I do staying home watching the kids while you go out prancing around."

"Oh give me a break really, who has watched these kids all their life and you're an ungrateful child as well. You never discipline the kids, it's always left to me. I am sick of this shit Trevor, I'm done I need a break I will find somewhere else to live and I'm taking the boys, and you can keep your daughter."

"Don't be so over dramatic."

"Overdramatic. No matter what Nancy does you take her side, whenever no one is around she treats me like shit, she won't do what I ask her to do, but she is little miss perfect whenever you or your family come into the room. I am always made out to be the bad one, you all make out that I am making it up. Is it any wonder that I want to go out and do something I love without constant criticism, something I'm actually appreciated for?" She strode off into the bedroom not even giving him a chance to reply, what was the point he didn't understand anyway.

Lilly moved out taking Mark and Jake with her, she found a small two bedroom unit that had some furniture in it, a lounge, refrigerator and a double bed. She worked a few days a week and sang two nights a week, she never asked Trevor for any money, she would do it on her own. They needed time apart to try and work out what had happened to the love they had shared, they had been together for ten years, and now it seemed like she didn't know him, she wanted more from life and she didn't want to be stuck in this town the rest of her life. Lilly wanted to travel, see more of the world and give their children more chances and opportunities in life.

After much talking, Trevor persuaded Lilly to move back into their home. She was trying to make it work but her heart wasn't really in it, she knew Trevor would never move away to the city, he wanted to stay here the rest of his life, he was a great father and she did love him, she just wasn't in love with him anymore. They had drifted apart, there was too much tension in the house, with Nancy now sixteen and Lilly feeling the way she did, things had reached boiling point. She and Trevor had a major blow up once again after Lilly had been called to the school to pick Nancy up after another incident. Lilly was trying to talk reason to this rebellious teenager, and once again Nancy was yelling back at her "you're not my mum I don't answer to you" and after ten years of this Lilly had finally had enough. She told Nancy to stay out of her way, if she was not her mum she could take care of herself, don't talk to me, don't ask me to take you anywhere or do anything for you, enough is enough. After ten years together they decided to end it while they were still friends and for the sake of the children.

Trevor moved out, and Nancy went to Sydney to live with her mother. Trevor had access to the boys whenever he wanted and would take them every second weekend. They were still friends but both realised it was for the best, Mark felt it the hardest, he didn't want his parents to separate, Lilly tried to explain, but how do you explain to an eight year old why his parents don't live together?

Years later when Lilly reflected back on this marriage, she came to the conclusion that there were really no major issues with Trevor and herself, they had just fallen out of love and had different goals for the future, he was, and still is a good Dad to all of his children. Trevor gave Lilly two beautiful children and for that, she would be forever grateful.

CHAPTER 14

1995

Lilly had known Michael for over ten years, he was the local Physiotherapist in town and when she had needed treatment over the years on her knee, shoulder and other troublesome parts of her body he was the one she went to. She had been on her own as a single mother for only two months when Michael asked her out. Lilly knew he was older than her but didn't realise how much older until they had started to date. Michael was very fit, he looked after himself and was probably just a little bit vain, he loved music, surfing and his kids. Lilly had been warned that he was a bit of a ladies man, but he swept her off her feet with his charm, she thought he was quite handsome, he had a bit of a Richard Gere look going on. The first five months of their relationship was just like in the movies, lazy days in bed with the sun streaming through the window, surfing, dining out, weekends away, he was a real gentleman and treated her like a princess, opening the car door for her, bringing her flowers. Michael was intelligent, and they would have great conversations, he opened her eyes to so many more possibilities that life could offer.

Even though he was fifteen years older than her, Lilly had fallen in love with Michael. Her family and friends were dubious, they knew of his past, that he had cheated on his wife, then cheated on his next two girlfriends and even on Lilly at the very beginning of their relationship. It was in the first month of their dating, his old girlfriend had called in to visit him, he was supposed to be seeing Lilly that afternoon but he called her to tell her he couldn't make it. Joanna was still in love with Michael, she wanted him back, she had cried on his shoulder, they'd had a few drinks and ended up back in bed together. Michael begged Lilly for forgiveness, it meant nothing, just two people saying goodbye for the last time, Lilly was the only one he wanted, he promised it would never happen again. Stupidly Lilly forgave him, thinking well they had only just started dating, and he promised it would not happen again, the seed of doubt had been sown in her mind, but still she forgave him.

Lilly had been working part-time for Rentokil selling hygiene products up and down the coast, they were making cutbacks and as she was the last one employed, her job was the first to go. Michael offered her work with his film company, doing the bookwork, answering phones, helping design brochures and video covers. Michael would attend physiotherapy conferences and film the two to three-day events, he would edit his work putting together a series of videos which showed all the new treatment techniques, the expert speakers and other interesting topics, he would then market it to the physiotherapists who were unable to attend the conference. Michael also taught her how to film, using the big video cameras and how to edit the footage. She loved this, it brought out her creative side, it was also the first time she got to see a cadaver, a dead body used for science. They used these in teaching, showing the layers of muscle. Lilly had to do the close-up shots of the arm and hand of the cadaver. The arm and hand were placed behind a screen with a doctor, her footage was streamed straight up onto the screen for the two hundred plus physiotherapists in the room to watch. It was very confronting seeing someone's arm just laying there on the table knowing that once it had been attached to a living body, but she took it all in her stride and focused on the job at hand (no pun intended).

Lilly still wanted more than the little town of Kempsey, she wanted new opportunities and challenges so when Michael suggested they move to Sydney so he could be closer to his ageing mother, she jumped at the chance. Lilly packed up all of their belongings and followed him to Sydney with Mark now nine years old, and Jake was five. Michael was great with her boys, and he spent a lot of time with them, teaching them to surf and sail, they would go on hikes and explore the coastline around the northern beaches.

The thing she loved the most about Michael was that he was so supportive of everything she did, he pushed her to sing and improve her talents, he encouraged her, no matter what she did and always treated her as an equal, he loved her children and encouraged them and helped them whenever he could. Finally, Lilly thought she had found her soulmate, the man she would spend the rest of her life with.

CHAPTER 15

LORD HOWE ISLAND 1996

The plane was small, a ten seater and everyone had to be weighed along with their luggage before boarding to make the flight to Lord Howe Island, a tiny crescent-shaped island east of Port Macquarie. Michael and Lilly were on their way to a physiotherapy conference and would be filming for the business. They had been dating for almost a year now, the conference itself was only three days, and they planned to have a week here with a few days holiday before and after the convention.

Lilly looked out the window as they approached the runway on Lord Howe Island. "Oh it's so beautiful, the water looks so clear."

"It does look great, the snorkelling in the lagoon is amazing, so I've been told, with its coral reef, fish and turtles, I can't wait to get in and have a look." Michael was squeezing her hand, he loved seeing the look of wonder on Lilly's face. "Once we get settled in our room we'll go exploring, the only way around the island is on pushbikes."

They had two days before filming was to start and would try to make the most of it. Once they had unpacked they grabbed a bicycle each and headed off along the road, the island was only ten kilometres long and about two kilometres wide in the largest part. Surrounded by sandy beaches, subtropical forests and clear waters and home to seabird colonies. Along the west coast there was a sandy semi-enclosed sheltered coral reef lagoon. The south was dominated by forested hills rising up to the highest point on the island, Mount Gower, with sweeping views, with most of the population living on the north of the island. Ned's Beach in the north had calm fish and coral-rich waters.

To the southeast was the volcanic and uninhabited Ball's Pyramid island and to the north a cluster of seven small uninhabited islands. Most of the island was virtually untouched forest, with many of the plants and animals found nowhere else in the world, here was the world's southernmost barrier coral reef, nesting seabirds, and the rich historical and cultural heritage it was stunning. Lilly loved riding the bike along the tracks, smelling the fresh tropical air, the sun filtering through the trees, the sounds of birds could be heard everywhere, a soft, warm, gentle breeze stirred the leaves scattered on the track as they rode from one destination to the other.

"You know because of its size they only allow four hundred tourists at a time on the island at any one time. They ship supplies in fortnightly from Port Macquarie, it's really quite isolated here." They had stopped at the end of the road and walked up to Mount Eliza to look back at Mount Lidgbird and Mount Gower which rose to eight hundred and seventy-five metres, the highest point on the island. The two mountains were separated by the saddle at the head of Erskine Valley. "Come on, let's head back and grab ourselves a drink and watch the sunset on the beach."

The next two days were spent exploring the island, snorkelling, bushwalking, canoeing and wandering around the museum and information centre, there were not many shops on the island only a bakery, butcher, general store, liquor store, restaurants, post office a small hospital, a nine-hole golf course, lawn bowls, tennis, and a bowling club. Then it was down to work for three days, filming the conference. On the final night, they were having a group get together with sunset drinks at Ned's Beach, a sanctuary zone where recreational fishing was not allowed, but you could hand feed the fish. They were running late and had taken the track across the island through the rainforest with its overhanging tree branches, palm trees and flowers and had just come out into the clearing. Lilly could see the beach ahead of them, and the sun was just starting to set, the sky had already begun to change colour, and the clouds were turning pink.

"Hurry up Michael, we will miss the fish feeding." Lilly was in front of him, he had been fiddling around behind her.

"Lilly just stop for a minute please."

Lilly turned to see Michael down on one bended knee behind her. "Come here please, I have something I want to ask you." Lilly took a few steps back to him, he reached up and took her hand. "I love you Lilly, you have such a beautiful heart and soul, and I want to spend the rest of my life with you. Lilly will you marry me?"

Lilly was dumbfounded; she had not seen this coming at all. It was so romantic, she was in love with Michael, he treated her like a lady and made her feel special and desired. She smiled at him, bent down and kissed his lips. "Yes Michael, I will marry you."

"I don't have a real ring yet, but this will do for now." That is what he had been doing behind her, out of a blade of long thin grass he had weaved a circle to make a ring, he slipped it on her finger, stood up, picked her up in his arms and swung her around before kissing her passionately on the lips. "Well come on then we're going to be late." They laughed and ran down the path to the waiting crowd at the beach to tell them the good news.

CHAPTER 16

1997

Lilly had returned home to Kempsey the first week of January to see her beloved grandmother. Her Nana had been in the hospital for some time now, she had been fighting cancer for six months, and the disease was taking its toll on her body. Due to work commitments, it would only be a quick visit this time, she had flown in from Sydney that morning and would be leaving on the last flight that day. When Lilly entered the room she caught her breath at the sight of Loretta laying in the hospital bed, she had been a large, jovial woman and now she was almost half her size.

"Hi Nana, it's Lilly." She bent down and kissed her clammy forehead. It was so hard not to cry seeing her this way, her once vibrant, funny Nana.

Loretta opened her eyes, seeing Lilly a small smile crossed her face "hello darling, it's so good to see you."

Lilly could not contain her tears any longer, she threw her arms over her Nana and cried, she loved her so much, she had taught her many things in life, to cook, sew and crochet. But most of all to be kind to people and help others less fortunate than yourself. She had always been so proud of all her grandchildren. Now she lay here dying, and there was nothing Lilly could do to help her except to tell her how much she loved her. They chatted for a while, until Lilly could see that grandmother was getting tired.

"Nana I love you so much, I wish now I had spent more time with you in the last few years, but I will always cherish our memories. Nana this may sound selfish." Lilly's throat caught on a sob "but I don't think I can come and see you again, I can't watch you waste away to nothing, I don't want that to be my last memory of you, I want to remember you as my happy, cuddly Nana dancing around the lounge room with me."

Loretta reached up and caressed her cheek. "It's okay honey, I understand, and that's the memory I want you to have of me, don't cry, it's okay I love you too, and I am so proud of you. You can do anything you want just believe in yourself, always remember that."

Lilly's heart ached as she left, knowing that this would be the last time she would see her Nana, she knew her mother would not understand that she could not come back, Lilly knew it was selfish of her, but she could not face the thought of watching the disease take her Grandmother. She had so much admiration for her own mother who had been by Loretta's bedside every day, making her mothers last few weeks on earth as comfortable as possible. Lilly knew if or when the day came, she would care for her mother with as much love and attention as her own mother was now doing for her mother.

Lilly opened the letter that had arrived that morning from her mother, she knew that she may not be

able to make it to her wedding and tears fell on the
pages as she read.

Dear Lilly,

*I received your invitation today and it's with regret
that I will not attend your wedding. What I have to say
I would like to do personally but circumstances prevent
that. Out of respect and love for my mother, I cannot go.
At present all is unknown, by the fourteenth your Nan
may have passed on or may still be here, we don't know.
Either way, I just can't plan anything at present just as
I wake each day, that is all I can count on.*

*One of us has to be with Nan all the time now as she is
so frail. To look after her, make sure she doesn't fall, give
her her medication, even give her a shower. I think that's
when it really hit home for me. Life has come a full
circle. I now have to do for my mum all the things she
did for me when I was a baby. I hope my love you never
have to experience the hurt and helplessness of watching
your mother slowly die. To see the hurt and pain in her
face. I'd love to be able to put my arms around her to
make it all better, to take the hurt away as she did for
me but I can't, so all I can do is to be with her, clean,*

get her meals etc. We will not let her last days, weeks be lonely.

I'm sorry I cannot be there to share the joy of your marriage, but you, I, everyone has their life ahead of them. Days, years. Nan has days, maybe a few weeks and I feel that everything else can wait, her needs can't. It's a time to put our own selfish needs and wants aside and to give love and care to the one who has the most need of it.

I know you will be upset by this letter, but this is how I feel. I love you as always, but there are times in our lives when our priorities and love have to be put in order. I love you, love all my children, grandchildren, my husband, my parents and because I love you all there are times because of one's special needs others are left behind for a while.

I hope you can understand my feelings. This is a very hard time and until it happens to you it's hard to understand. The one secure love and part of your life is going.

Bye for now my love, my thoughts and love will be with you.

Mum xxx

Lilly wept, she loved her Nana so much and wished to see her again but could not face seeing her wasting away and so close to death. She felt selfish that she was happy and that her life was going on while her Grandmothers was about to end. Lilly had an over-whelming love, respect and admiration for her mother and understood completely why she would be unable to be there.

It was Valentine's Day, and in a few hours Lilly would marry Michael, she woke early, the sun was just peeking out above the horizon. Michael was still sleeping peacefully, his face was so serene, Lilly looked at him and her heart filled with love, she slipped silent-ly out of bed and made her way out to the verandah to watch the sunrise over the ocean. Bright streaks of red, pink, and orange slowly overcame the dark blue and purple of the twilight sky with radiant colours, it's brilliant rays already shined brightly, Lilly marvelled at the glistening reflection of the sun on the ocean, and a thrilling feeling of awe swept over her. The air felt fresh and new, a gentle breeze caressed her skin, she was cast in crimson, bathed in a rosy glow, she closed her eyes and smiled and felt a cosiness to her core, what a glorious day to get married.

"Good morning beautiful." Michael had awoken and slipped up behind her silently wrapping his arms around her waist and kissed her neck, resting his chin on the top of her head. "Wow that view is stunning, it's like a flower opening." They stood silently, mesmerised by the beauty of a new day starting.

Lilly and Michael were married on the Mona Vale Headland with their close friends and family around. They arrived together in an old kombi with surfboards on the top, Michael wore black pants and a loose white cheesecloth shirt with long sleeves. Lilly wore a full-length hippy style dress in white with lace and ribbons, long flowing sleeves, with a fitted bodice and ribbons laced up at the back, her dark hair was pulled up with small wisps of hair framing her face and a garland of bright coloured flowers in her hair. The ceremony was short and emotional, then photos were taken on the headland with the beach in the background before the wedding reception at the surf club with the most amazing views across the surf and ocean. They flew to Tasmania for their honeymoon, hired a car and stayed in quaint bed and breakfast hotels for ten days while exploring the beautiful island.

They had moved into their own unit overlooking Mona Vale beach two weeks before the wedding and still had some work to do renovating. Lilly continued to work in the film company while Michael had set up his physiotherapy clinic nearby, he also worked at the hospital taking patients through exercises in the hydrotherapy pool. Jake had settled into this new life well, but Mark was having trouble adjusting and fluctuated between living with his mother in Sydney and his father in Kempsey. In March Loretta lost her battle with cancer and passed away leaving her mother, Lilly and the family devastated, but Lilly was determined to live up to her Grandmother's belief in her.

It was a shock to Lilly when her mother told her of the secret that Loretta had kept all these years about her mother's real father. Lilly was so excited to hear the news that they had finally accepted her mother as their sister and wanted to meet her. Lilly filmed her mother, sister and brother and their families and where they lived putting together a video introducing the Australian family to their new Italian family.

Lilly worked full time in the video production business taking and filling orders filming and editing, as well as singing every now and then in the clubs around Sydney. Jake and Lilly would also work as extras on television shows and movies. Lilly had scored a job on Mission Impossible 2 and had late night starts filming at The Rocks in Sydney, on the second night during one take she was bumped from behind just as the director yelled cut, turning she found herself face to face with Tom Cruise he smiled and turned walking back to his start position. When the film came out, there was only a quick shot of her from behind at the fire, but she didn't care it was fun, the pay was good, and she met some interesting characters on set.

It was New Year's Eve, Lilly and Michael sat cuddling on the outside balcony on the old wooden church pew that once had pride of place on her grandparents' verandah, she had sat on it almost every day of her childhood until the age of fourteen with her Pa. They sat silently reflecting on the past year. Lilly looked out over the ocean, the moon was rising above the water with a silver glow like a great luminous pearl, and the light shimmered on the waves as they rolled into the shore. The night was still, and she could hear the waves crashing on the beach mixed with the sounds of laughter and music from the houses nearby, celebrating another year coming to an end. What a year it had been, getting married, losing her Grandmother, her Mum finding out that her father was actually an Italian Prisoner of War and finding his family in Italy, her Dad having a heart attack and thankfully recovering. What a rollercoaster ride of highs and lows it had been, she looked up to the stars and sent love to her grandparents up in the heavens, whom she was sure were looking down on her and guiding her through life.

CHAPTER 17

1998

Lilly and Ruby were so excited and a little apprehensive as they stood with their mother outside on the viewing platform at Sydney International Airport. Their mother was about to board a plane for Italy to meet her Italian family in person, but first, she had booked a tour in Italy. Rose had only ever been on short one hour flights from Port Macquarie to Sydney, now she was going on a twenty-two hour flight to the other side of the world on her own. Her Italian lessons had paid off, and while she would not consider herself fluent in the language, she hoped she could understand and speak enough to get by.

"I can't believe you're doing this Mum, you've never been out of the country, and your first trip is alone to the other side of the world and you're taking a tour. Make sure you keep your passport safe and send a message when you get there." Lilly was almost in tears, she was excited her mother was going to meet her family in Italy, but she was going alone.

"Yes Mum, make sure you call us when you get there, you know we will worry about you." Ruby also was in tears.

"Stop worrying you two, I will be fine, I'm a grown woman and I will manage, besides the first week I am on a guided tour, and the next four weeks I will be with the family. Lucky I have learned a little of the Italian language and way of life, I can understand "poco" she laughed, and hopefully by the time I get home I will know a bit more."

Rose's flight had just been called for boarding, the girls embraced their mother again, kissed her and wished her well, she turned and headed down the walkway to customs, she stopped and turned, waved to her two crying girls and called "ciao" before taking the steps towards finally meeting her new family.

"I can't believe she is doing this and alone, I hope she will be alright." Lilly sniffled.

Ruby put her arm around her little sister trying to comfort her, but she too was apprehensive about her mother's trip. "She'll be fine Lilly, just remember all the things she has done in her life and what she has had to endure and overcome, our Mum is one strong woman." They waved a final goodbye as their mother disappeared behind the customs door.

Lilly had listened to her mother's tales of Italy over the past few months, and the fun she'd had with the family and how welcoming they were and had decided that she too would visit. Now she and Michael were about to land in Paris on the first leg of their journey. This was Lilly's first big overseas trip, and she was so excited to be going to France then Italy where she would meet the Italian family for the first time. They spent three days in Paris exploring and wandering the streets, hopping on and off the double-decker bus doing all the touristy things. They took the elevator up the Eiffel Tower to the second-floor viewing deck and admired spectacular views over Paris. Notre-Dame the famous cathedral, a masterpiece of Gothic architecture, a walk through the Louvre, home to Leonardo da Vinci's Mona Lisa, then a show at the Moulin Rouge where they enjoyed a French feast and fine Champagne while waiting for the show to start. The atmosphere crackled as the curtains opened to reveal an exuberant troupe of showgirls, dancers and musicians, Lilly sat mesmerised by the dazzling spectacle of drama, and dancers performing compelling choreography. Then they picked up their hire car and headed out of the city to Lyon, across the border into Switzerland to Geneva, a city situated along the banks of Lake Geneva at the foot of the Alps. Next stop was the seaside town of Nice for four days where they walked the iconic beachfront promenade, swam in the Mediterranean and soaked up the sun at the public beach. A day trip to Monaco, where the tour they had booked to the Old Town of Monte Carlo included free time to see the palace, the changing of the guard, the cathedral and the Cousteau Oceanographic Museum. They drove on the famous roads used for the Formula One Grand Prix. At Casino Square, they wandered the shops, marvelled at the stunning gardens and mega-yachts in the harbour and watched the beautiful people at play. A trip to Cannes where the film festival is held each May where stars pose in tuxes and full-length gowns on the red carpet. A walk among the designer bars, couture shops and palaces ofLa Croisette, there was so much wealth and glamour in this city with Ferraris and Porsches and celebrity-spotting on the beaches lined with sun-loungers, and marvelling at the liner-sized yachts moored at the port.

After two weeks in France it was time to head for Italy, across the border into Genoa, Italy's largest seaport, then up to Verona and finally to Ronco All'adige to meet the family. Lilly had called Angelica from Verona to let them know they were on their way, as they pulled into the street Lilly could feel the excitement building, she was about to meet her aunts and uncles for the first time, she did not understand much Italian so it would be interesting to communicate with them. Outside the house were people waving and clapping as they pulled up, Lilly recognised Angelica straight away from the photographs her mother had shown her. They were greeted warmly with much hugging and kissing and Marcus, Rosa's son translated for them. Lilly and Michael spent four days with the family enjoying the sites of Verona, a trip to Gardaland an amusement park, they took them to a local bar for dinner one night, and Lilly got up and sang with the Karaoke much to everyone's delight. On their last evening, they had a party with all the family there, and everyone ended up in the small swimming pool fully clothed, there was much love and laughter for these two families meeting for the first time. Lilly was sad to leave, she felt very at home here, but they must continue on their trip to Rome for three days then home to Sydney, just like her mother Rose she promised to return again one day.

CHAPTER 18

MONA VALE 1999

Mark's grades at school were not the best, his teacher had told Lilly he was a very bright boy but was easily led by others and talked a bit too much in school, he needed a stronger hand. Lilly had spoken with Trevor, and they agreed that Mark had to stop moving between them, Lilly had enrolled Mark in a boarding school in Goulburn for the start of year seven, she knew he would find it hard being away from family and she hated doing it, but she only wanted the best for her son. Trevor was in no position to help pay the school fees, so Lilly worked three jobs to cover the cost. The day she left him at the school and drove away was one of the hardest days she would ever face, watching the sad, bewildered lonely face of her eldest child staring at her as she drove away was torture, she cried all the way back to Sydney wondering if she was doing the right thing. Leaving him behind reminded her of when her mother and father left her alone with her brother on the farm at the age of fifteen and how she hated her father for leaving them, she just hoped that Mark would not hate her for this. It was hard on Mark, and he struggled the first three weeks with no contact with his mother. This was done to all the boys to help them adjust, or that is what the principal told Lilly, she thought it was mean not being able to speak with her son. Lilly would phone every other day to check on him, and when finally they were allowed to see him, they drove the two hours from Sydney to Goulburn to pick him up for the weekend.

The first term of school was coming to an end, and Mark's grades had improved dramatically, the teachers were all impressed with him. Mark seemed to have settled in well and enjoyed the sports and outings. Lilly knew it would be hard when he came home for the school holidays, she called Trevor and made him promise that no matter what, Mark would return from Kempsey after his week with his father and go back to boarding school, they had to keep a united front and stick together. Mark refused to come home from his fathers and would not go back to boarding school. Trevor had told Mark he didn't have to go if he didn't want to. Lilly had come to the end of her rope with both Mark and mostly Trevor for not sticking with their decision, enough was enough, she begged Mark to come back but to no avail.

"Okay Mark if that's your decision to stay with your father, I can't force you to come home. I am disappointed though."

"I'm old enough to make my own decisions Mum, and I'm not going back to boarding school. Dad said I don't have to, I can stay here with him."

"Fine, but I'm sick of you changing your mind every three months and going backwards and forwards between us. If you choose to stay with your father and not go back to boarding school, do not ring me in three months wanting to come home. If you stay now with your father you will stay with your father until you finish school, do you understand?"

"Yes, that's fine I don't want to go back anyway, I'd rather be here with my cousins and friends, I don't like Sydney. I do love you Mum, and Jake."

"I love you too son, put your father on the phone please," Lilly told Trevor precisely what she thought of him for backing down again and giving in to their eldest son. She was upset that he was not supporting her, but that was the way he had always been so why would he change now? Lilly made it quite clear that if Mark stayed now, that he would remain with Trevor and his girlfriend until he finished high school in four years. Lilly knew what would happen, they had been doing the same thing for the last few years, someone had to take a stand and stop it, and she knew it wouldn't be Trevor, so once again she had to take the hard line, she had to be the bitch.

Michael glanced over at Lilly frowning. "Don't you think you should do a bit more exercise and watch what you are eating. You seem to have put on a bit of weight lately" he was getting ready to go down to the ocean pool for his daily swim, he took great care of his body, he swam daily, surfed and ate well, he was very fit.

"I'm not overweight Michael, I'm curvy, I don't think there is anything wrong with my body." Lilly had listened to his criticisms for the last few months and was starting to feel uneasy with her body. At five feet two inches she was not tall, she was curvy and had a bit of a stomach, but she certainly was not overweight as Michael suggested.

"Well I'm going for a swim, I'll see you in an hour. Or you could always come with me and do some laps that will help burn off some of that extra weight."

Lilly was almost in tears, she didn't bother answering him and turned back to the fruit salad she had been cutting up, she heard the door close behind him as he left, over the last two months his constant subtle jibes about her weight had begun eating away at her. Lilly had noticed a change in Michael in the last few months, he was not as loving as he used to be and had become a bit secretive as well, sometimes cutting off phone conversations when she walked in the room, this did not help her insecurities at all. She remembered the cautioning words from her family and friends, that once a cheater always a cheater, but she believed he loved her enough not to do that to her. His ex-girlfriend Joanna had come to live in Sydney which added to her worries, he had cheated on her with Joanna in the first month of their relationship and she had forgiven him, but all her fears came flooding back. He had even met with Joanne and taken her to his mothers for lunch, Michael had not told Lilly about it, and she found out inadvertently from his mother who thought she knew and had made a comment about how good Joanna was looking. Michael's reaction when she confronted him was to say that he didn't have to tell her about everyone that he caught up with and he would see whomever he wanted and that she would just have to deal with it and get over her jealousy. Lilly didn't like the fact that they had caught up a few times and he never took her with him when they met, he would always tell her she should trust him, but how could she? She was becoming more jealous and untrusting which caused fights, she kept asking him to understand why she felt like she did, but he told her to "get over it" and stop throwing the past in his face.

Lilly was now working for a newspaper selling advertising in the local area as well as the occasional singing gig around Sydney, Michael had stopped coming to her shows and preferred to stay home instead. Jake was now nine and was doing well at school and loved his sport. Mark was still unsettled and still lived in Kempsey with his father and his girlfriend, as predicted he had wanted to come back a few months after he had refused to go back to boarding school, but Lilly had stood her ground, she felt terrible and as hard as it was, she had to show him that actions have consequences. Lilly missed Mark terribly but they clashed all the time, he was very much like her, determined, strong- willed but also very sensitive. Michael's approach often annoyed her even though he was great with her children he was very adamant about how children should be raised. That children should do as they were told, she had wanted to keep the peace with him, and that was why she had allowed Mark to go, but she felt so bad, she had put her husband before her own son, something she would end up regretting for a very long time.

Lilly had been having complications with taking birth control and had asked Michael to have a vasectomy after all he was fourteen years older than her and was adamant he wanted no more children. He had refused and talked her into having her tubes tied, this caused much more pain and suffering than the pill ever had, and Lilly was constantly ill and unable to work, some days she would end up in bed all day in pain. After putting up with constant pain and periods every few days and after seeing several doctors she was told that the only thing that may fix the problem was a hysterectomy, so at the age of thirty-five she underwent surgery.

They had been fighting a lot lately over silly things, she knew he was upset with his video business not working as well as he had hoped, and he had finally shut it down. At least when they fought he never said nasty, hurtful things, but he did make her feel inferior at times, whether it was unintentional, she was unsure, but her self esteem had taken a battering and she started to diet and exercise to lose weight so he would be happy and satisfied with her. Lilly would do anything to make this marriage work; she did not want to fail again. It had been a year of ups and downs but at least the year would end on a fantastic note. New Year's Eve Lilly had the best view of the fireworks, as she sang on one of the boats cruising on Sydney Harbour for the night, Michael came with her and as they stood on the deck watching the fireworks light up the night sky, he cuddled her and whispered in her ear how he loved her, maybe everything would be just fine after all.

CHAPTER 19

SYDNEY 2000

Lilly had just passed her motorbike licence test, and she couldn't wait to see her friend Jackie and tell her, they would often go for day rides out of the city up the back roads and had been planning a weekend away as soon as Lilly passed her test. Today was Jackie's birthday, and Lilly was going to surprise her with flowers and a bottle of wine and the good news. She knocked on the door and waited, she could hear noise from inside, it sounded like someone was crying. Lilly knocked again "Jackie are you there? Are you all right?" The door opened and her friend was standing before her dishevelled, crying her eyes out, Lilly reached for her "Jackie what's happened?"

They sat on the lounge and once Jackie had stopped sobbing and could talk, she told Lilly that she had found out her husband of twenty-five years Andrew had been cheating on her. She had confronted him and he had come clean, the affair had been going on for over a year, he told her he loved her, but he also loved the other woman. Jackie told him to get out, and he had only just left five minutes before Lilly had arrived. Lilly sat silently holding her dear friend, what could she say that would make this better, nothing could, she just needed to listen and help her friend through this. Lilly wondered if Michael knew about the affair. He was good friends with Andrew and they often went out together fishing, surfing or having lunch and had also had a few boys' nights. Lilly had an uneasy feeling about this, it bought her insecurities back to the surface.

"Let's go away for a couple of days riding the bikes like we planned, let's do it next weekend we could go down to Wollongong to the Buddhist temple maybe stay a night there, just us girls."

"Hmm I don't know," she thought for a moment "it would be good to get away, leave it all behind, the wind in our face, the freedom" Jackie smiled through her tears "what will people say about us two "old girls" on bikes?" They laughed at the image.

The following weekend, they packed up, jumped on their bikes and headed south out of Sydney. They turned off into The Royal National Park with its winding roads and beautiful forests, their first stop was Bald Hill, one of the world's best hang gliding locations. They parked their bikes and walked over to the cliff edge to watch the colourful hang gliders, they would start at the top of the slope jogging down to be suddenly lifted on the rising thermal air, gracefully moving around floating in mid-air, soaring above the sea, coastline and escarpment. The view from here was truly amazing from the steep drops, long coastline and beaches to the small town of Stanwell Tops. Lilly wanted a photo, so she pulled out the camera she had borrowed from Jake and asked one of the big leather-clad bikers who had also pulled up there to take a photo, he obliged and laughed when he saw the camera it was fluoro green camera with Bart Simpson's face on the front around the camera hole.

Back on their bikes, they headed down through Wollongong to their destination for the night, the Nan Tien Temple. The Nan Tien was one of the world's largest Buddhist temples in Australia with massive prayer halls, an eight-level pagoda and beautiful oriental gardens. They would be sleeping here for the night and taking part in some meditation, trying to find some calm and inner peace. They wandered around the temple marvelling at the architecture; it had been built using traditional techniques and materials by Chinese craftsmen, but with numerous modern features and it was set amidst award-winning landscaped gardens. The main halls had thousands of tiny statues of Buddha on the walls and the building housed large ceremonial bells. They were chatting and giggling about their adventure so far while waiting to be booked in for their retreat.

"Okay I have you booked in for the Peace Retreat, you will be sleeping in a dormitory with ten others, meals are vegetarian, and once inside there will be no talking for twenty-four hours, you will be taught meditation to help bring peace and calm into your life." The receptionist looked up at them smiling.

"You mean we can't talk at all?" Lilly didn't think she would be able to go that long without uttering a single word when she looked at Jackie. "What do you think?"

Jackie laughed "Us two being quiet for that long, that will never happen, come on let's get out of here."

"Okay let's go to Kiama for the night, we can get a room and have dinner then cruise around the markets tomorrow, you'll love it Jackie it's a beautiful seaside town."

"Lead the way, I feel a wine calling me."

They weren't having much luck getting accommodation for the night, the town was almost booked out. Finally they came across a pub that had one room left, the owner looked them up and down and smiled. "Well ladies the room's yours if you want it, it's a double bed and a single you don't mind sharing?"

Lilly knew what he was thinking, two women on bikes dressed in leathers. "That's fine we'll take it." They parked their bikes in the shed out the back and made their way to the room, once the door was closed they burst out laughing. "He thinks we are a couple, that's so funny." Lilly fell on the double bed causing the headboard to hit the wall making a loud thud, she jumped a few times making it bang the wall and started moaning, "Oh Jackie, yes Jackie."

"Stop it Lilly." Jackie fell on the single bed in fits of laughter.

They had an enjoyable meal with a few too many wines at one of the restaurants in the main street before stumbling back to their room and falling into a dead sleep. The next day they spent the morning wandering through the markets, the picturesque café scene set amid historic buildings housing unique shops, then rode out to the lighthouse and the famous Blowhole before heading back up the highway to Sydney and reality. Jackie had decided to give Andrew another chance, after all, they had been married for over twenty-five years and he was doing everything to win her back; he had told her the affair had really meant nothing. Lilly was sceptical; she hoped for her friend's sake that he was being truthful.

The Olympics were being held in Sydney this year, the city was abuzz with excitement. They sat and watched the opening ceremony on tv waiting to see who had been chosen to light the Olympic flame. It was Cathy Freeman, clad in her famous lycra suit. In 1990 she became the first Aboriginal sprinter to win a gold medal at the Commonwealth Games as a member of the 4 x 100 metres women's relay team, she had won two world championships, in 1997 and 1999 and was the favourite to win the gold medal in the women's four hundred metre race. Cathy ascended the staircase and stood atop a pool of water with the torch raised above her head, she lowered the torch to the pool and lit a flame that surrounded her, the ring of fire rose from the water and started to make its way upwards to meet the cauldron at the top of Olympic stadium, it was just above her head when it stopped. It seemed like an endless amount of time before finally moving and completing its journey, lighting the cauldron to signify the start of the games. Cathy Freeman went on to win the final of the women's 400-metre race, metres ahead of her closest rivals, wearing her iconic silver, yellow and green bodysuit paying testament to her country while her red, yellow and black sprinting shoes honoured her Aboriginal heritage. She was the first Aborigine ever to compete in the Olympics, and the first to wave the Aboriginal flag at a sporting event. This moment would become one of Australia's most famous moments in sport.

Michael had bought tickets to some of the events at Olympic Park, Michael, Lilly and Jake caught the bus out to the stadium and watched the hockey and swimming. Just walking around the park enjoying the excitement, buzz and atmosphere of an Olympic games was so much fun, meeting people from countries all around the world. It was a fantastic time, and a moment Lilly would never forget. In January she was booked to travel to Thailand to do some promotional filming for three hotels in Bangkok, Kon Kahn and Hua Hin, she would be away for twelve days, she had asked Michael to come with her, but he had said he couldn't, he had things to do. Lilly was upset, the trip was being paid for by the hotels it would not have cost them anything, and it would have been good to have a holiday together, things had been a bit rocky between them lately. It was five days to Christmas, and they were going back to Port Macquarie tomorrow to spend a week catching up with family and friends. Michael and Lilly had argued that morning, and he told her to go on her own, he needed space and time to think. Lilly packed the bags and Jake into the car and headed for the highway she had only driven half an hour and was too upset to continue on the five-hour drive, so she decided to turn around and go back, she needed to try to talk to Michael. He was not in their unit, but she could see his car at his clinic at the bottom of the hill, so she left Jake inside watching tv and walked down to talk to him. The door was locked, she used her key and opened it, she could hear soft music playing, and the lights were out, that's strange she thought.

"Don't come in here!" Michael shouted from behind the curtain.

Lilly reached up and pulled the curtain back and stood frozen to the spot, Michael was standing naked beside the massage table, on the table with a sheet pulled up to cover her naked body was one of his clients, Rachelle. Lilly had mentioned to Michael that she thought Rachelle was keen on him and they had

151

acted funny around each other whenever she was in the room, now she knew why.

"What the bloody hell is going on here?" Lilly looked from her husband to Rachelle with the realisation hitting her. "You bastard I've not even been gone an hour, and you're already in bed with someone else? How long has this been going on?" Lilly reached out and slapped him hard across the face.

"I told you not to come in, it's the first time honestly, I have feelings for her, and when we had that fight I called her to talk, and it just happened."

"Bullshit it just happened you had this planned all along, and this is why you wouldn't come to Thailand with me." Lilly turned towards Rachelle who was trying to get her clothes on as quickly as possible. "You fucking slut what does your husband think of this? Does he know?" Lilly lunged at Rachelle. She was so angry, she wanted to punch her in the face and pull her hair out, but Michael grabbed her and held her.

"My marriage is none of your concern, and my husband doesn't understand me like Michael does, besides if Michael was happy with you he wouldn't have come to me, would he?" Rachelle pulled her dress on over her head and stood defiantly looking at Lilly.

"He is married, and so are you, how could you do this to another woman, you ugly old hag, like he would want you over me."

"Rachelle get out of here, I'll call you later. I'm sorry."

"You're telling her you're sorry, I'm your fucking wife you arsehole, how could you do this to me? You promised you would never cheat on me." Lilly was trying to free herself from his grip but was not quick enough, Rachelle was dressed and running out of the door. It felt like someone had rammed a red hot knife through her heart and was turning it around and around cutting her heart out, the pain was unbearable she thought she would explode from the inside out. Michael was talking, but she couldn't hear a thing he was saying. Her rage was taking over, she grabbed the first thing in front of her which happened to be the fax machine and threw it up the wall, she ripped the curtain down, swiping things off the desk smashing everything she could. Michael tried to come to her, but she put her hand up. "Don't touch me you filthy bastard and don't speak, nothing you can say will stop this pain, and I won't believe you anyway." Lilly ran out the door and back to the unit, she rang Jackie and asked her to come over. While she waited for her friend to arrive, she stood at the edge of the balcony staring at the sea, the sun was starting to set, and the sky was changing colour to a beautiful glow of pinks, oranges and mauve reflecting off the clouds. Lilly glanced down from their third story unit at the hard concrete on the driveway below, and for a moment thought of throwing herself over the railing, ending this unbearable pain in her chest. How could he do this to her? She loved him so much. She had thought she had found the man she would spend the rest of her life with, what was wrong with her? Why wasn't she enough for him? Was this her fault? It would be so easy just to fall, but the only thing stopping her were her two beautiful boys, she could not do that to them? She had family and friends that loved her, and it would devastate them if she jumped, no man was worth it. There was a knock at the door, Jackie had arrived to comfort her friend, she knew all too well about the pain she was going through. Michael came a short time later and sat on the lounge waiting for Lilly to calm down enough for him to talk with her.

The next few days were a blur, Michael had convinced her that she was the only one he loved and it had been a horrible mistake. He only wanted to be with her, and he promised it would never, ever happen again. They went to Port Macquarie as planned, and Lilly put on a brave face, keeping what had just taken place from her family and friends. She felt so ashamed and embarrassed, they'd all warned her that he would cheat on her. Had she bought this on herself with her jealousy and insecurities? She couldn't let him touch her, it made her skin crawl, and she felt sick in her stomach. Just the thought of him touching that bitch and caressing her whispering in her ear. Had he been telling her what they had talked about? She could not get the image of them naked together on the bed out of her mind. Michael was bending over backwards trying to make it up to her, but she could not forget, and now she had to go away to Thailand alone next week, leaving him at home with that woman waiting on the sidelines. This did not help her peace of mind, no matter how many times he told her that he would not see her again. She had to be strong, she had to push through, she had to hope he would stand by his word this time.

CHAPTER 20

2001

Lilly sat on the plane on her way to her first stop in Bangkok, Thailand. Her mind was in turmoil, and even though Michael had promised her it was over with Rachelle, she could not trust him. What choice did she have? She would be away working for two weeks, maybe it would give her time to reflect and collect her thoughts and decide if she could ever forgive him or even trust him again. Lilly found it hard to concentrate on her job filming promotional videos for the three hotels she had been contracted to, her days were busy with filming and a little sightseeing in

Bangkok, Khon Kaen then Hua Hin. Thailand was a beautiful country, and the people were so helpful and friendly, Lilly wished she could enjoy her time there instead of the destructive thoughts going through her head. She spoke to Michael almost every day, and he kept reassuring her that he was being faithful and he missed her, but Lilly's gut instinct was telling her he was lying. The stress and worry of what he might be doing was taking its toll on her, and she hardly ate, losing weight, she felt sick all the time and could not get over the sinking feeling in her stomach.

The weeks passed relatively quickly, Michael met her at the airport with a bunch of flowers, hugging her telling her how much he had missed her, that he was so pleased she was back.

He made light conversation on the way home. "Wow you look great, you've lost weight while you've been away. Are you okay?"

"I'm as good as can be expected." Lilly stared out the window at the passing houses and people going about their daily business.

"How was the trip? Did you get all the footage you needed?"

"I think so, it was hard to concentrate with all that is going on in my mind." Lilly shot him a sideways glance. They drove the rest of the way in silence. Once inside the unit, he reached out and pulled her into his arms.

"I missed you."

"Did you really? Let me ask you something, have you seen her while I was away?" A flicker went across his eyes, and she knew he had, she pulled away from him. "Tell me the truth Michael, have you seen her?"

Michael could not look at her directly "yes I have but only to make sure she was okay. Her husband kicked her out of the house, and her children won't speak to her, I was worried about her."

"Are you kidding me? You're worried about her, what about your wife? I should be the one you are worried about, and you should be worried about our marriage. She bought this on herself playing around with a married man. Do you realise what this has done to me? Look at me Michael." He looked into her eyes, and she could see it, she knew then he had slept with her again. "You bastard, you had sex with her while I was away didn't you? When you talked to me telling me how much you loved me and asking me to trust you, it was all a lie."

"I'm sorry Lilly, it just happened, but I promise you it won't happen again."

"Really? It just happened? Your promises mean nothing to me Michael, just get away from me don't touch me, am I not enough for you? For Christ sake she's eighteen years older than me, do you want her and not me?"

"No, it's you I want. I'm sorry I just felt so bad for her, she's lost everything and it's my fault."

"You need to get your priorities right, make a choice Michael me or her? Now get out of my way, I need to get some fresh air." Lilly pushed past him and headed for the beach, she needed to clear her head, did she really want to try and save this marriage? How could she ever trust him again? The problem was she still really loved him, even though he had broken her heart and she could not imagine life without Michael in it, he had always been so supportive of her and everything she had done. It was also the fact that this was her second marriage she didn't want to fail again, how would she ever be able to face her family and friends?

As the months passed Lilly tried hard to trust Michael, she tried not to let her insecurities get the better of her and to make the marriage work. Michael was over attentive to her every need and kept reassuring her that he was not seeing Rachelle, but deep in the back of Lilly's mind she still had her doubts. Lilly and Jackie had been avoiding each other, their once close friendship had been shattered by the infidelities of their husbands, it had seemed that Michael and Andrew had been trying to keep them apart. Lilly missed her friend, so she had called her and today they were having lunch at Jackie's house. Jackie was the only person who knew of the betrayal, the only person she could talk to. Jackie had also taken her cheating husband back and was trying to make it work, but she too was struggling.

They sat out on the back deck enjoying a glass of wine and chatting when the conversation came around to their husbands. "Michael is trying really hard, and he is doing everything to make me trust him again, and he has promised me that it's over with that old cow. It will take some work but I think I can get past this." Jackie looked down at her glass and shook her head. "What is it, do you know something?" Lilly asked.

"Lilly, I've found out that Andrew is still seeing his bitch. He told me that he was going away for two days for work. I went down to the bay where we keep the boat, and he was out on it. With her, and Michael and Rachelle were with him, when I confronted him he told me the truth. Apparently our husbands are still carrying on with their lovers behind our backs and they are each other's alibi, they have never stopped seeing them."

Lilly sat staring unblinkingly at her friend, this can't be true. How could she have been so stupid? Of course he couldn't be trusted. "Are you sure?"

"Yes, I saw them with my own eyes, and Andrew admitted it to me. That's why they have been trying to keep us apart, to keep their dirty little secrets. I'm sorry Lilly but Michael's been lying to you all this time, I wanted to tell you but...... I've told Andrew it's over, I want a divorce." Jackie wrapped her arms around her friend, she knew what she was going through, no words could help, she just needed her to be there for her.

Lilly wanted to cry but she couldn't, she had shed so many tears over the past months she felt empty inside. It felt like someone was squeezing her heart tight and crushing the breath out of her. She knew this could not continue. She had to leave Michael, he would never change, he could never be faithful and the thought of him touching that woman, then coming home saying he loved her, made her feel like vomiting.

Almost a year to the day that Lilly had found him in bed with another woman, she picked up whatever dignity she had left along with her belongings, and moved out of their unit and into a three bedroom house.

CHAPTER 21

MONA VALE 2002

Lilly was working three jobs to pay the rent and support her boys, Jake had just turned eleven and Mark was fifteen, Mark who had been living with his father for the last few years had come back to live with her in the old house up on Mona Vale Headland. Lilly worked as a tour guide driving a tour bus from Sydney to the Hunter Valley two days a week. She would leave home at five am to drive across to the other side of the city to Clovelly to pick up the bus. Then drive into the city and pick up her clients and take them on a day trip to the Hunter Valley where they would visit five wineries. They would stop at a lookout in the hills before heading back to the city, by the time she dropped the bus off at the depot it was late and almost seven pm before she arrived home. She sang two or three nights a week around Sydney, as well as working at the local Marine shop in the mail order department four days a week. This left her little time to herself, Ruby's twenty-two year old daughter Liana had moved to Sydney and needed somewhere to stay so she came to live with Lilly. Liana was a great help with Lilly's two boys, her cousins, and if Lilly had to work nights or if she was late getting home Liana was there to take care of them. Liana and Lilly were close and had many fun times. Liana would make her go out to the local pub to watch a band with her and her friends trying to cheer her up after the breakdown of the marriage. They sang together and had many nights on the front balcony looking at the sea drinking wine and laughing. One night on the full moon, they took some wine and wood down to the beach and had a fire, howling at the moon and dancing around the fire.

Lilly still saw Michael occasionally, and he had told her he had started dating Rachelle, and they were now a couple, this cut Lilly to the bone that he could move on so quickly, did she not mean anything to him? Lilly wanted revenge on this bitch who had helped destroy her marriage and what better way than to give her a taste of her own medicine, not once but twice after all he still was legally her husband. Michael had called in to see her after finishing work at the hospital one afternoon, and they ended up in bed together. He made her promise not to tell Rachelle, as he was trying to make a go of it with her. As soon as he left Lilly rang Rachelle and told her what had happened and that he would never be faithful to her. Of course this upset Michael that she had betrayed him, but Lilly didn't care, his betrayal was far worse. Rachelle forgave him and told him that he could not see Lilly alone again. After a month Lilly called Michael asking could he do some physiotherapy on her shoulder and neck. Michael said he wasn't allowed to, Rachelle would not let him. Lilly made it quite clear that he was under the thumb and gutless and guilted him into seeing her so he came in to work on his day off on the Saturday afternoon.

"Thanks Michael for doing this, I have to drive the bus tomorrow, and I don't think I would have been able to." Lilly was laying face down on the treatment bed as Michael massaged her neck and shoulder.

"It's okay Lilly, but I don't think I will be able to do this again, it upsets Rachelle too much, and I am trying to make it work with her."

"Oh really? You want it to work with her but you didn't with me? How do you think that makes me feel Michael? You are still my husband by law." Lilly still loved Michael, and she knew that she could never take him back, she just wanted him to acknowledge how much he had hurt her.

"I'm sorry Lilly, I do still love you very much and I miss you all the time. If I could I would take it all back and try harder but I can't, and now I feel so bad that I've destroyed Rachelle's life with our affair. Her kids won't even speak to her now and she has no one but me." Michaels' voice choked up, and he fell silent.

Lilly lay quietly, a tear falling from her eye. She loved him so much, he had treated her like she was the most beautiful, talented, amazing woman when they were together, it was her insecurities and mistrust that helped end the marriage, but it was his betrayal that finally finished it off. As Michael massaged her she couldn't help but feel desire stirring inside her, his touch still made her tingle all over, he was the most amazing kisser and lover, and she didn't think she would ever find anyone that could do to her body what he could ever again. Michael also felt the surge of electricity that passed between them and they were caught up in the moment of lost love and lust, a final goodbye. As Lilly dressed she knew Michael would never be able to be faithful to anyone, could she ever believe anything he said to her, she knew that he loved her and he was genuinely sorry for hurting her. As they left the clinic Rachelle arrived, Lilly had wanted them to hurt as she had hurt, she wanted them both to go through the pain she had suffered. Rachelle seemed upset, it was apparent she didn't trust Michael, well how could she? She searched Michael's face then looked at Lilly.

"Hi, Rachelle we have just finished. I was just saying goodbye to Lilly."

"Will you tell her or will I Michael?" Lilly stared directly at Rachelle and smiled.

"Lilly please don't!" Michael's eyes pleaded with her.

"We just had the most amazing sex Rachelle, as you know he is good in bed," Lilly smirked at this woman in front of her, she could see the pain cross her face, now you know how it feels.

"Michael how could you? You promised me you would not sleep with her again. How could you do this to me?" Tears streamed down Rachelle's face.

Lilly laughed "How could he do this to you, he still is my husband and if you think he will ever be faithful to you, think again he is not capable of it, and now you know how it feels to have your heart ripped out?" She looked at Michael then back to Rachelle. "You two deserve each other I hope you will be very happy together, I don't ever want to see or speak to you ever again Michael." She shot a glance at Rachelle. "I'd say you wouldn't be allowed to speak to me anyway. Enjoy your day, I'm sure you have a lot to talk about." Lilly turned and walked away never looking back, sure what she had just done was cruel, but they both deserved it as far as Lilly was concerned.

Liana's boyfriend was coming down for work and would be staying the weekend, along with his boss Jeff who owned a furniture removal business and Dave one of his workers. Lilly had offered for them to stay in the boys' room as they were away at their father's for school holidays.

"You know Jeff is really cute and he is also single. He has split up with his girlfriend. Maybe you two could get together?" Liana was matchmaking.

"No I'm fine Liana, I don't want a man in my life, they are too much trouble, and they can't be trusted." Lilly could not imagine being with another man right now, not after what Michael had done to her.

"Well maybe it doesn't have to be serious, just a bit of fun, he is two years younger than you, you could have a toy boy!" Liana smiled at her and winked. "If you know what I mean?"

"I know precisely what you mean Liana and No!" Lilly laughed and gave Liana a playful smack.

Lilly had all good intentions of giving herself time to heal and not rush back into the arms of another man. She didn't need a man to be whole and worthy, but when you feel like you're not good enough and that no one would want you that's easier said than done, then along came Jeff, he was good looking, fit, charming and he made her laugh, and so the cycle began again. Jeff reversed the truck into the driveway and they all settled in for a barbeque and a few drinks. He was really cute and very polite, he made Lilly laugh and he was easy to be around, they talked late into the night, he had told her that he had separated from his ex-wife with whom he had two small children too, he had been living at his work shed for the last few months, the conversation was so easy and comfortable, they were very relaxed in each other's company, one thing led to another and they ended up in bed together, but Lilly made it quite clear she was not interested in getting into a serious relationship with anyone right now and he agreed. It was a whirlwind romance and after only three weeks Jeff was practically living with her. Whenever he could, he would stop in and stay while he was in the area working, always arriving with flowers and a big cheeky grin. Jeff treated her like a princess, Lilly would go with him on some of his delivery trips, working during the day and sleeping in the bunk in the truck.

Jeff had taken her to Port Macquarie for a few days; he wanted to show her his depot and to introduce her to his family. Lilly was sitting outside his depot drinking a cup of coffee in the sunshine while Jeff was upstairs in the office with his office manager when a black four-wheel drive pulled up and out jumped a slim dark-haired woman who made her way straight to where Lilly was sitting.

"So you're the slut who broke up my family!" she spat the words at Lilly, her eyes were full of hate.

"You must be Darla?" Lilly replied calmly.

"Yes I am, I'm the mother of Jeff's children and he would still be with our kids and me if it weren't for you." Darla was standing over Lilly shouting, her fists were clenched, and she was trembling with rage. Lilly stood up to meet her eye to eye.

"Your breakup had nothing to do with me, he had already left you when we met, don't blame me for your problems." Lilly turned to walk away, but Darla grabbed her arm and yanked her back. At that moment Jeff came out through the door, he had heard the shouting from upstairs.

Darla laughed. "Is that what he told you? He's a liar."

"Let her go Darla!" Jeff pushed himself between the two women and guided Darla away back towards the car. "Get off my property and don't come back, your issue is with me, not her." Darla argued with Jeff for a few more minutes then got into her car and drove off with tyres screeching. "I'm sorry Lilly, she just can't get it through her head that we are over."

"Tell me the truth Jeff, were you already separated when you met me and there was no chance of you getting back together?" Lilly wondered at the comment Darla had made, was it truth or just a vengeful ex wanting to cause doubts?

"Lilly there was no chance we would get back together, I don't love her anymore, I'm not sure I ever did, but we had kids together so I stayed trying to make it work." He pulled Lilly into a tight hold "don't let her get in your head, she's good at that."

Lilly had her doubts, but she had to learn to trust again and give him the benefit of the doubt. They returned to Sydney and Lilly continued to work driving the tour bus and singing, she had a singing tour coming up with another girl Cassie, they would be performing seven shows in two weeks from Sydney up to the Sunshine Coast in Queensland. Cassie was slim and a bit taller than Lilly with long blonde hair, she had been performing around Sydney in cabaret shows. They had put together a "Blondes Have More Fun" show performing songs of some great female artists, they had three costume changes, Lilly had to wear a long blonde wig. Even though Lilly was quite slim she was curvy, Darla and their manager told her she had to lose more weight for the show, Lilly refused she was proud of her curves, she told them "take me as I am or forget it".

Jeff accompanied Lilly on tour, helping with the setup and sound. He kept telling her how he loved watching her on stage performing, and he felt so proud that she was his girlfriend. A few days before Christmas and six months into their relationship they moved back to Port Macquarie into a rental house on the canals. Jake would be starting high school next year, and Lilly wanted to be settled before then, and she wanted to be closer to her family. Mark didn't want to move, he had a job now and had made some great friends, so he stayed in Sydney with Liana. Lilly was helping out in the removal business taking care of the bookwork, and she would go away with Jeff in the truck occasionally.

It was New Year's Eve, and Lilly was performing at the El Paso Hotel in town. They had booked a room for the night and had invited a group of friends to come and have dinner with them. It was a great evening and while Lilly packed her gear up Jeff disappeared back to the room, by the time she got back he was asleep on the bed, beside him was a bunch of red roses and a ring box, inside was a beautiful yellow gold ring with brilliant cut diamonds. Lilly stood staring at the box, surely he wasn't going to propose they had only been together six months.

"Jeff, wake up! Jeff, what is this?"

Jeff opened his eyes and smiled. "Sorry I was trying to stay awake, so I could do this right. I know it's only been a short time, but I love you, and I want to marry you, will you say yes?"

MARIANNE DELAFORCE

Lilly thought for a moment about the promise she had made to herself to wait, oh the hell with it, life is short. "Yes Jeff, I will marry you."

Jeff pulled her down onto the bed, placed the ring on her finger and kissed her. "You have made me the happiest guy alive."

Lilly was in love again. Jeff was so attentive, he could not do enough for her, he was romantic bringing her flowers and organising to take her out for dinner, buying her jewellery, leaving little love notes around the house and in the pockets of her clothes for her to find. Lilly started working full time in his removal company keeping the accounts, Jeff employed eight staff, had a storage facility as well as two trucks for long distance removals and a smaller truck for around town. Lilly would also go with him on some of his trips. He taught her how to fill out the inventory, and how to pre-pack household items, she also started driving larger trucks. Lilly enjoyed seeing other places and meeting people.

CHAPTER 22

Jeff wanted to marry as soon as possible so in March they had a small intimate wedding in the backyard of their rental house on the river bank. They had put up a small marquee for the reception, folded the clothes-line up and wrapped it in brown paper and placed real palm leaves at the top to make it look like a palm tree. Lilly had made all the decorations for the tables and set up the music. They arrived on a small flat pontoon boat decorated with flowers and palm leaves, and Lilly sang as they arrived. Jeff wore a dark purple suit and white shirt while Lilly wore an off white strap dress with a small train, her hair was up with a cascade of curls falling down her back and crystal hair pieces that reflected the sunlight. It was a short ceremony followed by a roast dinner and music. They danced into the small hours of the morning before finally falling into bed exhausted; they would be leaving in two days for their honeymoon.

They landed in Paris, picked up their bags and went to the metro station to await a train into the city and their hotel. As Lilly entered the train she was shoved from behind, she checked her bag, someone had stolen her travel wallet with their passports and their cash. They jumped off at the next station and reported it to the police but there was nothing they could do, this happened all the time and now they had to spend the next few days at the Australian Embassy replacing their passports. Luckily Lilly had photocopied their passports and other documents and had them in her suitcase. They would not let this setback ruin their holiday, they spent three days in Paris visiting all the "must see" tourist spots, eating fresh baguettes with cheese, tasting the local wines and sitting in the parks drinking coffee.

Then it was off to Egypt, a place Lilly had always wanted to visit, she had always been fascinated by Ancient Egypt, and now she would finally be going. They had a stopover in London for eight hours before boarding their flight, they put their suitcases into a locker at Heathrow Airport and caught the train into town. They rode a lap around the city on a double decker open top bus seeing the Tower of London, Trafalgar Square, St Paul's Cathedral, The London Eye, guards in their red and black uniforms and big fluffy hats, London Bridge and Big Ben. Crossing the river twice, they had spectacular views of London's stunning scenery along the Thames before returning to the airport for their flight to Egypt.

Lilly had organised an Egyptian sites tour for the twelve days, and they were met at the airport by their English speaking guide and taken to the hotel. Lilly was aware of the customs here and made sure she was always dressed in long sleeves and long pants or skirts to respect local traditions. The next morning they were awoken at five am by an unearthly sound, coming from the mosque calling the Muslims to prayer, it was loud and persistent, Lilly looked out the window, the smog obscured the city, Cairo was noisy and dirty. The first stop was to be the Pyramids, Lilly burst into tears when they turned the corner, and the Pyramids appeared for the first time, her childhood dream was finally a reality. The defining symbol of Egypt is The Great Pyramid of Giza, the last of the ancient Seven Wonders of the World. Cheops pyramid rose up one hundred and forty-six metres and was two hundred and thirty metres around the base, comprising of over two million blocks of limestone. It used to be covered in white limestone that shone brilliantly in the sun and would have been visible from every direction for miles around the site, but the limestone fell away a long time ago, now it was a yellow colour in a significantly weathered state, but still very impressive and mysterious. Their guide ushered them to enter the pyramid, they scrambled up the stones to the entrance and once inside made their way up the narrow passageway with some rope to hold on for balance. It was hot, dark and dusty with no ventilation, it was an eerie feeling as they made their way up inside, even a little claustrophobic, at the top of the passageway it opened into the burial chamber where the King would have been laid to rest to await the afterlife, it was built from huge blocks of granite. The spirituality of the place struck Lilly.

They walked around the Great Sphinx, a large human-headed lion carved from a mound of limestone. It was placed there to guard the tombs and temples. They had their first ride on a camel, what amazing animals they were. Over the next few days they visited Alexandria, the Roman Amphitheater, the Catacombs and the Citadel, the Cairo museum was unbelievable, there is nothing in Australia as ancient as the many historical artefacts contained in these walls. The three thousand-year-old mummies in the Egyptian museum were unwrapped; they still had some strands of hair, teeth, and fingernails. Lilly looked at the mummies of Seti I and Ramesses II, the most powerful men on the planet at one time. But physically they were so tiny about the size of a twelve-year-old confirming that size really didn't matter after all. They visited calm mosques and lively night markets, sat in a coffee shop trying the robust bitter coffee watching the men play backgammon, dominos, and smoked a shisha, a water pipe with flavoured molasses-based tobacco, the smell was wonderful it was like incense.

Their next stop was Aswan; they were delayed for three hours at the airport because of a massive dust storm and the lack of visibility. It was eerie to see so many men and young boys standing around inside the airport with guns, the war had broken out in Iraq only weeks earlier, and a lot of people had cancelled their trips to Egypt for fear of safety but at no time during their stay did they feel threatened. Finally arriving in Aswan, they visited the High Dam, the Philadelphia Temple and the unfinished Obelisk. Then to Abu Simbel and the Great Temple of Ramesses II standing thirty metres high and thirty-five metres long with four seated colossi flanking the entrance, two to each side, depicting Ramesses II on his throne; each one twenty metres tall, beneath these were smaller statues. Lilly stood staring up at these massive statues in awe the sheer size was astounding and to think these had been built so long ago without modern technology was a monumental feat, inside was just as impressively decorated with engravings.

The Small Temple stood nearby at the height of twelve metres and twenty-eight metres long. Colossi across the front facade also adorned this temple, three on either side of the doorway, depicting Ramses and his queen Nefertari at the height of ten metres. The prestige of the queen was apparent; females usually were represented on a smaller scale than the Pharaoh but at Abu Simbel, Nefertari is rendered the same size as Ramesses. The temples were aligned with the east and twice a year, on 21 February and 21 October, the sun shined directly into the sanctuary of The Great Temple to illuminate the statues of Ramesses and Amun.

What was even more amazing was that in the 1960's when the Aswan High Dam had been built on the Nile that the government undertook to move these temples from their original place to higher up so the rising water would not submerge them, it took over four years to dismantle and rebuild them up on the plateau. Lilly and Jeff watched a short film at the entrance of the temples on how the project had been completed. The temples were sawn into blocks, the cuts were made to be least noticeable when reassembled. The interior ceilings and walls were suspended from a supporting framework of reinforced concrete. When the temples were reassembled, a mortar of cement and desert sand were used in the joins. It had been done so discreetly that today it was impossible to see where the joins were made. Both temples now stand within an artificial mountain made of rubble and rock, supported by two vast domes of reinforced concrete.

At the end of the week they embarked on a three day cruise heading for Luxor on the Nile, the world's longest river, Lilly was up at dawn on the top deck, the breeze felt fresh and clean and everything was wet, from the handrails to shining green foliage on the riverbanks as they glided along the Nile. Disembarking along the way at Kom Ombo temple, it was a double temple that's devoted half to Horus and half to the crocodile god Sobek. This stretch of the river used to be infested with vicious crocs, preventing locals from using the water to wash or cook – this temple was a way of appeasing them. The cruise along the river was beautiful with palm trees, bougainvillaea flowers, sugarcane and wheat fields, mud huts and happy smiling people waving from the banks as they watered their stock on the river's edge, a lone fisherman rowing slowly home, oars cutting cleanly into the water. They laid back on sun lounges on the top deck relaxing and watching the world float by; the scenery would change from green on the riverbanks to dry, yellow hills and the air was hot and sometimes heavy with dust. A stop at Karnak Temple with its intricately carved pillars, obelisks and walls, the sheer scale of this ancient temple complex gave Lilly a shiver down her spine. Their guide told them that the main area was the earthly home of the Egyptian sun god Amun-Re, and the temple is the largest religious building ever built. Soon they would be in Luxor; they enjoyed a refreshing drink on the top deck under the shade enjoying the last of the cruise catching glimpses of men sitting on plastic chairs in the blazing sun, enjoying their coffee and smoking a shisha pipe.

At Luxor, they sailed between the east and west bank of the Nile on a felucca, a traditional wooden sailing boat. In ancient times, the east bank, the first to see the morning light, was the home of the living and the west bank of the Nile, where the setting sun's last rays touched over the golden sands of the desert, was seen as the home of the dead. They travelled in an air-conditioned van to the hills west of Luxor to the Valley of The Kings; the valley was known to contain at least sixty-three tombs and chambers. From the outside, the tombs looked plain, simple entryways carved into the rock, but once they stepped inside, they were decorated with scenes from Egyptian mythology, hieroglyphics and interesting scenes carved into the walls. Many of the ancient temples they had visited had only small specks of paintwork left on them, but here inside the tombs that had not seen the sunlight, there were bright paintings of birds, snakes, boats and many other symbols still in vibrant shades of red, yellow, blue and white. Inside the burial chamber of King Tutankhamun, the room was coloured a vibrant yellow with different paintings on the four walls of the pharaoh showing from his death to his afterlife journey.

They arrived at Deir el-Bahri with its dramatic rugged limestone cliffs which rose almost three hundred metres above the desert plain and at the base, beneath the peak of the mountain was the dazzling

Temple of Queen Hatshepsut, she was the second historically-confirmed female pharaoh. The temple itself was almost modern looking and blended in beautifully with the cliffs from which it had been partially cut into. Entering the complex through the great court they could see original ancient tree roots still visible as the guide described how it used to look in the Pharaohs' time, Lilly could imagine people wandering around in here going about their daily business, the beautiful gardens and palm trees, ponds and water features.

At the entrance to Luxor Temple sat two enormous seated figures of Ramses II, they wandered around taking a close look at the beautiful carvings of people clapping, beating drums, dancing and performing acrobatics, while boats are carried to the Nile under the shouted instructions of captains and the remains of frescoes, belonging to the Roman Imperial cult. They strolled through the markets with all their brightly coloured clothing, spices and ornaments. Stopping to buy mementos of their trip and enjoying a meal of Fiteer, an Egyptian type pizza made from thin layers of flaky pastry and stuffed with different ingredients and cooked in a brick oven before heading back to Cairo to fly to Venice, Italy for the start of their two- week Italian holiday before heading home.

They wandered the streets of Venice for two days immersing themselves into the atmosphere and the magic, walking labyrinth-like streets and the quiet lanes, crossing quaint bridges, admiring the goods in unique stores, sipping coffees in a tiny square listening to the beautiful sounds of Italian music and admiring the ornate buildings with arched walkways. The Grand Canal was alive with energy, from the gondolas full of tourists to the water buses chugging along and the beautifully crafted timber taxi boats giving a feeling of the luxury of times gone by. They visited the beautiful Rialto Bridge which spans the Grand Canal, St Mark's Square, the most famous piazza where several important buildings were also located. St. Mark's Basilica with its ornate detail, sculptures and artwork of the front facade and beautifully painted frescoes and Byzantine works of art on the inside of the domed ceiling, the pink and white marble building of Doge's Palace with its grandeur as well as its sumptuous decorations, marble sculptures, reliefs and oil paintings.

Two days passed quickly, and they were soon on a train heading to Verona in Northern Italy at the foot of the Lessini Mountains on the River Adige. They would be meeting up with Lilly's Mum Rose and Liana who had also arrived to see the Italian family. The four days spent here with their Italian family was fun and a highlight of the trip. It was amazing to meet them all and get to know them. The family took them on a tour into the ancient city of Verona with its cobbled streets, ancient buildings to see the Colosseum and the famed Juliet's balcony.

Jeff hired a car and with Lilly in the front, Rose and Liana in the back they set out to explore the surrounding countryside. Jeff was a competent driver but really had to concentrate, as now he was driving on the opposite side of the road to what he would normally drive back home. Once he turned from the main road onto a smaller country road and found himself confronted by a car coming straight at him, he was on the wrong side and with three screaming women in the car he pulled off onto the grass. When they had calmed down, they all laughed seeing the funny side of what could have been a catastrophe. They passed vineyards, cypresses, olives, cherry trees, persimmons and traditional marogne dry-stone walls, hilltop villages and historic villas. The surrounding hills were green, and on the top of the nearby alpine mountains, they could see snow. They got lost and ended up somewhere on a small country road in the Alps, joking that they would soon be in Switzerland. It even snowed a little while they were there, the family had organised a party for Lilly and Jeff, a late local wedding reception. There was so much laughter, dancing, food and vino and on finally retiring to bed they found that their bed had been short sheeted and filled with pasta, Mama's sister Angelica was a prankster.

Lilly was sad to say goodbye to the family, but they had to continue on their trip. They drove down through the mountains and stopped at Florence and then onto the leaning tower of Pisa before driving into Rome where they got lost and drove around and around in circles before finally finding their way and dropping the car off. They explored the city for two days on the hop on and off tourist bus at all the main attractions before flying to Sicily, landing in Palermo with its Norman architecture surrounded by what's left of ancient walls that once surrounded the city. The islands scenery was inspiring, surrounded by turquoise seas, views of craggy mountains, ancient Greek and Roman ruins and mediaeval towns, the smell of orange blossom, oregano and mint, they enjoyed a local meal at a small fishing village and tasted Marsala's most famous product a sweet dessert wine, before wandering around its gracious squares. The highlight was the view of Europe's largest volcano, Mount Etna which was still active with a faint puff of smoke rising from its crater.

They travelled across to the mainland by ferry, driving along the Amalfi coastline with its dramatic cliffs, winding road and sweeping ocean views. There was a constant flow of traffic along this very narrow road, an endless stream of cars and coaches heading towards them with motorbikes, scooters and cyclists overtaking them often on blind bends and heading straight towards them on their side of the road. Further along the coast, the road became increasingly narrow, until it was only as wide as a small alleyway, they had to pull over as far as they could a few times to let the buses coming the other way to get past. Finally arriving in

Naples late afternoon they had an early night ready for the adventure that awaited them the next day.

An early morning thirty-minute hike up a steep gravel path to Mt Vesuvius, the volcano that entombed the ancient city of Pompeii. They walked around part of the crater admiring the stunning views across the Bay of Naples, then spent the rest of the day exploring the fascinating city of Pompeii which had been preserved just as it was when the volcano erupted and instantaneously covered the city in 79AD. They visited numerous buildings in which residents had gone about their everyday life, including some temples, the basilica, the forum and baths, as well as some of the most lavish homes decorated with frescoes, mosaics and paintings all which were still intact. The eeriest part for Lilly was seeing the bodies of the victims of the explosions, they were fossilised, and you could see the terror and pain they must have felt just as they died. Lilly and Jeff returned to Rome to board their flight home. It had been a fantastic trip with some beautiful memories, one that Lilly would always remember.

CHAPTER 23

2004

Lilly and Jeff worked hard and long hours, working towards their dream of owning their own home. They had found the perfect place at the end of a quiet cul-de-sac, it was a large house, with five bedrooms, three bathrooms, a rumpus room, small verandah and a pool in the backyard. It was perfect; they set about painting the interior in a soft tan getting rid of the outdated peach colour all through the house, they had new carpet laid on the floors and lino in the kitchen. They chose the back half of the house as their retreat, turning the rumpus room into their bedroom;

the other two rooms became an office and a dressing room. There were three bedrooms at the front of the house, and Jake moved into the front room which had an ensuite and the other two rooms would be for Tara and Craig when they came to visit. Lilly had plans for renovating more, but that would have to wait until later on. When they could afford to, they planned to extend the verandah, put in a new kitchen and a modern bathroom.

Lilly and Jeff had expanded the business, purchasing another prime mover truck and trailer, adding to the storage facilities which were now overflowing, they would soon have to start looking for bigger premises. Lilly had some money invested, and Jeff had saved some money as well from the business, so they had enough for a deposit on a large block of land in the industrial estate and started to build a specially designed shed and expanded into shipping containers for storage. Jeff was having a lot of issues with his ex Darla, who would not let him go, she still believed that Jeff would come back to her one day and continued to blame Lilly for taking him from her. Whenever he could, or more to the point whenever Darla would let him Jeff would have his two smaller children Tara and Craig. Darla used the children to get at Jeff, and sometimes they also had Kelly, her daughter from her first marriage. Kelly looked at Jeff as her Dad, as he had helped raise her from a very small age.

Both Lilly and Jeff were hands-on with the building of the new depot, and they tried to save as much money as possible, Fred had come to help with his backhoe and had levelled the block he would come back and dig the footings once the earth settled and compacted. They hired a roller and would take turns in driving it over the ground to flatten it out ready for the excavations to start. It was exciting watching the building taking shape. Lilly's friend Miranda was an architect in Port Macquarie and they worked closely together to design a purpose-built shed that would meet all their needs for storage and the running of the business. Lilly took control of all the building construction acting as the site manager, making sure everything was done on time and budget. They worked long hours trying to realise their dream, but they always made time for each other. Jeff was such a romantic he would bring home flowers every week for Lilly, they would go out for coffee and walk on the beach to chill out.

Lilly was turning forty, and instead of having a party she chose to take a trip to Bali, a romantic getaway with Jeff, they would have ten days away. They arrived in Bali, collected their bags and passed through immigration walking out into the hot, wet, heavy air of Denpasar. Their first stop was their hotel in Kuta, after checking in and dropping their bags they walked through the streets looking in all the shops and stalls, continually being approached by street people trying to sell them something. It was a different world than they were used to, that was for sure, dinner on the beach to watch the sunset and drinks at a local bar before falling into bed happily exhausted.

For the next ten days they explored the island, from the beaches and bustling villages to the rice terraces cut into the hillsides reaching down into the lush valleys. Stopping at a high scenic viewpoint which was cool and breezy and a great spot to take photos. They wandered along the markets on the side of the road stopping to buy a canvas painting of a buddha head. Then onto Ubud specialising in handmade crafts and woodcarving, along the main street were art studios, local craft markets and galleries, shops selling antiques, woodcarvings, crafts, textiles, paintings and jewellery. Ulun Danu Beratan Temple set on a smooth reflective lake which surrounded most of the temple's base created a unique floating impression, while the mountain range of the Bedugul region encircling the lake provides the temple with a scenic backdrop. Lilly marvelled at the dramatic volcanic landscape of Mount Batur, an active volcano which actively spills molten lava. They stopped for a bite to eat at the lookout, enjoying the beautiful mountain scenery and the fresh, crisp air. On their way back to Kuta they stopped at the Sangeh Monkey Forest a sanctuary, six hectares of lush forestland with primordial, giant nutmeg trees which grow to a height of forty metres, the grey long-tailed macaques monkeys clustered in the towering trees and would come down to sightseers for food and photos.

Lilly and Jeff explored the cheap shops and bought gifts to take home, cheap summer clothes, sunglasses and nic nacks, they walked the beaches and relaxed in the coffee shops. For Lilly's birthday they made the trip out to Tanah Lot, the sea temple with its black lava towers and rushing waves, the temple was located on a rock just offshore, an ancient Hindu shrine perched on top of an outcrop amidst continually crashing waves. Before returning home, Lilly sat on the beach while a local girl braided her hair while adding material to make it longer, it was down past her waist. The time passed so quickly, and soon it was time to head back home to Australia and back to work to finish the building of the new depot, they were hoping to move in before Christmas.

CHAPTER 24

2006

The last two years had been hectic, they had moved into their new depot, purchased another removal company with a depot on the central coast which added another eight employees, three trucks, trailers and more storage, they had bought two more prime mover trucks and trailers and two small rigid trucks and another forty shipping containers. The business had expanded quickly with their new government contracts, and they had started servicing the Northern Territory. They were now making regular runs to Cairns and Melbourne and were becoming one of the largest companies on the mid-north coast. Mark had moved back home to live with them and was training to be an air conditioning and refrigeration mechanic, Jake was now fifteen still at school and showing great promise as a football player, he was the fullback for the local team. Jeff's ex-wife Darla was still being difficult, it was hard to deal with her, and it upset Jeff that he rarely saw his children. Jeff always paid child support and would drop off fresh vegetables and food now and then to make sure his children were eating properly. Kelly had refused to see them, her mother had poisoned her mind against Jeff, this hurt Jeff, but he knew that in time the children would come around.

Their workload was massive, so they had decided to close the depot on the central coast and bring everything back to the main depot, some staff stayed with them and Daphne whose job it was to book in work and organise truck runs to Cairns, moved to Port Macquarie with her husband and two children to continue working for the company.

Lilly and Jeff would go away every two months or so on jobs, they were away from home for up to three weeks at a time, making the long haul drives up the coast. Lilly had passed her Heavy Combination driving test and was now driving bigger trucks, taking turns with Jeff they would two up drive, one would sleep in the truck's bunk while the other drove swapping over every few hours so they could cover more distance in a shorter time. Lilly also helped pack up the houses, load the trucks and check the inventory. They would sleep in the truck in the sleeper cab and occasionally they would book a hotel. Their truck had a small refrigerator, a TV and DVD player above the bed, their little home away from home. Lilly loved driving and seeing new places; they would often unhitch the trailer and drive around in the truck sightseeing when they were in a new location with time to spare. Most of their work was now using shipping containers, and it saved on double handling the furniture. They would load the furniture into a shipping container on one truck and then lift it off with the big forklifts to store at the depot or transfer to another truck to go to its final destination.

This trip they were driving into the Northern Territory to a remote community in West Arnhem Land in the outback of Australia, they had to cross the East

Alligator River at the eastern boundary of Kakadu at Cahills Crossing to reach the small community of Oenpelli to deliver a teacher's furniture. They had to time the crossing of the river at the causeway with the low tide, and it was notorious for its crocodile-infested waters. Even though the crossing is fifty kilometres from the mouth of the river, the tides can be over six metres high, and on the change of the tide, the water comes rushing in extremely fast bringing mullet and other fish with it making it a smorgasbord for the crocodiles. After crossing the river, they drove slowly on the dirt road passing red, dusty rock formations, brilliant green wetlands and spectacular escarpments which lined the road. Lilly loved their work, and it was a great way to see the country. She and Jeff were together twenty-four hours a day, they got along so well and enjoyed each other's company, and even though they were away working they always found time to go out for dinner or see a movie.

They headed towards Darwin for their final delivery and spent two days looking around the city. They had decided to set up a depot here as there was so much work coming up this way, it made sense, and they had been accepted to the Toll board which meant they could now bid on Australian defence work coming in and out of the territory. They found a small shed on a corner block in Berrimah not far from the train freight depot, the rent was reasonable, but the yard needed some work. They spent the next few months sealing the yard with bitumen and began bringing containers in, two of the smaller trucks and a new container forklift. The shed was small, and they could fit five containers side by side for storage, and there was a small upstairs room for the office. Two of their most reliable and trustworthy workers from Port Macquarie came up and lived on site in a portable building with a bedroom, bathroom, kitchen and lounge area; they employed two locals to help with the day to day work of removals.

"I don't think I can do it Jeff."

"Yes you can Lilly, you are more than capable, you have been driving trucks for years now, and this is the next step up to a multi-combination licence you will be able to drive the B-double with me." Jeff knew Lilly was more than competent; he just had to convince her.

"I believe in you baby. You can do this, we will do more practice before your test on Thursday."

"Okay, I guess I can try" Lilly sighed, she was apprehensive about the test and driving such a large truck with two trailers.

"You will blitz it. I know you will." Jeff grabbed her and hugged her tightly. He loved this fiery, beautiful woman who would have a go at anything, even though she lacked confidence in herself at times. As predicted Lilly passed the four-hour driving and knowledge test with flying colours and just as well because they had to make a run to Cairns leaving tomorrow, it would take them two weeks to return, by the time they made all the unloads on the way north and reloaded on the way back.

They had been working so hard for the last few months, they decided to take a trip to Tasmania for two weeks and hired a motorhome to get around to see the sites. It was fun pulling up on the side of the road anywhere to have a cuppa or to spend the night without the worry of trying to find a motel. Tasmania was beautiful and green with its stunning scenery, and they loved the small motorhome so much that they decided to buy one of the older models from the hire company that were selling off older stock to make way for new vehicles. They flew down to Hobart two months later to pick it up and drive it home, crossing the Bass Strait on the Spirit of Tasmania to Melbourne then back up along the coast to home.

Jeff was still having problems with his ex and was only able to see his children Tara and Craig when it suited her, she was very demanding, and as they were getting busier with the business, she expected more money from him in child support. Just because they had a company and had now bought a home didn't mean they were rich, they had borrowed heavily from the bank and worked long hours trying to pay back the debt. It rankled Lilly, she had worked hard with Jeff to build the business up, and now his ex wanted the money from their hard work. She had no qualms about supporting his children, as long as the money went to the children and not spent on their mother. Lilly was fed up with being abused by Darla whenever she saw her. She had even spat at her once and called her a whore and a home wrecker in front of the children.

Whenever the children came over they were wearing old clothes which reeked of cigarette smoke, Lilly would get them to undress and change into the clean clothes she had purchased for them, which she kept at the house. On several occasions when they arrived they had nits in their hair, so she always had treatment products on hand just in case. One time when Tara was five she came with her head shaved to almost nothing because her mother didn't want to deal with washing it and getting the nits out. Jeff went ballistic when he saw his little girl with a shaved head and too embarrassed to go outside. Kelly had stopped coming over, her mother had filled her head with lies about Jeff, and she rarely saw him now.

It was a lovely winter's day in August when Lilly and Jeff stood at Nora Head Lighthouse on the Central Coast watching Jackie and Kendrick exchange their wedding vows in a beautiful, emotional service in front of their closest friends and family. The guests then hopped onto a big red double-decker bus to take them to the reception at the surf club.

"I'm so happy for you Jackie, you look so happy, and you are such a beautiful bride." Lilly hugged her friend tightly, finally Jackie had let someone into her life, and it was apparent to everyone that they were very much in love and very well matched.

"I didn't think I would ever trust again or find someone that I would love after what Andrew did to me, but Lilly seeing you and Jeff so happy together, you kept telling me to have faith and one day someone would come into my life. Who would have known it was someone I had known for over twenty years." Jackie was absolutely glowing with happiness, she looked so glamorous in her champagne calf length pink satin dress, with its fitted bodice and sheer elbow length sleeves with crystal and sparkles on the sleeves and bodice.

"We have been through a bit together Jackie, bad times and good times, but look at us we have come out the other side, both of us with men who love and adore us." Lilly giggled remembering their trip down the coast on the motorbikes.

"Yes look at us Toots, two amazing, beautiful, confident women pursuing our dreams, we are lucky that's for sure." Jackie had nicknamed her Toots after Australia's first female truck driver, Thora "Toots"

Holzheimer, a strong, tough woman who was more than capable in her own right. Working in rough country and able to outwork some men while still being a true lady with a heart of gold. "Come on, let's go have a glass or three of champagne to celebrate."

CHAPTER 25

2007

Jeff was turning forty this February, so they had organised a trip to New Zealand for his birthday. He wanted to bungy jump from one-of the bridges in Queenstown. Lilly thought he was mad; there was no way she was going to jump from a bridge with a rubber band attached to her ankle. Lilly had found out that her cousin Jase was working in New Zealand as one of the instructors at the bungy jump and had decided to surprise him, they had not seen each other for over twenty-five years and he had no idea she was in New Zealand. They arrived at the jump site half an hour before it closed, Lilly recognised Jase as soon as she saw him. She stood and watched him waiting for him to finish work, he kept looking across at her, and she'd smile, Lilly could tell that he was trying to work out whether he knew her or if she was some weird stalker, when they started to pack up Lilly approached Jase.

"Hi Jase how are you?"

"Hi I'm good thanks, do I know you? You look familiar." his eyes crinkled in thought.

"Well you should know me. We got up to a lot of mischief a few years back." Lilly was enjoying stringing him along; he was probably trying to work out if he had dated her.

"Oh really! Umm, I'm sorry I simply can't place you, but your eyes remind me of someone, but I just can't think who."

"Well we were very close" Lilly laughed "It's me, Lilly, your cousin you silly bugger."

Realisation set in, he hugged her and spun her around, "Oh my god, I knew you looked familiar, you have Aunty Rose's eyes, how are you? What have you been doing? How did you know I was here?"

"Okay one question at a time, are you free for dinner? We can catch up over a few drinks, we're here for a few days." They went out for dinner and reminisced about the things they had gotten up to as kids and laughed late into the night.

The next day being Jeff's birthday they lined up at the desk to book his jump from the Kawarau bridge with a drop of forty-three metres to the river below. Jase met them there and was taking the booking. "Come on Lilly, don't be such a chicken, do a tandem jump with Jeff if you don't want to do it by yourself." Jase was egging her on. "The Lilly I knew as a kid was not a scaredy cat, she would have a go at anything."

"Yeah come on Lilly, you can get strapped to me and we'll jump together, it will be fun." Jeff had now joined in trying to get her to jump.

"No bloody way am I jumping off a bridge with only elastic holding me from falling to my death."

"It's fine Lilly, I've done it hundreds of times it's safe, think about it just come out with Jeff and you'll see, if you don't want to do it, you don't have to."

After much talking, Lilly followed them out onto the old wooden bridge area which was surrounded by steep rocky walls with the turquoise river running underneath. Finally, after Jase had shown her how it all worked and assured her again it was safe, she decided to give it a go. Jase attached them together in a double harness and placed the cord around their legs. The adrenaline had really kicked in now, they shuffled forward to the jumping platform, the last few steps to the edge were not easy and her legs were shaking. Lilly's heart was pounding, her nerves had kicked in, her mind racing, sweat started to form on her brow, why the bloody hell had she decided to do this? Jumping off a bridge, she must be mad, she looked down at the river below. It seemed such a long way down to the water and the boat waiting to collect them.

"I can't do it Jeff, I just can't. I think I'll die from a heart attack before we even jump off."

Jeff put his arm around her "We'll be fine, let's take a leap of faith beautiful, everything will be just fine, and I think you will love the adrenaline rush." Lilly didn't have time to think Jase yelled out three, two, one, JUMP. They fell forward together heading towards the rushing water below, she screamed all the way just closing her mouth before they were dunked into the water up to their waist, they bobbed up and down, waiting for the boat to come out and collect them. Lilly laughed, it had been a mixture of fear, thrill, excitement and anxiety. Jeff was right even though it had scared the hell out of her, she loved it and wanted to go again, she felt so happy and proud but mostly relieved.

They booked to do the Nevis Bungy jump the next day, they were taken out to the jump site by a four-wheel drive bus. It was a forty-minute drive to reach their destination up the narrow and steep road that climbed the mountains, and the scenery was spectacular. Upon arrival, they signed the paperwork, put on their harnesses and had their weight checked, then a quick briefing before boarding the small cable car which would take them to the jumping pod that was suspended by wires in the middle between the two gorges. This was scary in itself as it kept moving with the wind as it was only hanging on the ropes. Lilly's turn had come, and she was seated in a massive chair, to have the cables attached to her ankles, Jase joked with her as he tightly fitted the straps, he could see she was becoming anxious, Lilly was wondering if she had made the right decision or had she lost her mind. Jase checked her harness and rope for the last time and showed her again how to release the cord so that she didn't come back up hanging upside down.

Lilly shuffled her way out to the small platform that she would then have to launch herself from. It was hard to move with the elastic cord wrapped tightly around her ankles, her legs were shaking and she thought her legs would buckle from the sheer fear, the blood was pumping so hard through her veins and the thought of what she was about to do. She got right to the edge and looked down at the canyon floor below, there was a small river of blue green water flowing through the base of the canyon and rocks either side, could she really do this? This was complete lunacy. A last smile for the camera then three, two one JUMP! Lilly took a deep breath and fell forward into the void, no time to think about it, she screamed so loud she was sure that they would have heard her back in Queenstown. It took eight and a half seconds of free fall to drop the one hundred and thirty-two metres. The river Nevis underneath was fast approaching then the rope started to stretch and she was pulled back up towards the platform, bouncing up and down a few times before she pulled the cord and moved into the seated position. It took a while to be pulled back into the cabin, Lilly looked out at the astonishing scenery below and in front of her as she was winched in, she felt very proud of herself, she had stepped outside her comfort zone, she had done something she didn't think she would have ever done in her wildest dreams. Lilly was now addicted to the adrenaline rush.

In April Jeff and Jake brought home a six-week old Australian Cattle Dog. She was the cutest little thing with floppy black ears, black patches on both eyes and a white diamond on her forehead. They called her Elly, and she soon became the boss of the household, she grew so quickly and bonded tightly with Lilly, following her everywhere, she would even go to work with her every day, they became inseparable.

Lilly and Jeff had expanded the business even more through a lot of hard work and long hours. They were now moving furniture all over Australia into every state. In August they had been to a four- day industry conference in Fiji and had taken a few extra days to look around the island. They had a wonderful time and were still very much in love. Jeff was thoughtful and considerate and romantic; they enjoyed exploring and seeing new places, Lilly felt blessed. They had been so busy with work and the children they hadn't had a lot of time alone lately, so it was a well deserved holiday.

"Come on Mark it will be fun, what better way to celebrate your twenty-first birthday than jumping out of a plane with your mother? It's a tandem jump. You will have an instructor strapped to your back."

"You have to be kidding Mum. You want me to skydive on my birthday. I don't think so." Mark was sure his Mum had gone mad, ever since she had bungy jumped in New Zealand she wanted to do more and more wild and dangerous things.

"I'm game if you are. You will love it, besides it's my shout for your twenty-first birthday." Lilly wanted to share this experience with her eldest son. It took some convincing, but Mark finally agreed to skydive on his birthday.

They had filled out their forms, completed the safety briefing, met their tandem instructor, kitted up into their harnesses and loaded onto the plane. As they took off up the runway in the little plane the excitement was building, Lilly looked at Mark and smiled, she was so proud of both her boys. Mark was an air conditioning refrigeration mechanic and had started dating a lovely girl Lori, she was the same age as him, and Jake was an apprentice plumber.

The plane took off and started its climb, circling around until they reached ten thousand feet, the view was breathtaking, and everything below looked so small. It was almost time to jump. Mark gave his Mum a nervous smile, the instructors were doing the final equipment checks before shuffling towards the now open door, the sound of the air rushing past was so loud Lilly couldn't hear anyone talking. One by one they shuffled to the door and disappeared over the edge into the open air, it was now Lilly's turn, the blood was pumping through her veins, and she felt euphoric. It was only a few seconds that she sat on the edge waiting to fall but it seemed like minutes, then she leaned forward and fell out of the plane. Lilly let out a scream of excitement and fear as they started to accelerate, it was so fast, free-falling towards the earth below, the force of the wind pushing up at her as she fell was so strong and intense. She couldn't hear anything; it was so loud but at the same time, utterly peaceful and serene. The cameraman came into view and started floating around her, waving and giving her a thumbs up. A few more seconds and the instructor pulled the chute, and they were pulled back up and then slowed as the parachute filled with air and they started to glide to the ground, spiralling around heading towards the drop zone. The view was astonishing and she felt so free, now she knew what a bird must feel like as it glided around on the wind currents, it was so beautiful and peaceful, Lilly's ears popped as they came closer to the ground, she lifted her knees up to her chest as the instructor had shown her as they glided down and slid forward onto the grass. Lilly could not put her feelings or sensations into words. She was unstrapped and turned to watch as Mark came floating down to the drop zone, the smile on his face said it all. Lilly felt tears come to her eyes as her eldest boy came over and grabbed her in a big hug.

"That was awesome Mum, thank you, I'm so pleased you talked me into it, I loved it, BUT I won't be doing it again." Lilly laughed, she knew he would love it, now to convince Jake now to do it for his twenty-first birthday.

CHAPTER 26

2008

Jeff had surprised Lilly with a romantic weekend away at a retreat in the mountains, and they had a cabin to themselves with a spa bath out on the balcony overlooking the valley and the mountains; it was just what they needed. It had been a hectic few months, and Jeff was still having trouble with his ex and getting to see his children, it didn't matter what he did she would find an excuse to argue with him and tried to fill the kids head with lies, telling them their father did not care about them. It had finally taken a toll on Jeff, and he was starting to become agitated over the smallest things. They made a vow not to talk about work or children on their weekend away. They spent time laying in bed, riding horses through the forest and just relaxing. Jeff had even organised a massage for Lilly then a romantic candlelight dinner for them. They came away feeling totally renewed and still very much in love, they were inseparable, they enjoyed being together, they rarely argued and when they did it was usually about work or his children.

Jeff had started to do general freight with his truck, and they now had a road train. Once the road train was hooked up with all of its trailers, it was almost fifty metres long. Jeff had driven over to Perth in the truck to make deliveries, and Lilly had now flown in to meet him to help drive back, it would be the first time she had driven a road train, and she was feeling apprehensive.

"My god it's so long, I don't know if I can drive this Jeff." Lilly stood at the back trailer taking in the length of the truck with trailers. It was daunting for her. She had driven the B-doubles at nineteen metres but nothing this big.

"You will be fine, it's no different to the trucks you have been driving Lilly, it's just longer, so you have to remember about the length and weight, it will take a lot longer to stop." Jeff stood behind her with his arms wrapped around her waist, he was proud of his little pocket rocket, she would have a go at anything, and he knew once she got going she would be fine.

"Well if you think I can, let's go then, just don't give me any corners!"

Jeff laughed "The back trailers will follow the front trailers around Lilly, trust me it will be okay, come on then you can have the first drive it's fairly straight going, so it will be easy."

They climbed up into the cab and Lilly turned the ignition on, checked her mirrors and slowly released the clutch, she was rolling, she felt so much pride in herself that she could drive such a large vehicle and it didn't feel too different to driving her regular trucks. As she rounded the first bend she watched in the side mirror as the trailers all followed each other around, she felt relieved, it wasn't so bad after all. It would take them three days to drive the four thousand or so kilometres back to Port Macquarie. They only made stops for fuel and to eat and shower, then continued on their way two-up driving, taking turns at the wheel while the other one slept. This would be the first of many trips this year. They would only have three weeks at home before they had to make a three-week trip.

Jake was now eighteen and working so he was able to take care of himself while they were away. Once again they were on the road heading for Queensland, they had deliveries to make in Mackay, Townsville and Cairns before heading across on the Flinders Highway to the Northern Territory, up the Stuart Highway to Darwin to unload and reload with another job that would take them across to Broome in Western Australia. They had never made a trip across the top end of Australia before, so it was all new and exciting crossing into Western Australia. They turned at Kununurra onto the Great Northern Highway through Halls Creek and Fitzroy Crossing before finally making it into Broome. The scenery was stunning all the way. They would have two days in Broome and had booked a motel for a night. They had been sleeping in the truck for two weeks now, even though it was comfortable, Lilly craved for a big bed and a clean shower. The truck stop showers left little to be desired and sometimes Lilly had to use the mens' as there were no separate showers for women and she always showered with her rubber thongs on so as to not have bare feet on the well-used shower floors. There were a few women on the road driving trucks but not many, that would change in the years to come. They completed their work and looked around Broome for a day. Lilly wished they could have stayed longer but they had a time schedule to keep and had to get back on the road. Back across the Great Northern Highway into the Northern Territory before turning back onto the Stuart Highway at Katherine then straight down the centre to Port Augusta in South Australia then across through Broken Hill and home to Port Macquarie. They had been away for three weeks, had driven through five states, three different time zones and driven over fourteen thousand kilometres.

Lilly and Jeff had become very friendly with one of their office staff, Daphne and her husband, who had children the same age as his kids. Lilly had a sneaking suspicion that Daphne had a bit of a crush on Jeff, and she would go all coy and laugh a lot, whenever he was around batting her eyelids at him. Lilly felt pretty secure in her relationship with Jeff but from past experiences she never totally trusted anyone. Jeff would sometimes go around to Daphne's and have coffee when Lilly was at work, mostly when he had his kids with him, and they would play, swim in the pool with her children. Lilly tried not to let her past demons of mistrust and jealousy get to her, but sometimes it was hard, especially knowing that Daphne's husband was away working at the time.

Lilly and Daphne had become close friends and they would discuss their husbands and issues with each other. Lilly confided her troubles with Jeff to her, and Daphne had also seen that Jeff could be a bit unpredictable at times. He was changing somehow, Lilly could not put her finger on it but he had become a bit distant of late and had even started to make trips without her in the truck. His knee had been playing up a bit, and he had been booked in for a knee reconstruction early next year.

CHAPTER 27

2009

Jeff had been acting strangely for the last few weeks and had become secretive and obsessed with keeping his mobile phone near him. He would disappear for hours giving no explanation of where he had been. He often snapped at Lilly for such silly things, questioning every decision she made at work, and he had started to be very condescending to her in front of their staff. Lilly had become uneasy and had that sinking feeling in her stomach, she had seen this behaviour before in Michael, and she knew where that ended. She hoped she was wrong and put it down to the fact that his knee operation was coming up in a few weeks, maybe he was worried, and that was making him upset. It meant he would be off work for at least six weeks and would be resting up at home. Jeff had been trying to lose weight and Daphne would bring him shakes and snacks to work and they would sit in the corner at her desk speaking softly and laughing, and whenever Lilly approached they would stop, this did nothing to help Lilly's growing concerns.

Lilly waited in Jeff's hospital room waiting for him to return from physiotherapy, she spotted his overnight bag and couldn't help herself, she pulled out his cell phone and checked his messages, they had all been deleted. This, of course, made her even more suspicious, once he would not care about her looking at his phone but these days he would growl at her if she asked who he had been talking to. He had not wanted her to stay with him at the hospital, he'd become cold to her and told her he was fine; he didn't need her to take care of him. Lilly felt like she didn't know this man anymore, he was not the man she fell in love with and married. For the next few weeks he recuperated at home watching tv and resting while

Lilly ran the company, they were getting bigger and busier, and the business in Darwin was going ahead in strides. Whenever he would call the office he always spoke to Daphne not her, and Daphne would whisper and giggle whenever she talked to him, even she had become funny towards Lilly also acting like she knew something more and was better than her. Jeff had changed so much in the last two months he had gone from a loving, affectionate, caring partner to a man she hardly recognised. One minute he was nice the next he would be nasty as all hell, bringing her to tears on many occasions.

Jeff was now back at work and was going away in his truck to take a load to the Darwin depot. He left the house at seven o'clock that night telling her he was leaving to go on the trip and would call her tomorrow. Lilly had become more suspicious of his relationship with Daphne; she knew in her gut something was going on. She had to find out so the next day she downloaded his phone records, it showed he had not left until midnight that was five hours unaccounted for and there were multiple messages to Daphne right up until four am in the morning. What was going on?

Why would he be texting her at that time? Lilly said nothing and over the next week checked his messages he was texting and sending videos and photos from his phone to Daphne at all hours having conversations that lasted over an hour, yet he would hardly phone her, his wife.

How could Daphne do this to her? Lilly called her into the office and confronted her, and she wanted to know what was going on with Daphne and her husband. She had trusted Daphne and she had told her of the problems they were having. Daphne had consoled her even saying that he treated her badly. Standing before Lilly in her office Daphne was crying, saying she was just there to listen to him and was trying to help, yet she didn't bother to tell Lilly about all the calls or what was said during those calls. Lilly did not trust her. Her intuition told her to watch her back. Of course, Daphne called Jeff and told him that Lilly had called her into her office and asked her what was going on. Jeff called Lilly and abused her, he told her to mind her own business and to leave Daphne out of it. When he returned, she confronted him wanting to know what was going on between them, she received the usual response, that it was all her fault she shouldn't be checking his phone records, at least he could talk to Daphne, she understood him. Of course she did, she didn't have to live with his constant changing moods, one minute he was yelling abuse at her the next he would be asking if she wanted to go out for coffee. Lilly wanted to sack Daphne, but Jeff would not allow it.

Why did she stay? She no longer trusted him; this wasn't the first time she had doubts about his fidelity. Once again she let things slide and tried to get back to normal, well as normal as she could. Lilly pulled into the driveway to see Kelly sitting on the steps in tears, she'd had a big fight with her mother and ran away from home it had become physical. Lilly rang Jeff to tell him he came straight home and rang Darla to tell her that Kelly was with them and would stay until they both calmed down. An hour later the police were at their door asking what was going on. They had been informed that Kelly was being held against her will and was not allowed to return to her mothers. After a brief conversation with Kelly, they decided it would be best for Kelly to stay with them for a few days until they could all sit down and work it out.

Kelly didn't return to her mothers; instead she moved in with Lilly and Jeff. Lilly went out and bought her new school clothes and casual clothes, she refused to talk to her mother, and things soon settled down again. Even though Kelly wasn't Jeff's biological daughter, he had been the only father she had known since she was one year old and called him Dad. Jeff had a strained relationship with his ex-wife, and they continually fought about the kids, she would not let him see them, then when she needed money she would call and be as nice as pie. Jeff always gave in to her. Jeff knew the kids weren't being looked after well, sometimes going to school in dirty clothes and not enough food to eat. The last straw came when the education department contacted him to tell him how much school they had missed and that they were taking Darla to court for neglect, it was then that Jeff decided he would go for full custody. He didn't discuss it with Lilly. He told her that was what he would be doing. Lilly didn't mind but it was hard, their relationship was already strained and having two more kids in the house would not make it easier, they would have to set rules and stick together.

Daphne had been very smug with Lilly at work, refusing to do anything she asked her to, saying that Jeff was her boss and he was the one she answered to, not her. Lilly had finally had enough, and she took control. When Jeff was away working, she let Daphne go with the explanation that business was quiet and they could not afford her anymore. Jeff called not long after and went ballistic at Lilly demanding that she rehire Daphne, she stood her ground and told him it was either her or Daphne at work, make a choice. He relented knowing that she meant it. So finally Daphne was out of her face every day with her smug attitude and stupid knowing smile.

Lilly was close with Miranda and her partner Monique, they had been together for thirty years and were still very much in love, they complimented each other in so many ways and were a perfect match. Miranda was a very successful architect, and Lilly would come to her for advice about her own business, she'd also confide in Miranda about her troubles with Jeff, she was always there to listen to her problems with a comforting shoulder to cry on. Lilly loved the parties that Miranda and Monique threw at their riverside home, there was always so much fun and laughter, with all the girls getting together for dinner and drinks and then to play poker or pool. Now it was Lilly's turn to help her friend, Monique had been diagnosed with breast cancer only a few months ago, it had taken hold quickly and there was nothing the doctors could do, she had passed away in Miranda's arms, leaving her devastated at the loss of her soul mate. They had an amazing love story, meeting in Sydney at a Pyrmont pub, Miranda had told Lilly that she knew from the first time she laid eyes on Monique she was the one she wanted to spend the rest of her life with. Monique would laugh recalling how she thought that Miranda looked like a wild child and she knew that Miranda was younger than her, at first Monique didn't accept her offers of a date, but Miranda would not take no for an answer, she persevered, and finally Monique relented. They'd had a wonderful life together, work-ing hard, travelling the world and setting up a home together on the banks of the Hastings River. Lilly knew it would take a long time for Miranda to get over the loss of her beautiful Monique, Lilly would be there for her whenever she needed her.

CHAPTER 28

2010

Lilly and Jeff sat in the courtroom listening to the defence put forward against Darla by the education department. The children had missed one hundred and twenty days of school in three years. Jeff made his statement and pleaded to the judge to take custody of the children. Lilly felt like a hypocrite sitting there pretending they were a happily married couple, she had come today to support Jeff, she was unsure about this, they had been sleeping in separate rooms now for the past three weeks after the last blow up, how could bringing two young children into this relationship be better for them? Jeff promised her things would get better and that he loved her and they would make it work and asked her to give him another chance. The judge awarded full custody to Jeff, and the children were to be picked up by him that afternoon, Darla would have them every second weekend from Thursday night to Sunday night, but was given a strict dressing down by the judge that if she failed to send them to school at anytime that her privileges would be revoked.

It was hard trying to organise school, sports and tutors for the kids with them working so much, so Jeff decided they needed a nanny to help. He called Josie and asked her to take on the job which she accepted, she would work from twelve to six each day, picking the kids up from school, running them around to appointments and help clean the house and cook dinner so it took some of the workload off Lilly, who was flat out in the office. This worked well as Jeff and Lilly still went away for work, driving the truck sometimes and flying in and out of the Darwin depot for work and to check on the business, especially in their peak periods.

Josie would stay over whenever they went away for work taking care of the children and Elly.

They were at the Darwin depot working for the week and had been to the pub to have dinner and a few drinks. They now sat watching television at the small accommodation unit they had on site in the yard. They both had had a bit too much to drink, and Jeff was in one of his moods, then the arguing started, Lilly could not bite her tongue she had changed in the last year or two and was becoming someone she didn't like very much.

"Oh, so it's my fault then?" Lilly screamed at Jeff.

"Yes it's always your fault, you're a selfish bitch especially when it comes to my kids."

"Are you kidding me, I've bent over backwards for your children for the last seven years, it's been me who has had to deal with your ex, you always vanish whenever she is around, and you leave me to do your dirty work for you. You put your kids before me every time."

"Of course I do, and I always will so get used to it." Jeff stood up and walked over to where she was standing at the door. "You're a fat fucking ugly cow who only cares about herself, you have done nothing for my kids."

"Bullshit, I'm the one who feeds them and cleans up after them not you, all you want to do is be their mate. You didn't bother with them for so long because it was too hard dealing with their mother, and now you have taken them away from their mother you realise that you have to step up and actually be a father, good luck with that."

Jeff shoved her, and she fell against the door, Lilly reached out and slapped him across the face, he hit her in the face, just below her eye, then grabbed her arm in a tight grip, she could feel his fingers digging into her bones, she would have a bruise tomorrow.

"Let me go you pathetic piece of shit, what a big man you are pushing a woman around."

Jeff pushed her out the door, and she fell, landing heavily on the step and deck, pain seared through her arm and it began to swell, she was unable to move it, she lay there crying, did she deserve this? Why didn't she just keep her mouth shut?

"Get up ya fucking sook, stop bunging it on. I'm sick of your fuckin bitchin."

"I'm not, look at my arm! I think it's broken. What is wrong with you?" Lilly sat on the deck cradling her arm and cried, Jeff turned and walked back inside leaving her there. The next morning Lilly had a swollen black eye and could not move her arm, Jeff took her to the hospital and waited in the car, he refused to go in with her. When the nurse asked how this had happened Lilly told her she had been at the bar when a fight broke out, and she had been pushed off the chair that's how she got her injuries. She had become just like her mother all those years ago telling lies to cover up the awful truth. Lilly knew by the look on her face that the nurse didn't believe her. Luckily her arm was only sprained and needed rest, they wrapped it up and placed it in a sling. Jeff was full of regret and promised it would never happen again and he went out of his way to make things better. Was she so desperate to be loved that she would put up with anything? It seemed so.

This was the last trip away for work that they would take together for some time. Jeff refused to go to work saying he needed to spend time with his kids, even though they had Josie there to help, he had worked long and hard and wanted time off, she could run the business. Lilly was left with no choice but to pick up the slack, and he would only come to work for an hour or so each day barking orders and then disappear to go surfing or fishing. No matter what decision Lilly or the staff would make it was always the wrong one, he would tell them to do something and then when they did it he would ask why they did it that way, forgetting his orders and refusing to believe he had said it. The staff were getting very frustrated, Lilly was becoming more and more unsettled and was turning into a nasty, uncaring person but she didn't see it, she was becoming more like him.

Lilly hated the business, it had become too big, they were getting further and further in debt, she worked long hours and had to deal with the staff, as well as running the truck operations and finding the money to pay the bills. It didn't help that Jeff just wanted to be a part-time boss, changing everything she did but he didn't want to be there. He spent money on surfboards, fishing gear and kayaks and everything had to be a designer brand not from Kmart or Target for his kids and himself. The business had come between them, and the stress was pulling her apart, she started to gain weight and didn't like the person she saw in the mirror. Lilly had been drinking way too much, a bottle of wine or more a night by herself, it helped relax her and to fall asleep. She had tried to talk to Jeff about scaling the business back or selling it to try and save their marriage he was uncooperative he didn't see a problem, his idea was to buy more trucks, go bigger, but Lilly refused and he didn't come to work at all now, and she wasn't going to keep doing it by herself.

This December was a busy period for defence removals in and out of Darwin and the remote islands. Jeff refused to go away to work, so Lilly boarded the flight to Darwin to work the peak period, she stayed in a motel in the city and worked three weeks straight for up to eighteen hours a day. There was paperwork to take care of staff to organise, trucks to send out, she even went out with the boys working in the remote communities, hiring a charter flight to get them to the outlying islands, the shipping containers had been sent out already on the barge and would be waiting for them. Once they had landed, they would go to the job, do the pre-pack, inventory and load the containers ready to be sent back on the barge to Darwin. They would leave at first light and return at last light. They stayed out on some of the islands for two or three days when they had a lot of jobs to complete. Lilly worked tirelessly right alongside the boys for three weeks, while Jeff stayed home and helped with the office work when the surf wasn't up. When Lilly returned home a few days before Christmas Jeff seemed to be in a better mood and was even happy to see her, maybe the time apart had done them good. Lilly had missed her dog Elly and was greeted with a big sloppy wet kiss as she walked through the door. At least the dog loved her unconditionally and was happy to see her.

CHAPTER 29

2011

Today was their eighth wedding anniversary. Lilly sat at the table with pen and paper wondering what had happened to their love, where did it all go wrong, she was finding it hard to cope with Jeff's mood swings, for the last week he had been quite vicious with his comments. She was not perfect and partly to blame, she knew she could be strong-willed and stubborn at times. She looked at the blank page in front of her and she needed to write down how she was feeling. It was time to let go, she had to for her own sake, he would not change, she had also changed, and there was no trust, and without trust, there is no marriage. Every time she decided to leave, he would talk her into staying. She wondered if it was because he loved her or because he wanted someone to help raise his kids?

Jeff,

Today is our 8th wedding anniversary, and just like last year you have said nothing, I have stupidly been waiting for a sign from you to show me that you actually love me and want to make our marriage work. Once again I am disappointed. Last year when I asked you at the end of the day about our anniversary you said you remembered but as far as you were concerned there was nothing to celebrate. I guess it's the same this year. Your pride and your stubbornness have gotten in the way again. I'm sick of being the one who always tries to organise something nice for us cause no matter what I do it will be wrong.

The last two years with you have been the worst of my life, I cannot remember the last time we had fun, or when we laughed together, I cannot remember the last time you told me you loved me or that I have even felt love from you. I will not live through another two years of this. You say it's because you are standing up to me and you won't take my shit BUT does that give you the right to treat me like a piece of worthless shit?? I'm tired of being verbally abused of being called a fat fucking whore, an ugly fucking cunt, a lazy fuckin bitch who does nothing all day but sit in my office playing with myself with my head up my arse, you say I have done nothing for your children and that I haven't raised my own children. Tired of you telling me that I was a slut when you met me and I'll always be a slut, that I am a sympathy fuck that's why I fuck you from behind so I don't have to look at my fucking ugly face. You call me a fucking fat whale and an ugly fuckin whore. You yell at me that you wouldn't stick your dick in me until you've had an aids test and you accuse me of sleeping around. I have been faithful to you from our very first day together, can you say the same? You tell me I've destroyed the business, do I need to go on? My god Jeff, these are true words of love aren't they?

I know I'm not perfect, I never said I was, but I do the best I can, and I try to change the things I can. We cannot talk because it always ends with you calling me names and being nasty whenever I say something you don't like. We keep going around in circles, and nothing gets resolved. Your mood swings are over the top. I don't know what your demons are but don't blame me for the person you are today when you met me you loved me because I was so outgoing, I was strong, independent I was singing and driving tour buses, and I was who I was. The only thing that has changed in me over the past eight years is I've become less tolerant of selfish, nasty people. I am still the same person. You told me not so long ago you had women queuing up waiting for you, well go find one.

We do not trust each other and without trust you have nothing there is no love in this marriage at all anymore I have been stupidly clinging on to that man I fell in love with the one who would looked at me from across the room with love and respect, the man who would just touch me on the arm or back as he went past with love, the one who would talk to me as an equal, the one who thought I was beautiful and talented, the one who would cuddle me all night, the one who said he would never let work or kids come between us, the one who said don't put yourself in a position that will put doubt in someone's mind. That man is gone and he will never come back. Just sit down and really think about what you have said and done over the past two years. I mean really think about it.

I will no longer sit back and take your crap. I am not going to do this anymore. I don't like you, I don't trust you, and I will not be here to be your punching bag emotionally anymore. So Happy Fucking Anniversary my present to you is us separating and going our separate ways.

Without Love Lilly

Jeff begged her to stay and managed to talk her around once again with a promise to change this time. And yes, Lilly fell for it, she didn't want to fail again, this was her third marriage she had to fight to keep this marriage working. Josie stood by her side even though she could see that her best friend was changing and not for the better, she would listen to her problems and offer a shoulder to cry on and be there for her just like Lilly had been there for her.

Lilly looked down into the serene perfect little face of her first grandchild, Jackson, a boy born six weeks early. She breathed in the sweet baby smell, tears of joy fell on her cheeks at the beauty and wonder of this new life she held in her arms, and her emotions overcame her. This small precious child in her arms had a little bit of her in him. Lilly looked up at Mark and Lori.

"He is so beautiful, he's perfect, Mark now you know how I felt the day that you were born and they placed you in my arms for the first time, it's a feeling you cannot explain."

"I know Mum it's pretty amazing." he placed his arm around Lori and kissed her forehead "This is one amazing woman that helped create this little fella, and I'm feeling pretty good right now."

"I can't wait for him to grow up and come to Grandma's and I'll give him red cordial and lollies and then give him back to you." Lilly laughed "paybacks a bitch son."

Mark laughed at his mother's joke, but he knew his life had now changed forever.

It was to be a busy few months travelling for Lilly and Jeff, with a holiday in July to Hawaii, an annual conference on Hamilton Island in August, and then back to Hamilton Island in October for their friend's wedding.

"You know it has always been a dream of mine to own my own restaurant lounge bar Jeff, but I won't do it without your blessing and a promise that you'll support me." Lilly had discovered a restaurant that had been recently closed by the owner due to illness, she could buy it for a reasonable price and fix it up, but she needed Jeff to agree, they had been getting along so well lately, they had both been trying hard to make their marriage work, she didn't want to jeopardise it.

"What about the removal company?" Jeff's voice was hard.

"Well we don't agree on how that should be run, and I hate the place you know that. You could take it over and have full control, run it the way you want, I'll keep doing the accounts and wages."

Jeff thought about it and smiled "Okay, as long as I have total control, and whatever I say goes."

"Within reason Jeff, I will support you if you support me. Promise you will not use the restaurant against me, as much as I want it, it's not worth destroying us over."

Jeff pulled her onto his lap and gave her a big bear hug and kissed her firmly on the lips. "I promise, I know you have always wanted to do this and besides, I'll be able to come out and get a free feed." Lilly laughed; she was excited that she could fulfil one of her dreams and get away from the trucks.

The restaurant had been a Greek Taverna, and she was turning it into a Mediterranean Restaurant with food from Italy, Greece, France, Turkey, Spain and other European countries. Lilly worked hard for the next two months renovating the restaurant, employing staff, advertising and deciding on the menu. She did most of the painting herself, inside was white and blue, with large murals for the walls, one of Mykonos the other Santorini. She pulled out the old bar and replaced it with a new one. On one side of the restaurant were tables and chairs to seat fifty people, on the other side a lounge area where they would have live music and dancing. The restaurant overlooked the Hastings River with amazing sunsets everyday. As Lilly sat on the back step only five metres from the river with a glass of wine she felt excited, finally she had something of her own, something that she owned just for herself. She couldn't have done it without her good friend Miranda's help, she had encouraged her, helped her set up the finances and backed her all the way. Tomorrow they would open the restaurant, and her dream would be realised.

CHAPTER 30

2012

It started as a conversation over dinner and a few glasses or maybe bottles of wine. The next thing Lilly knew Jeff had signed them up for a trek across the Simpson Desert with the Hanley's who had made this trip seven times already. Lilly's idea of camping was a Formula 1 motel, they left Port Macquarie four days before Easter and headed for Dubbo where they were to meet Viv and Jan. Jan was so prepared she had emailed a full itinerary of their trip and a list of things they would need to take, so with the 4wd packed they headed out. The second night was Broken Hill, on arriving Lilly and Jeff found out that Jan's Dad had passed away in New Zealand, so this trip was dedicated to him. He was with them in spirit as they headed out to Maree in South Australia with a last stop at Petersbourgh for supplies then out on the Oodnadatta track with a stop at the ochre cliffs with their vivid colours of oranges and yellows before arriving at the Maree Pub for the night.

On Easter Friday they made the two hundred kilometre trip to William Creek with a stop at Lake Eyre for a look at the vast salt pan. Next, it was a stop at the bubbler and Blanche Cup springs, amazing ponds of water coming up from the underground artesian water table. Strangways Springs was a heritage site and was an Overland Telegraph Repeater Station which relayed signals along the route from Adelaide to Darwin, its ruins were well posted with descriptions of what the houses were like and historical information plus there were several walks around the ruins to learn the history of this isolated remote place. It made Lilly realise how isolated and lonely it must have been for the first settlers out here in the middle of nowhere. That night they stayed at William Creek.

There were so many ruins to stop and explore along the way as they followed the Old Ghan Railway Line and the Overland Telegraph Line. On reaching Oodnadatta Pink roadhouse they refuelled the cars and their bellies, while enjoying a coffee, they were approached by the local police officer who explained that the road ahead to Dalhousie Springs was shut so instead of one hundred and sixty kilometre trip they had a six hundred and forty kilometre diversion out to the Stuart Highway and back in to Mt Dare. Arriving late in the evening it was straight to the pub for dinner and drinks.

For the next three days, they cruised across the red sandhills of the Simpson Desert averaging twenty-four kilometres an hour, they got bogged and broke a shock absorber on the car, luckily Jeff was very mechanically minded and soon had them back on the road. The dingoes stood and stared at them as they passed, they saw camel tracks, then made their way up and over the famous Big Red Sand Dune and onto Birdsville pub for a hot shower, a cold beer, steak and a good night's sleep before heading to Innaminka the next day. Lilly had a new app on her IPad, the Hema

4wd maps tracks you live via satellite. So with great hesitation Viv let Lilly lead the way, following the track on her maps, all was going well until someone moved a fence and forgot to tell Hema. Then it was on to Bourke for their final night together before heading for home. It had been an unbelievable adventure and Lilly could not wait for the next trip, Jeff had been so happy and easy going all the way, he was always better when they were on holiday. In ten days they had travelled six thousand kilometres and been in four states.

Lilly was at the office doing accounts when a text came through from Kelly. Can I borrow your car today please, I'll clean it up later? Lilly looked at the message and shook her head, Jeff had discussed this with her last night. Since Kelly had turned eighteen she was not helping as much around the house and was going out all the time, he would constantly whinge to her but say nothing to Kelly. That was always left to Lilly to do, he wanted to be the good guy and Lilly had to play bad cop. Even though Kelly was not her daughter she still loved her and had lots of good times with her, she had always wanted a daughter. Kelly had also been there and supported her when Jeff had abused her. Kelly had used her car for two weeks and had promised to clean and wash it as well as fill it up with fuel, she had still not done this also there was a scratch on the side that wasn't there before. Jeff had told her not to lend the car to Kelly again. She had to learn some responsibility. Lilly texted back 'No you cannot borrow my car, you said you would clean it and fuel it up a week ago, and you still haven't. You should be helping all the time, not just when you want something.'

It had been a long day at work, Jeff was away in the Darwin depot and would be back in a few days until then she had to work late to keep up with the busy season they were having as well as work at the restaurant at night. Kelly came out of her room when Lilly walked into the kitchen sulking.

"Hi honey, how was your day?"

"Well, I had to catch the bus downtown because you wouldn't let me use your car."

"It is my car Kelly, and I don't have to lend it to you every time you ask. If you'd cleaned it and fueled it up like you promised to do a week ago then it may have been a different answer, but you didn't." Lilly was tired and had a headache. She didn't need this right now.

"I said I would do it!" Kelly snapped at her.

"Yes, but when? By the way, there is a scratch and dent on the driver's side back door. Do you know what happened there?"

"You're always complaining, I didn't do it, you probably did it yourself and now you're blaming me. Jeff would have let me take it."

"Are you for real? It was Jeff who told me not to give you the car and how dare you speak to me like that. Who is the one who's been taking care of you all this time, you're not even my daughter yet I choose to help you out and now you're trying to make out like I'm nasty because I won't lend you my car? It is my car!"

Kelly turned and stormed back to her room muttering to herself, Lilly followed her "What did you just say?"

Kelly turned around and yelled at her "You're a selfish bitch!"

Lilly stood looking at this girl she had taken into her home with disbelief. "Get out, I won't be spoken to like that, you are ungrateful and nasty, just get out of my sight. How dare you, after everything I have done for you in the past three years just because I won't lend you my car I'm a bitch."

"Well, actually bitch is an understatement." Kelly grabbed her bag and walked out slamming the door behind her.

Lilly needed a hot bath and a drink. She hoped that once Kelly had time to think about her actions she would realise how wrong she had been and would apologise. As she lay in the bath with a glass of red wine she mulled over her life, was she even happy? All Jeff's children showed her no respect; it didn't help that he wouldn't pull them into line and he undermined everything she did. Their marriage was like a roller coaster up and down; it was taking its toll on her.

The phone was ringing as she dried herself and dressed, it was Jeff "Hello."

"What the fuck is going on down there? Kelly has called me and told me you kicked her out of the house and told her not to come back."

"Jeff calm down, it's all over the bloody car, I wouldn't let her take it, and she called me a bitch, so I said get out, I didn't tell her not to come back."

"Why didn't you just give her the car?"

"Because you told me not to, she had to learn to respect things."

"No I didn't."

Oh god here we go again, he's said one thing then changes his mind and blames someone else, of course he would be taking her side now so he could look like a good guy, Lilly knew there was no point arguing, he had selective memory. "I've had enough of being treated like shit by your kids Jeff."

Jeff's tone was filled with a dark rage spewing down the line. "Don't push me when it comes to the kids. I promise if anything happens to her while I'm away god fuckin help you, you fuckin big hero." That was the end of the call, Lilly knew she would cop an ear full when he returned home, but she would stand her ground.

When Lilly got home from work the next day Josie was there as usual preparing dinner, she told her that Kelly had been to the house earlier and taken all her clothes and belongings from her room and to tell Lilly that she would not be back. This was going from bad to worse, well one bright side she could now clean the room and repaint it like she had planned to do. If Kelly wanted to go, let her. Lilly spent the weekend painting and cleaning the room and was painting the skirting boards when Jeff arrived home; she could tell he was not in a good mood by the slamming of doors, he stormed into the room and glared at her.

"You phone Kelly right now and apologise you self-ish bitch. You tell her to come home."

"I will not. I have nothing to apologise for. She's the one that called me a bitch, she should be apologising."

"It's all about you isn't it, grow up and pull your head out of your arse." He took a menacing step towards her.

"Piss off Jeff I'm over it I won't take any more of this shit from your kids or you."

Jeff picked up the bedside table and threw it at her hitting her in the shoulder. "You're a fat fucking whore, a selfish fucking bitch, why don't you just fucking leave?" He grabbed his car keys and left, leaving Lilly crying on the floor. Jeff didn't speak to her for a week, he helped Kelly get a flat and bought her all new furniture and even a cheap car. Kelly was telling everyone that Lilly had kicked her out and told her not to come back. Lilly messaged her to tell the truth and to stop being disrespectful. Kelly texted back, "I haven't been disrespectful to you, all I said was you were a horrible person for kicking me out. I haven't even done anything bad to you except call you a bitch. You're wasting your time trying to pick fights haha I have a sick home, everything I want and it's all because of you. I'm glad you kicked me out. It's the best thing that's happened to me so thanks. I still care about you. I hope that one day this can all be water under the bridge bye."

Over the next month things calmed down, but there were still issues with Tara and Craig and how much time they were spending on their iPods and face-book. They were not doing their homework or help-ing around the house, and when Lilly asked Craig to clean his room, his response was "that's what Josie gets paid to do." Lilly gave him a dressing down over his attitude and told him Josie was not the maid but there to help with their school work and run them around and that they should be grateful and not disrespectful. The problem was they had no idea of hard work or money because their father would give them whatever they wanted, he wanted to be their best friend, not a father. Jeff would ground them for a week but then turn around two days later and let them go out and do whatever they wanted. Lilly tried to explain that this was sending the wrong message, they knew they could do wrong, get in trouble and that it would all blow over and they could get whatever they wanted from their Dad.

The last two months had been hell for Lilly, firstly Tara had gotten too close to Elly's face and Craig had hit the dog on the back just at that moment, so Elly struck out and bit Tara on the lip and she had to go to hospital and have three stitches. The next thing they had the police on the doorstep saying they had a complaint from the children's mother that there was a savage dog there that needed to be put down. Lilly was beside herself Elly was her dog; it wasn't the dog's fault, and she wasn't savage. Everybody knows not to get right into a dog's face, especially a blue heeler. Then a week later Lilly had just arrived home from work at eleven pm when the police were on the doorstep again wanting to check on the children, Craigs mother had informed them that Craig had been on Facebook and stated his father had punched him in the head. Craig had been banned from Facebook as well as had his iPod taken from him for back chatting his father, but he had found it and was still using it. The police then checked both children's rooms to make sure they were fine and informed Jeff that Craig was indeed still awake and had his iPod with him, Jeff promptly took it away. Jeff and Lilly checked his iPod to find that he had posted his father had hit him over the head for back chatting, he had messaged his girlfriend telling her he hated his father, calling him names and a selfish bastard.

Once again Jeff did not follow through with any punishment and then complained that the kids didn't do as they were told. Lilly refused to discipline the children anymore and made Jeff deal with any issues, she didn't see the point, they didn't listen to her and besides Jeff never backed her up.

Jeff's moods were growing more and more unpredictable and Lilly never knew what mood he would be in, she had also started to become short- tempered and was extremely stressed. Even though she had let Jeff take over the running of the removal business, she still had to go to work most days to help, as well as work in her restaurant. Even though Jeff had promised to support her, every time they had a fight it was thrown in her face "well you're living your dream with your restaurant" the removal business was struggling financially, and Lilly had to try to make ends meet while Jeff's idea was just to spend more money and go bigger. Just like at home Jeff wanted to be everyone's friend and would not make the hard decisions at work. He would bitch about the staff behind their back constantly but never say anything to their face.

Lilly's happy place was her restaurant, she wasn't making lots of money, enough to pay her debts and she was happy with that. It was more about having something of her own. She loved sitting on the verandah at the restaurant overlooking the river, enjoying a coffee or a glass of wine watching the sun set over the river, it was so peaceful. This was her place to escape the turmoil of her unhappy home life. Lilly enjoyed being in the kitchen with Chef Sam helping to prepare entrees, sides and desserts, she loved cooking, and Sam was an amazing chef and so easy to get along with. Lilly would work the front of house, wait tables, cook and sing on some nights. She loved being here. It was such a shame that every so often Jeff had to have a dig at her about her 'living the dream".

They landed in Queenstown, New Zealand. It was the middle of August and extremely cold, they had flown over for their annual association removal conference and decided to have a few days off first before the meetings started. They spent the time looking around and trying to learn to snowboard. They had gone out for dinner then off to a bar for a few drinks, and it had been going surprisingly well. They chatted and laughed over dinner, Jeff had a bit too much to drink, his mood had suddenly darkened, and he was trying to provoke her. This is crazy she thought, it's like she was living with two different people. Lilly tried to get him to leave with her around nine pm to go back to the hotel. Jeff refused to leave, so she went back without him. She drifted off to sleep around midnight and woke again at three am. Jeff had not returned, she became concerned and called his cell phone but he was not picking up. Lilly became very worried, what if something had happened to him, she was about to go out looking for him when he stumbled through the door, pushing her out of the way and face planting on the bed promptly passing out. The next day Jeff offered no explanation and told her she should have stayed out with him instead of going back to the hotel and sulking.

Mark had been working with them in the company for a year now and was flying in that afternoon to join them for the conference. Jeff was still being a total arse; it seemed like he was going out of his way to upset her, undermining her in conversations and being cold towards her. Lilly decided it was best to just stay out of his way and keep quiet, if she had learnt anything about living with Jeff in the last few years, it was that she was never right and whatever happened it would be her fault so better to shut up and simply agree. Lilly had hoped that this trip would bring some romance back to their marriage, that was not to be. It just pushed them further apart. It was like Jeff was jealous of the fact that everyone wanted to talk to her and asked her questions about the business, not him. The band wanted her to get up and sing with them, but she knew from the look on Jeff's face that it would only antagonise him, so she declined. Lilly was glad when it was time to go home, and she hadn't enjoyed this trip at all.

CHAPTER 31

2013

It had been raining now for over a week and the river behind the restaurant was rising fast. There was a large amount of debris floating down the river, large tree branches and rubbish bobbing along in the dirty, fast flowing current. The water had started to lap at the bank and as Lilly stood looking at the rising river she wondered if she should cancel tonight's function. The food had been prepared, the restaurant decorated in the Priscilla Queen of the desert theme, they had fifty people booked in for the dinner and show. Hopefully, the river would not break its banks until tomorrow, they had been on flood alert now for the past twenty-four hours. There was a knock at the door she opened it to find two police officers, the road in would be closed and they would have to evacuate the building. Lilly had no choice but to call all her clients and tell them that they had to postpone until the river dropped. Chef Sam helped her move things up onto table tops just in case the river came into the building and then they left and hoped for the best.

It was two days before Lilly could return to the restaurant to find that the water had come up level with the top step on the back verandah, almost entering the building. All around the verandah where the water had receded were branches and logs, caught amongst the piers, there was thick, brown mud surrounding the whole area it would take days to clear it all. Lilly was thankful that they had not lost anything or had any major damage and she set about rescheduling their function for the following weekend.

Jeff had been even more difficult lately and kept changing his mind about attending Mark's wedding in Fiji, finally, he had agreed to go and Lilly, ever hopeful, thought it might give them a chance to reconnect as they would celebrate their tenth wedding anniversary the day before the wedding. Arriving at Nadi International Airport, they collected their luggage and caught a shuttle bus to Port Denarau Marina. They then boarded the boat for the one and a half hour trip to Mana Island. It was encircled by clear turquoise seas, coral reefs and beautiful white sandy beaches. They enjoyed relaxing days of swimming, snorkelling, exploring the island on foot and resting on a beach chair in the warm sun.

Lilly and Jeff enjoyed a beautiful breakfast together at the waterfront restaurant before walking along the beach and taking a swim. Jeff was a different person when they were on holidays; he was very loving and affectionate and kept telling her how much he loved her. Lilly was hoping that this would continue when they returned home and back to work, but he had done this so many times before that she didn't hold out much hope.

Lilly stood looking out at the beautiful setting for her eldest son's wedding, they were to be married on the beach, the sand was white and the ocean was blue-green. There was an arch covered in flowers and a small white cover over the bamboo. Lilly prayed that Mark and Lori would have a wonderful life together, they were such a great match. Lori was a fantastic mother to their two- year-old boy, Jackson, Lilly's first grandchild and they complimented each other in so many ways, they had been together for almost six years. Lori walked down the beach accompanied by her father and two bridesmaids with traditional Fijian warriors leading the way. The ceremony was beautiful, and Lilly cried tears of joy, this was followed by photos around the island then back for dinner at one of the waterfront restaurants. Jake made a fantastic speech for his brother which had everyone in tears at the love and sincerity of his words: they all danced and laughed late into the night.

As Lilly settled into her seat next to Jeff on the flight back to Australia the next day, she prayed things would change. She wanted to work things out with Jeff, she didn't know how.

Their annual work conference was being held in Alice Springs this year, Lilly had already organised all the airfares and accommodation but she was concerned Jeff's mood swings were getting worse, one minute he was going the next he wasn't.

"Jeff we leave tomorrow the flights, hotel and conference are all booked and paid for, you can't pull out now?" Lilly was frustrated with his constant swinging moods and changes in Jeff.

"I don't want to go, it's as simple as that." He grimaced and frowned at her.

"But Jeff it's all paid for and Mark will be disappointed if you don't go." Mark had been working in the business for a while now and he, Lori and Jackson were coming with them. It had all been planned, and Jeff had agreed to go, they would spend four days in Alice Springs then fly to Darwin to spend another four days checking out the running of the Darwin depot before coming home.

"I want to fly home after the conference, not go to Darwin." his frown deepened.

"Jeff, we need to do some work at the Darwin depot and catch up with the staff."

"Well, you can do it, change my flight or I'm not going."

"Fine, I'll change it then." Lilly knew not to argue; she wouldn't win. Maybe if he came and started enjoying himself he would change his mind, if not she would change it while they were away.

It was six am, and Lilly was up and dressed and doing a final check that she had everything. "Come on Jeff, get up, the taxi will be here in thirty minutes to take us to the airport."

Jeff rolled over in the bed and gave her that look "Did you change my ticket to fly back after the conference?"

"No, I didn't have time. I'll do it once we are there now come on, hurry up."

"I'm not going then. I told you to change my ticket."

"I will, I'll do it tonight. Mark was looking forward to this trip with you, come on, please. It's too late to cancel your flight this morning, and there is no refund on it or the accommodation and conference fees. We will have a look at flights when we get into Alice Springs."

"I don't care, and besides I don't want to go and see that pack of arseholes, they all think they are so good and better than me, you can go by yourself and play the big woman. I told you to change the ticket, and you didn't, so fuck you." Jeff stared at her with such hatred Lilly couldn't help herself, she reached out and slapped his face.

"You are such a selfish, spiteful arsehole Jeff. It's always about you. Stay home then if you're going to be in this mood no one wants to be around you." Lilly picked up her bags and walked out the door to wait for the taxi. Why did he have to make life so hard? Nothing she did seemed to please him. It was like he enjoyed pushing her buttons, he liked to upset her, he fed on her hurt and tears. Once again she was left to take care of the business side of things even though she had stepped back from it so he could be in charge. She was so thankful that Mark was there to help her. Jeff only went to work when he felt like it and wouldn't make any decisions, that was left to the staff or her. Old patterns were emerging, and she had the feeling that maybe he was being unfaithful, it was just a hunch, but she was learning to listen to her gut.

The conference was a great event, and she told everyone that there had been a last minute family emergency which meant Jeff had to stay home. Lilly had a wonderful time with Mark, Lori and Jackson exploring around Alice Springs before they headed up to Darwin for a few days work and a look around before returning home. Lilly only spoke to Jeff three times while she was away, he would not return her calls or texts, the office staff said he hadn't come into work much at all. This didn't help her suspicions. Jeff acted like nothing had happened when she returned home, she was sure he had dementia or was bipolar or something, it was like she was living with two different people, you never knew which one was going to be there when you arrived home.

CHAPTER 32

Lilly sat on the verandah of her restaurant overlooking the river. She was still trying to digest what Lana had just called to tell her. Lana and Lilly had been friends for a long time; they were just like sisters, Lilly had been the MC at her wedding to Troy and had sung for them to dance to their bridal waltz. Lana and her husband Troy would help her out sometimes at her restaurant waiting on tables or behind the bar. Troy's health had been deteriorating over the last couple of years. Troy had Cystic Fibrosis, he'd had it since childhood, it had always been part of his life and had restricted him from doing many things as he grew up, but it didn't stop him from enjoying his life.

Troy's lungs were now failing him, and he was finding it hard to breathe, he had a persistent cough and would tire quickly, making it hard for him to work. Three months ago his doctor had told them that he had only about six months to live. Lana was beside herself, she knew when she had fallen in love with Troy that he may not have a full life ahead of him, and to have children they would have to go through IVF treatment, but she loved him. Lana had been trying for two years to get him onto the Lung Transplant list; finally, he had been accepted. Troy would go to Sydney every six weeks to have treatment to help with his condition at the Royal Prince Alfred hospital, today was their son's first birthday and tomorrow was Father's Day, so Lana and the children had gone to Sydney to have a family weekend.

Then they got the phone call from St Vincent's Hospital, a donor had become available, and he would need to be on standby in case the other recipient could not make it on time. Luckily for Troy, the fact he was in Sydney and close to St Vincent's Hospital, he was now the number one candidate to receive the lungs. But he had to be at the hospital within half an hour.

Lana bundled Troy and the kids into the car and drove as fast and as safely as she could in the Sydney traffic. Pulling up outside the emergency door the transplant team were waiting with a wheelchair, he was given a handful of tablets to take as they rushed him away to prepare for theatre. As the emergency doors closed behind him, Lana stood staring in disbelief, they were taking her husband away, and she hadn't even had time to say anything to him, it had all happened so quickly. After Troy had been prepared for surgery and was about to be taken into the operating theatre, Lana and the children were given two minutes with him to say whatever they needed. Lana looked down at her husband, laying on the hospital gurney, this may be the last time she ever saw him alive.

Troy looked at his wife and whispered: "I just want to wake up."

With the two children clinging to Lana screaming and crying, she took his hand, "You have too, you can't leave like this. I love you." She could see the terror in his eyes, the uncertainty. It had all happened so fast. There had been no time to think about what if it all went wrong.

Lilly realised her problems were small compared to what Lana was going through right now, she looked up at the heavens and said a silent prayer for Troy, he was an amazing, beautiful person, a wonderful father and husband, she prayed he would pull through and recover.

It would be a lengthy operation; firstly they would remove his diseased lungs, then transplant the donor's lungs, one at a time. Then if the transplant was successful, Troy would be moved to ICU and monitored closely, he would be taking a host of medications to keep the new lungs healthy and to help stop his body rejecting them. All Lilly could do now was to wait and hope, she would be there if Lana needed her.

It had been an agonising twenty-four hours waiting for word from Lana. Finally, the call came, Troy was recovering in the ICU, his operation had lasted eight and a half hours and so far all was going well, his body was accepting the new organs, the future looked promising. He would have to remain in ICU until he was stable enough to be moved to a ward before transferring to a rehabilitation house at Bondi for another two weeks. This had hit close to home for Lilly, she now realised why organ donation was so important, and when her time came, she would want her organs donated to help someone else have a chance of life.

CHAPTER 33

OCTOBER 2013

The debts were mounting at the removal company, and Jeff would not listen to Lilly that they should cut back on spending, he just wanted to buy more trucks and employ more staff. It was left to Lilly to find the money to pay the bills, money they did not have. She hated it when the phone rang, and she knew it would be someone looking for payment. It didn't help that Jeff would only go to work when it suited him, you can't run a business that size when you aren't there to make decisions, leaving it to the staff. The mood in the office was always strained, and they would constantly be bitching to Lilly. It had been a long week at work between the restaurant and helping with the transport company Lilly was exhausted mentally and physically.

Lilly arrived home coming in through the side door, Josie was cooking dinner and looked up at her as she entered. "Bad day?"

"You have no idea. I'm sick of this shit. Did you pick up that parcel for me?"

"Oh sorry I forgot, Craig's football practice went longer than normal, I wanted to get home to get tea on."

"For fuck sake can't anyone do what I ask?"

Josie stopped stirring the pot and looked at Lilly. "Really! It's only a parcel, Lilly I can get it tomorrow."

"Don't bother, I'll do it myself." She dropped her bag on the floor with a loud thud and kicked off her shoes.

"You know what? You're lucky I love you Lilly because right now I don't like you very much." She stopped what she was doing and wiped her hands. "You have become so nasty lately, everyone is walking on eggshells around you. This marriage is toxic, look what he has turned you into, where is the fun-loving, happy caring Lilly we all know and love, where has she gone? Jeff is destroying you, and it breaks my heart to watch it happen, but you won't listen to anyone. Go take a good long hard look in the mirror, see if you can find Lilly because I don't know who you are. I'm going home." Josie grabbed her bag and her keys and left slamming the door behind her.

Lilly stood for a moment staring at the door, her words were like a slap in the face, what the hell, stuff her what would she know, Lilly poured herself a glass of wine and went out the back to sit on the old church pew, Elly curled up at her feet. Why could no one see she was struggling to keep it all together, there was nothing wrong with her, they could all go get stuffed. Lilly went to the bathroom and washed her hands, she looked up at the mirror and stared at her reflection. Who was that woman staring back at her? Could that really be her? My god she looked haggard, there were dark circles under her eyes, her face was puffy and she had put on quite a bit of weight in the last few years. Lilly stood there and stared at the sad woman looking back at her, and the tears fell down her face. Josie was right, she had changed, she had become critical and nasty, she was turning into the same person as Jeff, and that had to stop. Lilly picked up her phone and rang Josie in tears apologising, begging for her to forgive her, they had been friends for so long, it took someone who truly loved her to make her wake up to herself. From then on Lilly would not listen to the whingeing in the office instead telling them to sort it out themselves, she would no longer be doing the dirty work. She refused to sort out any issues that Jeff was supposed to be dealing with, forcing him to take control, but of course, he didn't, he just left it to the staff to sort it out. Lilly started to take control of herself and mentally pulled herself up before she said or did anything.

Jeff took her to the Gold Coast for her forty-ninth birthday for the weekend, once again it was the nice Jeff. They went out for dinner, went shopping and strolled along the beach. Lilly wished he could be like this all the time, it made it hard for her to leave, he could be so loving one minute giving her a glimmer of hope, then he would turn into nasty Jeff again, and she would be in tears wondering why the hell she was here.

They had to leave their weekend getaway soon and head off to the airport to return back to work. Lilly sat in the bed having a cup of tea as Jeff lay beside her, his arm across her lap, he looked up at her with a smile of love and happiness.

"You are so beautiful, I love you so much." He kissed her hand.

"I love you too Jeff." Maybe, just maybe this time would be different.

Jeff became distant again as soon as they went back to work, he didn't show her any affection at all, and it was like he was repulsed to touch her. Lilly spoke to Lucy, her friend and secretary about Jeff many times about his mood swings. Lucy had known him for many years and she'd seen a real change in him over the past five years, and she even confessed to her that he had had an affair with her sister when he was with Darla. She too had been on the end of his anger. Lucy had been with her at the office late one evening when they had been catching up on book work when Jeff had come in yelling at Lilly, getting so angry he punched a hole in the wall and the office door.

This craziness was getting out of control. How much longer could she tolerate this continued abuse? What choice did she have? Like the old saying goes. It's better the devil you know, so once again she shut up and just got on with life.

"Craig can you come here please" Lilly was in the laundry about to do the washing, Craig had placed a pile of his clothes on the floor to be washed, she had only washed two days earlier there was no way he could have worn all these clothes in that time.

"What?" Craig slumped up against the door frame.

"Craig, have you even worn these clothes? They look like the ones I washed the other day and put in your room on your bed to put away."

Craig just shrugged "I don't know they were on the floor, so I just put them all out."

"I don't wash for fun you know these clothes are clean, fold them and put them away now." She handed him the clean clothes, Lilly was so tired of the laziness of Jeffs' children they expected everyone else to do everything for them.

"I'll do it later. I'm going surfing with Dad," he smirked at her.

"You will do it now please Craig."

"I'll do it when I get back; don't get your knickers in a knot."

"Don't speak to me like that you ungrateful child, I'd love to go to the beach too, but I'm stuck here cleaning and washing. How about a little help."

Craig just walked away from her going outside to where his father was tying the surfboards on the roof racks of the car. "Jeff, Craig needs to fold and put his clothes away before he goes anywhere."

"He can do it when we get back," Jeff shouted to her.

"No Jeff he can do it now, he just put all the clean clothes I washed two days ago back out to be washed because he is too lazy to put them in the cupboard. I'm sick of this, please back me up."

Jeff looked at Craig who stood there with a smug look on his face. "Come on, let's go buddy. See you when we get back."

That was it, Lilly was left standing there as they drove away. Fine, if no one else was going to help her, she wouldn't do it either. She went back to the laundry, got all of Craig's clothes clean and dirty and dumped them on his bedroom floor. No longer would she do his washing. Of course, this caused a fight between her and Jeff; he accused her of doing nothing for his kids. What did he think she had been doing the last ten years? She had cooked, cleaned, taken them to appointments, cared for them when they were sick, she did everything for them. This time she stood her ground and refused to do anything for Craig. Lilly had had enough of being treated like shit by these two teenagers that were only nice to her when they wanted something from her. Jeff slept in the front bedroom for the next two weeks. He usually sulked for a few days then came back to their bedroom but not this time he hardly even spoke to Lilly. This is being a bit over dramatic, Lilly thought, and she went to the bedroom where he was laying on the bed watching tv.

"Jeff, what's going on? Are you coming back to our room?"

"No, I've had enough of your constant bitching; this marriage is over." He never took his eyes from the tv screen.

Lilly stood there stunned had she heard him right. "What?"

"You heard me, we are over, the marriage is finished, I don't want to be with you anymore."

"Are you serious? All because of your lazy children, I'm not a maid you know? Are you seeing someone else?"

"Fuck off bitch, of course you blame it on every- one else. You're the one I can't stand being around now fuck off out of my room."

"Fine then if that's the case, you can do all the cooking, washing and cleaning for yourself and your kids. You need to grow up Jeff." Lilly grabbed her handbag, ran outside and jumped in the car. She drove to the beach. She needed to clear her head. As she walked and watched Elly bound in and out of the waves, she made herself a promise. It was time to think about her future, her happiness. She was desperately unhappy and kept hanging in there because she didn't want another failed marriage. Her unhappiness was affecting everyone around her. It was time to let go, but it would not be easy, they had a lot of property and debt to sort out. She made the decision to put herself first, enough is enough!

Lilly had a sneaking suspicion that Jeff was cheating on her, so she pulled up his phone records online and scanned through them. There was one number that had a lot of calls, and late at night, he had even phoned this number within half an hour of returning from their romantic weekend. The number was Lucy's! Lilly felt her heart sink; surely Lucy would not be sneaking behind her back with her husband. Lucy had been cheated on herself and was very verbal about how much she hated women who took other women's husbands. It would explain why for the last few months Lucy had started dressing up more and wearing makeup to the office. Lilly never thought twice when Jeff went to help Lucy, she was a single Mum with two kids, and she was sixteen years younger than Jeff. Lilly checked further back on the phone records, and sure enough, there were many calls and texts going back to just before he refused to go away with her to Alice Springs. Lilly could see where he was when he had made phone calls, and a lot were from Wauchope where Lucy lived and at times when he had told her he was surfing or fishing. The realisation hit her, he was having an affair with Lucy, the one person she thought she could trust, Lilly had told her so many private thoughts and had even discussed how their marriage was in trouble with her. Lucy was envious of Lilly's lifestyle, Lilly thought for a moment, as hard as it would be, she decided not to say anything just yet, she would wait before confronting Jeff, she wanted to be sure.

Over the next month, Lilly kept a check on where Jeff said he would be and compared it to his phone records and sure enough he was lying to her. He would go out at night leaving her at home with his children, when Lilly asked him where he was going and that he needed to take care of his kids not leave them with her, he would yell at her telling her "it's none of your business and it's not like you're going out anyway."

It was three days before Christmas and Lilly had just returned home from work at the restaurant. It was ten pm. Jeff's car was not in the driveway; she decided to drive out to Wauchope to see if he was at Lucy's and sure enough, his car was out the front. Lilly felt sick in the stomach, her heart pounding, she had to know, she marched up to the door and knocked. Most of the house was in darkness; she knocked again. It took a few minutes for the door to open. It was Lucy's niece.

"I want to see my husband. Let me in please." Lilly could feel her temper rising. She knew she had to keep in control. She grabbed the door handle and tried to open it, but it was locked.

"Wait there I'll get him." She closed the door and Lilly could hear the whispers and shuffling inside.

It was five minutes before Jeff came to the door. "Hey what's going on?" He acted like it was normal to be at a single woman's home at eleven o'clock at night.

"Let me in! Where is Lucy? What the hell is going on?" She tried to keep her voice calm, but her stomach felt like there were elephants doing cartwheels in there.

Jeff unlocked and opened the door "we're just having a few drinks, nothing else."

"Well why did it take so long to open the door? Don't lie to me Jeff. I'm not stupid." Lilly barged past him and out the back, Lucy was sitting at the table her clothes were all dishevelled and she had a guilty look on her face. "What's going on Lucy?"

"I don't know what you're talking about, we are just chatting." Lucy's face was turning red, and she would not look Lilly in the eye.

"Are you two having an affair?"

"How dare you, you fucking fat cow, I need someone to talk to, I can't talk to you. Besides, I told you a month ago. We were over."

"This has been going on for more than a month Jeff. I checked your phone records it's been happening since August. That's why you didn't come away with me, you have been lying to me for months. It was you who said to me, don't put yourself in a position that will cause doubt in your partner's mind, what do you think this is?" Lucy sat quietly. Lilly could see her shaking as she went to pick up her drink. "You of all people Lucy after you were cheated on, I didn't expect this from you. So all those times you sat and bitched about Jeff were just a lie, you want my life well you can have it, trust me it's not as good as you think. You both deserve each other. I no longer want you in my office, you can move your things out to the front desk. And you will no longer have access to the bank accounts that I trusted you with. That's if you have the gall to show up at work. Jeff, you go on about how much you take care of your kids, yet you leave them with me or alone at home late at night while you're out with this tart. You both make me sick." Lilly held her head high and turned and walked out to her car, she drove around the corner, pulled over to the side of the street and burst into tears, she knew the marriage was over but why did he have to cheat on her? What was wrong with her that a man could not remain faithful, she did everything for them, and they still treated her like crap. Tomorrow she'd go to see the lawyer and start the process of settling their finances.

Lucy called in sick the next day obviously not having the guts to show her face and when she did return to work she walked around like she owned the place, she felt that she could do what she liked. Jeff and Lucy denied the affair at the start, but it eventually came out months later that they had been seeing each other for over six months while Jeff and Lilly were still sharing the same bed. Jeff wanted Lilly to move out of their house. She told him to go to hell, if he wanted to be with someone else he could get out and take his kids with him, she had done nothing wrong and would not be leaving so he could move his bitch in. Lilly put things into motion, contacting her lawyer and getting advice on her next move. She placed the restaurant up for sale and started to plan a new life for herself, alone.

When Lilly told Jeff that she had sold the restaurant his response was "Good at least now you don't have your dream." Lilly tried to work with Jeff to try and get the business on track, but it was too hard, once again he wouldn't show up to work, and she was left to try and fix the mounting debt he had put them in. The staff all knew what had happened; they didn't like Lucy before this all happened. She was sarcastic and rude to them. The staff only tolerated her now because she was sleeping with the boss. When Jeff moved out of their home on Friday into a unit, Lucy stayed with him all weekend. Kelly had told Lilly that she was always there, and she was not happy with her Dad for what he had done and that Craig and Tara didn't like Lucy. Lilly didn't care. It was no longer her problem.

CHAPTER 34

2014

Jeff only stayed at this unit for two months, before renting a house and moving Lucy and her two children in with him. Jeff had agreed to buy her half of the business, the house was to be sold, and they would go their separate ways. Jeff would be nice when he wanted something, and then turn on her when she would not agree to the terms of the settlement. They would agree on a price then he would offer her less, this dragged on for over nine months until exhausted, Lilly finally decided to take half of what she should have received. Jeff had abused her so much that she was close to a nervous breakdown, she couldn't eat, sleep or think straight, her sanity was more important than money, she had to get away from him before he finally destroyed her.

"What will you do now?" Josie was concerned for her friend, she had watched what Jeff had done to her over the years, and Lilly had always worked. She was always helping everyone else and not taking care of herself.

"Oh, I don't know. I'll buy a caravan and go travel around Australia, just the dog and me." Lilly laughed. "I'll become a gypsy."

"Oh, that sounds like fun. Why don't you? You could sing all over the place; maybe find a nice fella one day."

"I don't want a fella, I can't seem to pick a decent one. It's silly, and I don't know what I'll do." Lilly had been out on several dates and had a few one night stands, for which she hated herself for the next day, why did she feel she needed a man to want her to make her feel whole?

Lilly sat on her old church pew with a glass of wine looking up at the stars, asking her Pa for help and guidance. She thought about the caravan, why the hell not? What else was she going to do? She would be turning fifty that year, and she could travel and call it her "Free Fabulous and Fifty" tour. Lilly knew she needed to get away from all the reminders, the house had sold, and she needed somewhere to live. Lilly decided she would go out and buy a caravan and travel Australia by herself until she could be comfortable with living alone and happy with herself again. Until she could find peace within, she would never be able to have a happy relationship. Not that she would be able to trust a man again for a very long time. It would still be a few months before final settlement, but she needed to get away now.

As Lilly drove down the Hume Highway on her way to Pambula to surprise her friend Lalicia for her fiftieth birthday, she reminisced about their school days. Lalicia had been her best friend at school, since she was fourteen and she had moved to Coonabarabran. They had met on her first day at school. As Lilly was new and starting near the end of the year, the teachers had asked one of the smart, posh girls to show her around. As they walked through the yard

Lilly had noticed a group of girls over in the corner. They looked like they were the cool girls of the school. One stood out; she was tall and slim with light brown hair, she smiled at Lilly as she walked past. At recess, she had introduced herself as Lalicia and asked her to come to join her and meet the group, from then on they were best friends. Lalicia lived in town, so when they played in the basketball night competition, Lilly would stay at her house, that way her mother didn't have to drive the hour round trip into town to pick her up late at night. They would stay at each other's house some weekends, doing the usual teenage things, doing each other's hair, talking about boys, walking around the streets meeting up with other friends and getting into a little mischief.

They had remained friends all these years, Lilly had been a bridesmaid at her wedding, they had watched each other's children grow, and caught up when they could. They would go a long time without talking or seeing each other, but no matter the distance or time, it was a friendship that had lasted for over thirty years. Lilly had told Lalicia she couldn't make her fiftieth birthday party because it was too far to drive, it was a thousand kilometre from Port Macquarie, also because of all the drama happening with Jeff, Lilly didn't feel like socialising. A week before the party she decided that life was too short, so Lilly phoned and organised with Lalicia's husband to surprise her. Lilly hid in a small room at the back of the pub where the party was being held, and when Lalicia arrived, Lilly called her on her mobile phone telling her that she had sent a special present and where to find it. Lilly was excited as she heard her footsteps getting closer to her hiding spot, and was trying hard not to giggle and give it away. The door swung open, and Lalicia seeing Lilly before her stopped in shock, she was speechless for a second before screaming and grabbing Lilly in a big hug. They were inseparable all night. Lilly enjoyed her weekend away, and there was loads of laughter and way too much wine. She promised that she would make sure she would stop and appreciate the simple pleasures of life and be grateful for her friends and family.

CHAPTER 35

A NEW START

At eight am on the fourth of September 2014, Lilly drove out of Port Macquarie with her twenty foot off-road caravan hooked up behind her Land Rover, heading off on her adventure to travel around Australia. Tears flowed down her face as she left the town limits, she had mixed emotions, she was excited, scared and felt apprehensive, what the hell was she doing? Was she even capable of doing this alone? She had talked herself up to everyone about doing the big lap of Australia; now it was time to do it. Lilly was not sure of what to expect or even if she would like it or how Elly would cope with the travelling. She just knew she had to do this for herself, to find herself again, to be happy with who she was, not what she thought people wanted her to be.

Jeff had eroded her self confidence over the past twelve years to almost nothing. She had something to prove; she could do this alone; she was strong and more than capable. Her mother Rose had given her a big hug before leaving telling her she had nothing to prove to anyone but herself, and if she went out and found that it was not for her, she could always come home, she wouldn't fail because at least she had tried.

Lilly headed for the winding Walcha mountain road, glancing in the rear vision mirror she could not see the caravan only the road, her heart stopped, she panicked. Where was the van? Then she remembered she had put a camera on the back of the caravan so she could check traffic behind her and for when she was alone and reversing, she giggled with relief. She felt so silly, she looked ahead at the road and smiled. A new chapter in her life had begun. She headed for Northern Queensland, stopping at Goondiwindi for the night. Lilly loved driving with the music playing, the window down, singing along the wind blowing her hair. It was a learning curve with stopping and setting up the van each night. Luckily she had drive-through sites each time so there was no need to unhitch the van, this way she could get away early each morning. Then it was on to Cloncurry where she stocked up on groceries and fuel before heading to Karumba in the Gulf of Carpentaria, this is where she had planned to really start her trip . It took four days to drive the two thousand seven hundred kilometres to her destination, and she would spend four days here to rest and look around.

The Point Sunset Caravan Park was beautiful. It was right on the water's edge, Lilly spent her days laying on the soft sand and soaking up the sun, watching the spectacular sunsets, the Tavern was only a five-minute walk away. There were plenty of walking tracks along the river connecting the point to the main township. Lilly had heard that the prawns were amazing here, so she decided to buy some fresh ones from the fish co-op and try them. She wandered over to the fish cleaning area to place the shells in the bin, on approach she could see two men who appeared to be in their seventies cleaning their catch for the day.

"Hello love how are you? I'm Glen, and this is my mate, Nifty Nev." He gestured to the other man cleaning fish who looked up and smiled.

"Hi, I'm Lilly, and this is Elly, I'm good thank you, looks like you had a good day fishing." She pointed at the fish they were cleaning.

Nifty Nev stopped what he was doing and looked at her then the dog. "You here alone or are you travelling with someone love?"

"No it's just me and my dog Elly." Lilly reached down and patted Elly.

"Oh, so you don't have a man then?" he asked with a slight grin, his face was warm and gentle with laugh wrinkles around smiling eyes.

"No I don't, it's just me and Elly travelling Australia, we've only been on the road for six days."

Nifty Nev's lip curled in a cheeky smile "Are you looking for a man?"

What a strange question Lilly thought to herself, was this old fella hitting on her? She could not be sure.

"No I'm not looking for a man, I just got rid of one, I think I'll stay single for a while."

"Oh well if you are looking for a man love you should go to the library and find one."

Lilly pondered this she didn't understand why you would go to a library to find a man, were they smarter there or something? Nifty Nev could see her confused expression and chuckled.

"Yes love, go to the library if you want a man" he paused "why buy when you can borrow, and if you don't like it take it back and get another one." He laughed at his own joke, Lilly giggled, she chatted to them for a few minutes before waving goodbye to head to the beach to watch the sunset with a cold beer. As she sat and watched the sun sink over the ocean and the sky dancing with colour she pondered what the old man had said, maybe he had the right idea, she would treat men like fishing. From now on she would Catch, Kiss, Tag and Release.

Next stop was King Ash Bay on the other side of the Gulf in the Northern Territory, to get there she had to drive across the Gulf on the Savannah Way, it was going to be an adventure taking her through remote areas in the footsteps of the ill-fated explorers Burke and Wills. The trip through the Gulf Savannah would take her through rocky river crossings, past endless savannah woodlands and into historical mining towns. The majority of the road was unsealed, and there were creek and river crossings along the way. With a quick stop at Normanton to take a photo of the purple pub and with the replica of Krys the Savannah King, claimed to be the largest recorded saltwater crocodile captured in the world at 8.63 metres long. It had been shot by a female croc hunter in 1957 along the Norman River.

As she moved west, the country varied from scrubby and gently undulating to grassy and flat. During the wet season, the vast coastal wetlands between Karumba and Burketown were home to a huge range of water and shorebirds. First stop was Leichhardt falls, there was no water running over the long concrete causeway, and there were plenty of places to pull over. Lilly and Elly wandered around and looked at the astonishing drops and rock formations, even though the volume of water falling over the cliff face was not huge, it was still an impressive sight, she could just imagine the raging torrent of water flowing through here in the wet season when it became impassable.

Lilly learnt a valuable lesson here. Do not have glass bottles of beer in the fridge on rough roads; the jarring and shaking of the corrugated road had made the beer blow its top and the van smelt like a brewery. So there would be no cold beer tonight. She would have loved to camp here, but there were only two other couples there and she had promised her mother and her boys that she would only free camp if there were at least five other couples around. Besides, she didn't feel comfortable enough yet to free camp, so it was back on the road to Burketown for the night.

Burketown was the oldest settlement in the Gulf, boasting a rugged frontier history of "Gulf Fever" thought to be typhoid devastating the pioneers, there were also apparently lots of Barramundi here to be caught and many historical sites including the old cemetery. It was only an overnight stop. Lilly had planned her whole trip and knew how far each day she would travel and what she would see. Old habits die hard, after organising trucks for the past twelve years she had created a run sheet for her adventure. As she drove out early the next morning at dawn, bizarre cigar shaped cloud formations called "Morning Glory" where in the sky, they looked astounding.

Through the scrubby savannah woodland to Gregory River crossing, a large tropical river with clear running water between banks lined with lush vegetation and abundant wildlife, Lilly knew not to walk through the water up here, there could be crocodiles lurking. Lilly drove slowly through the rocky crossings loving the excitement of it all, she hadn't seen many cars at all on her trip so far and enjoyed the serenity of the isolation. She made her way across the broad rocky bed of the Nicholson River into the Aboriginal community of Doomadgee then onto Hells Gate Roadhouse with a stop to top up on fuel and a cold drink. Elly was travelling well and enjoyed sitting up looking out the window as they drove along. They crossed the border into the Northern Territory driving through plenty of creek and river crossings. Some were deep and fast flowing others shallow. The water crossings helped wash some of the red dust from the car, but the fine red aeolian dust known as bulldust covered the road. It was hard driving through this, and at times the car would swerve when she hit a deep patch. It also covered dangerous potholes, and when a car came the other way, it made it almost impossible to see through the large choking red cloud.

Lilly had been warned to be careful at the Calvert River crossing with its steep embankments on both sides, and it was deep and rocky. Lilly stopped and placed the Land Rover into high clearance, this lifted the car up higher off the ground to make it easier to make the crossing. She edged forward and crossed easily. It was rough and bumpy, but luckily she had been told to keep to the left side as there was a deep hole on the right where a car had gotten stuck last week in the middle of the crossing. It was then on to Borroloola and into King Ash Bay where she planned to stay for the night, pulling into the caravan park late in the afternoon. On opening the van she was horrified to find the whole inside coated in red dust, the kitchen draws had fallen out on the floor, and one of the shelves in the fridge had broken. This is not what she wanted after a long, hard day driving, and now she had to clean the van before she could have a well-earned rest. Lilly was swearing to herself and muttering about the fact she had bought an off-road van so she would be able to do the rough roads and now it was a total mess inside, and she was not happy at all. As she was cleaning and tidying the van, picking up the broken items from the floor and sweeping the dust, she heard a man's voice from outside.

"Hello?" Lilly popped her head outside, standing before her was a man with a shaved head, beard and a big grin on his face.

"Hello" she replied.

"Hi I'm Greg, I'm camped just over there." He pointed behind him. "I was wondering if you would like to come and have a drink with us?"

Oh god, she had been here five minutes, and already someone wanted to have drinks. "Thanks but my van is a mess, and I need to clean it up, maybe later." Hopefully, he would get the message she wanted to be left alone, she wasn't sure if he was hitting on her or not.

"Ok, but if you change your mind, I'm just over there. Do you need a hand with anything?" Lilly shook her head "ok maybe later." He turned and headed back towards a cottage and a caravan not far from her.

Was she being oversensitive, she was so used to being mistreated by men she figured they were all the same. Lilly continued to clean and swear, turning on the air conditioner to help with the stifling heat. Now the air conditioning wasn't working properly either and was blowing out warm air, but to top it off the hot water system wasn't working either. Luckily, it was so hot she wouldn't need hot water to shower. The television seemed to have gone out in sympathy as well. An hour had gone by, and Greg appeared at her door again.

"How's it going? Would you like a cold beer and come sit in the shade. My friend Lea sent me over. She said you sounded like you needed a beer with all the slamming doors and swearing." He chuckled.

Oh what the hell Lilly thought to herself, he is only being friendly. "Sure sounds great, and my beer is warm because the fridge hasn't been working properly, along with a lot of things." Lilly followed him over to the cottage where a woman and man were sitting at the outside covered area. They introduced themselves as Lea and Rob, Lilly enjoyed their company for a few hours chatting about her trip so far. They were locals and had been here for many years, and when they found out that Lilly was a singer Lea rang the bar and organised for her to sing the next night, she would get free camping, drinks and a meal. Even though Lilly was only going to stay for one night, the offer from Greg to help fix up her van the next day was too good to pass up.

Lilly performed at the fishing club bar and was well received, so much so, they asked her to stay for a week and do some more shows. Lilly declined; she was on a schedule; she still couldn't help herself after all those years organising trucks she still kept herself to a plan even though she was now not working and there was no need to really be anywhere by a set time. The next morning when she came out of the van the Vice President of the club was waiting outside for her, asking again would she stay for a week and perform at the club again. He offered to take her Barramundi fishing, and there would be a trip out to Vanderlin Island to stay the night and watch fireworks, free camping food and drink. Lilly was about to refuse when she thought to herself why not? I don't need to be anywhere in a hurry. She was on her way to Darwin to see Mark, Lori and Jackson, how often do you get an opportunity like this? Slow down and enjoy the journey she thought. Lilly stayed for a week and had the most amazing time, they treated her like a rock star. They took a boat out to Vanderlin Island in the Sir Edward Pellew Group in the Gulf of Carpentaria, it was a two-hour boat ride through the river system with mangroves on either side. She saw crocodiles lazing on the river bank, brolgers in the shallows, fish jumping, then it was into the gulf past the many islands before landing on the sandy beach to make her way up to an old shack where she would be sleeping the night on a camp bed in her sleeping bag. People were so friendly here, and down to earth. After dropping their things at the shack they went out fishing, the rock formations as they circled the island were astonishing. Lilly caught a huge cod, and it took her ten minutes to pull it onto the boat; it was just over a metre long. She posed with her catch for a quick photo, and then threw it back into the sea, watching it dive deep into the ocean. Lilly felt happy and content, and she was so pleased she had stayed now, look at what she would have missed out on.

Lilly sat on the beach watching the sunset. It was so beautiful and calm. She was glad she had decided to stay, it was time to throw the schedule out and just let her trip evolve as she went along, not so much planning, take each day as it came, she felt truly blessed and lucky. She had dinner of fresh fish and salad sitting by a bonfire on the beach and enjoying the fireworks before returning to the shack to sleep. There was no door on the cabin so Lilly could see down to the beach from her bed, she fell asleep with Elly curled up at her feet, contented and happy.

Lilly did two more shows at the bar that week and went out fishing catching her first Barramundi fish. It was seventy-six centimetres long, she kept this one but threw two more back. That night she cooked up a feast of fresh fish which had never tasted better. King Ash Bay was just a small fishing club with a bar, grill, caravan park and some permanent residents, it was forty-two kilometres from Borroloola and seven hundred kilometres to Katherine it was remote, and people came there to fish. Lilly loved it here and when it was time to leave she knew she would come back again and spend some more time with her new friends.

An overnight stop at Mataranka and a swim in the hot springs then on to Darwin for a week to see Mark, Lori and Jackson, who had been living in Darwin for over a year now, they had room for her to park the caravan in the front yard. It was a busy week with repairs being made on the caravan, three of the four brakes on the dual axle had broken, this explained why Lilly had trouble pulling up the van, it was the car brakes doing all the work. They went out fishing in Mark's boat on Darwin harbour and had dinner together at the waterfront. Lilly loved having time with her grandson Jackson, they swam in the pool, sipped cups of tea and played with Elly in the nearby park. Soon she was on the road again heading for Western Australia. She did have to stick to a bit of a schedule here as she had organised to have her fiftieth birthday in Perth with family and friends flying in. After a stop at Lake Argyle and Wyndham, it was onto The Gibb River Road, stopping at El Questro for the night. People were so friendly on the road, they were happy and loving life. Lilly was enjoying her new found freedom and seeing so many new places. Fires had been through only a few weeks ago, and a lot of the landscape had been burnt, there were still spot fires burning as she drove along the red dirt road. The going was hard with bad corrugations on the road making it a bouncy, bumpy ride. She could only drive at sixty kilometres an hour, finally making it to Derby for two days to look around before making her way down to Broome where she would stay for a week. Lilly had booked herself a flight to the horizontal falls as an early fiftieth birthday gift to herself.

Lilly needed someone to look after Elly while she took her flight, and all the kennels were full in Broome, she may have to cancel. Luckily one day on the beach, she'd pulled up beside a couple who also had a dog, she asked if they knew of anywhere that could mind her dog. Jo and Bill were from Perth and were staying in the same caravan park, they caught up later for happy hour and offered to take care of Elly while she went on her seaplane adventure.

Lilly left at five thirty in the morning leaving Elly in the van, and Bill would come and get her at seven and would feed her then take her for a walk and watch her until she returned later that afternoon. Lilly had managed to get the front seat on the seaplane, as she was the only single person everyone else had partners. They took off from Broome airport circling out over the ocean then along the coastline up to Cape Leveque with the breathtaking beauty of dramatic Red Sea cliffs, turquoise water of the Indian Ocean, and the pristine beauty of the Kimberley. It was incredible flying low over the stunning islands of the Buccaneer Archipelago before landing on the calm waters of Talbot Bay right near the Horizontal Falls. It was then onto the fast speedboat for an adrenaline-pumping ride to race through the narrow opening between the cliffs with the fast rushing water, a few water doughnuts in the bay before heading back to the pontoon to swim in a glass tank, with the friendly resident sharks on the other side. Then a laid back cruise through the amazing river with dramatic, majestic cliffs and wildlife, then back to the luxury house-boat for lunch before the return flight to Broome.

When she returned to get Elly, Bill had a story to tell her of Elly's adventures for the day. Lilly had left the window beside the bed open so there would be fresh air flowing through the van. Elly had become distressed at her leaving and had jumped through the gauze smashing it and the blind out the window. Bill had come across to check on her, and she was out the front of the park sniffing around where Lilly had hopped on the bus, he wasn't game to leave her after that and spent the rest of the day with her at the caravan reading a book. They could laugh about it now, but it could have been a tragic situation if he hadn't come across her when he did. Lilly would stay friends with Jo and Bill and catch up with them again a few times over the next few years.

Lilly spent the next ten days driving down the west coast to Perth pulling into some of the pretty spots along the way. She needed to be there to meet her family and friends for the week holiday for her birthday. Fred's son Lucas lived in Perth and Fred, Victoria, their daughter Amelia, Miranda and Jenavieve, Mark, Lori, Jackson and Jake had all flown in to join her, they had a fantastic time for five days looking around Perth and down the coast. The only downside to the week was as she arrived in Perth she received an email from the bank saying that they were recalling all joint loans due to the fact the payments had not been met. When Lilly left the business, Jeff had agreed on a price to buy her out, but he'd kept changing the amount for settlement and had been trying to knock her down even further on the money. Lilly was still the director of the company even though Jeff was running it. He had made her agree to walk away from the business until the final settlement came through, he wanted total control. Lilly didn't mind she couldn't have worked with him anyway, but in hindsight, she should have stayed, but stupidly she trusted him to do the right thing, another mistake she would learn from in the years to come.

Jeff's response was "well I didn't have the money to pay it, and I didn't want to talk to the bank." Once again he had buried his head in the sand and not dealt with the problem, so Lilly had booked a flight back to Port Macquarie the day after her birthday to sort out the issues and hopefully stop the bank shutting the business down. She organised for a friend to drive her car and van back for her, there was no way she could have driven back, she was too angry with Jeff for once again leaving her to sort out the mess he had created, but still, he blamed her even though she wasn't there. Jeff had been wasting money and would turn up to work only when he felt like it.

It took two months of pleading with the banks not to put the business into receivership and to sort out the mess, and she even helped organise the loans for Jeff to pay her out. Lilly ended up taking even less than agreed to three months earlier. She didn't have a choice. Jeff had threatened her to take it, or she'd get nothing at all, he was still trying to control her even though he was now with someone else. Lilly didn't care anymore; she just wanted to be away from him and the toxic vibe that came from him. Lilly hardly recognised this man she'd once loved. He had become so nasty and self-centred, the best thing she could do was to cut all ties with him, and keep searching for her own happiness within herself. The few months on the road alone had proved that she could do it and she only needed to believe in herself. Finally two days before Christmas it was all settled. Lilly looked at the cheque in her hand. It wasn't much but what price could you put on your freedom and sanity? She folded

the cheque and put it in her wallet, smiled and for the
first time in a long time finally she felt free.

CHAPTER 36

2015

It had been a busy three months with the start of the new year and a trip to Tasmania on board the Spirit of Tasmania for the voyage across Bass Strait to spend three weeks exploring the island. Lilly had been to Tasmania on several occasions, but this would be her first trip alone and with Elly. She looked at Elly sitting in the back seat, Lilly had given her medication from the vet an hour ago, she hoped that it would help keep her calm for the crossing, she didn't like it, but she had to leave Elly in a kennel below decks for the ten-hour trip.

When it was her turn to board she drove slowly up the gangplank and onto the ship, guided by the staff to her spot right at the front, at least she would be first off when they arrived in Devonport. Lilly placed Elly into the cage with her soft bed, crocheted blanket and water. She felt terrible leaving her here alone, at least it would be a calm crossing. Lilly sat up on deck and watched Melbourne disappear as they headed out into the bay and the open ocean. The time passed relatively quickly, and she was pleased to be finally allowed back down to the car and Elly. On approaching the cage, all she could see was white stuff everywhere, Elly had been distressed and ripped her bed up. It looked like it had snowed in her cage, her blanket was also shredded to pieces, this did not make Lilly feel very good especially when they had to do the crossing again in three weeks. The gangplank lowered, and she drove out into the fading light of the day, making her way to the caravan park where they would spend the night before setting off early the next day to explore.

They had a great time exploring the breathtaking beautiful island with its rugged mountains, spectacular coastlines, native forests, sweeping bays, picturesque beaches and sparkling lakes. Lilly ate some delicious food and fell in love with the cheese from Ashgrove, as well as sampling a cold beer at the Cascade Brewery. She spent four days in Hobart and wandered around Salamanca Markets and drove up to the top of Mount Wellington. Then a stop at Richmond Bridge and the Museum of Old and New Art. The Port Arthur historic Site sent a shiver up Lilly's spine. It was almost like you could feel the ghosts of the convicts who had died here. She paused at the site of the 1996 massacre and said a prayer for the thirty-five lives that had been lost. Port Arthur was dog-friendly as long as you kept them on a lead and picked up after them, Elly loved wandering around with her rather than be left in the car alone. There were so many beautiful places to see and enjoy; Penguin, Stanley, Launceston, the beautiful seaside towns of Bicheno, Binalong Bay and St Helens. Her final stop was a drive out to Cradle Mountain with its picture postcard views before boarding The Spirit of Tasmania once again for Melbourne.

The Great Ocean Road was two hundred and forty-three kilometres long. It winds alongside the wild and windswept Southern Ocean, it traverses rainforests, as well as beaches and cliffs composed of limestone and sandstone. The road had been built by returned soldiers between 1919 and 1932 and dedicated to soldiers killed during World War I, it is the world's largest war memorial. There were many beautiful spots to stop and admire the scenery, the towering 12 Apostles, Loch Ard Gorge, The Grotto, London Arch and amazing, friendly towns. Then it was back to Port Macquarie in time for Miranda and Jenivieve's commitment ceremony.

Lilly was the MC and would be singing at the wedding, it was a fantastic evening full of love, laughter and dancing. Lilly watched as her friends danced their first dance together. She had worried that Miranda would not let anyone in again after losing Monique six years ago. It took her a long time to put herself out there again, but then along came Jenivieve, a warm, loving caring woman with so much love to give. Lilly was so happy that Miranda had found such a beautiful person like Jenivieve to spend her life with, it was there for everyone to see the special bond of love they had for each other. It was such a shame that they couldn't be married legally yet, but hopefully, that would all change soon, and same-sex marriage would become legal in Australia after all love is love.

Lilly had been booked to sing at King Ash Bay for a month in April and was looking forward to heading back to the Northern Territory and to do some fishing again. Her Mum Rose was turning seventy, and they had organised a family get together to celebrate on Saturday. Lilly would be leaving straight after the party to drive north. Lilly was busy packing up the caravan getting ready for the long trip when her phone rang.

"Hello."

"Hi honey it's Dad, your Mum has been taken to the hospital by ambulance they think it's her heart." Tom's voice was shaky as he spoke to Lilly.

"What? Is she okay? What happened?" The tears welled in her eyes.

"I don't know love, they are taking her to Kempsey Hospital, she felt dizzy so she laid down and her heart was beating really fast. Can you go over to the hospital?"

"I'm on my way Dad. Don't worry it will be okay. I'll call you when I get there." Lilly tried to reassure him; she knew how much he loved her mother; they were inseparable. Lilly tried to drive as calmly as possible but the forty-minute drive seemed to take forever. When she entered the emergency ward, her mother was sitting up in the bed, grinning sheepishly.

"Hi honey." Lilly burst into tears "it's okay I'm going to be fine, they have checked my heart and it's all good." Rose cuddled her youngest daughter trying to comfort her.

"What happened? Dad said it was your heart."

"I was out mowing the lawn."

"You were what?" Lilly was gobsmacked. "Why are you mowing the lawn for god sake Mum, I know you're healthy but you're not a spring chicken either."

"I always mow the lawn. I got dizzy, and my heart was racing, so Tom called the ambulance. When they put me on the heart monitor it showed a minor heart attack, so they brought me here to do more tests, and my heart is clear it's not a heart attack. They think it's because I was dehydrated and pushing the mower up the hill and the heat made me feel faint. I'm going to be fine. Stop worrying."

"I won't stop worrying, and you won't be mowing the lawn again." Lilly stood with her hands on her hips. Rose could see the tears in her eyes and the worry she had caused her. "I'll cancel going away and stay with you."

"No don't be silly, I'm fine, and you have commitments, I promise I won't mow the lawn again. You go and enjoy yourself. I promise I'll behave."

Rose thought about arguing the point but realised she would not win this fight with her daughter. She nodded faintly, there was really no choice at all. Lilly drove Rose home and gave her a good ear bashing all the way about mowing the lawn at her age, and if she didn't organise someone to mow the yard she would, she made her promise she would not do it again. Rose gave in; she knew not to argue with Lilly, and she was sure Ruby would also give her a piece of her mind too when she called.

"Lilly, maybe we should cancel my birthday party."

"Don't think you're getting out of it that easy Mum, I know you don't like a fuss but it's organised, and everyone is coming, after giving us all that scare you will be having a party." Lilly was quite firm, and Rose knew there would be no changing her mind.

Lilly left for the Northern Territory straight after the party, with a promise from her mother that she would not overexert herself again, and to call her if she needed her to come back. It took five days to drive the three and a half thousand kilometres to King Ash Bay where she would stay for the next month singing three times a week. The average daily temperature was around thirty-eight degrees and took a bit of getting used to, the month passed quickly with fishing and chatting to people even Uncle Max called in to see her on his fishing trip to the Gulf. Lilly packed up after her month to head off to Darwin to stay with Mark again, and this time she would spend a month with him. First, she stopped at Daly Waters Pub to sing for three nights, they enjoyed her show so much they convinced her to stay. Lilly sang sixteen nights straight at this iconic old pub. The atmosphere was great, everyone was happy, they would dance and sing along. The Pub was unique, and it had bras and knickers hanging from the ceiling and money stapled to the walls, drivers licence, business cards, anything you could think of the travellers would leave behind to mark they had been here. It was here at the pub that she first encountered the tradition of the backpackers dropping their pants and dancing when she sang Eagle Rock, she was laughing so hard she almost couldn't sing.

Lilly made a lot of new friends here and would end up catching up with many of them at their home towns as she continued to travel. But there were two, in particular, she would keep meeting and travelling with, Lou and Cathy, they had ridden in on motorbikes towing little trailers, they were trikes actually, and they were initially from Wauchope only fifteen minutes from where Lilly had been living. Cathy was very thin and tall with curly light brown hair to her shoulders. Lou had a big white beard and the most beautiful blue eyes, they were travelling around Australia on their own adventure, this would be a friendship that would continue into the years ahead.

She stayed a month in Darwin exploring and playing with Jackson, fishing, going to the water park and spending time watching the sunsets at Mindil beach.

Jake flew in to spend a week with them. Lilly, Mark and Jake went to the Casino to watch the sunset and try their luck on the pokies and gambling tables. It was here that Lilly met Doug and Bev, an older couple from Nelson in Victoria, they exchanged numbers and would catch up again in Karumba. Lilly had completed her Marriage celebrants course last year and would perform her first wedding ceremony here in Darwin for her close friends Seth and Amanda on Mindil beach, they had organised it before leaving Port Macquarie, and they surprised their family on the day with the wedding. Seth and Amanda had been together eighteen years, engaged for eleven of them and had two beautiful girls and Seth thought it was about time he made an honest woman of Amanda.

Lilly had organised ahead to do singing gigs as she travelled to help with the cost of her adventure so the next stop was back to Daly Waters for a few nights singing. Then on to King Ash Bay for a night, back across the Gulf on the Savannah Way to Karumba where she was booked in for three weeks to perform at the pub and the caravan parks around town. Lilly had been interviewed for Meraki TV about her travels; it appeared on Foxtel a few weeks later, and she was asked to do some freelance filming for them as well. Aunty Daphne was also staying at Karuma in another caravan park.

Lilly and Elly were coming back from watching the sunset on the beach when she started to chat to the people walking beside her. They were from Nowra, they were here on a family trip with their parents and Lilly spent the next week hanging out with them. The younger brother Paul was cute, and Lilly thought he looked about forty-five, she found out later he was only thirty-nine, he was medium height with short dark hair with flecks of grey coming through, he had a ripping body with a six pack, he was also hilarious. They had been having drinks back at her caravan after her show, it was quite late, and Lilly was ready for bed. She liked Paul and thought he would be out of her league, she didn't want a permanent thing, but she had an itch that needed to be scratched.

"Well, I'm ready for bed, it's been a long day, thanks for the drinks and the laughs. I enjoy your company." Lilly smiled at Paul, should she ask him to stay the night?

"I enjoy your company too Lilly, it's good to relax and laugh." Paul stood up and came over to give her a hug goodnight.

Oh, bugger it Lilly thought, you only live once so what he was ten years younger. "Would you like to stay the night? No strings attached. I'd like some company if you get my drift?" She giggled nervously; she felt like a teenager.

"I get your drift, and yes I would like to stay." Lilly took his hand and led him up the steps into the van, grinning she just realised she was now a "cougar." The next day as they sat and enjoyed coffee, Lilly talked about her upcoming Cape York trip and how she was a bit apprehensive about doing the drive up to the northernmost tip of Australia alone. Paul was envious of her trip up to Cape York hoping to do it himself one day, Lilly enjoyed his company and invited him to join her. She told him the date she would be leaving from Lions Den just near Cooktown in Queensland and he agreed to meet her there.

It was great to have some company as she travelled, even though Lilly didn't mind driving alone it was nice to have someone to share the sites with, someone to talk to as they drove through the countryside. Paul was excellent company and easy to get along with, they left the tar road behind them at Laura following the wide dirt Peninsular Development Road which was badly corrugated, the going was slow for a while until the road became smoother, singing along to the music as they bumped along the rough road. They had decided to head straight to the tip of Cape York and would explore some more on the way back. After stopping a few times to take in the sites and scenery, and enjoy a cup of coffee from the thermos and some biscuit's, they arrived at Bramwell Station, a Brahman cattle station for the night and enjoyed a home cooked meal and listened to the live music.

The next morning they left early, leaving the caravan there and taking the tent and camping gear for the final leg. First stop would be Fruit Bat Falls, but to get to the falls they had to cross a creek, it was about thirty metres across to the other side. Lilly pulled up at the top of the road leading down to the creek, she was doubting her ability to drive across the dirty muddy water, she had driven across creeks before but not as deep as this one.

"You don't have to do it if you don't want to." Paul could sense her hesitation. "Let's just watch for a while and see what the other cars do."

They watched as several 4wd cars made the crossing. It was deep in the middle with water coming halfway up their doors, it seemed the best way to cross was to stay over to the right side. Lilly made her decision she hadn't come all this way to chicken out now over a bit of water.

"Well Paul, I didn't get the snorkel fitted to the car for show. It's there so I can do this sort of crossing, so let's do it." She took a deep breath.

"Are you sure?"

"Yes, come on, make sure you take photos. I want proof that I did this." Lilly jumped into the driver's seat and raised the car with its airbags to the high position, she put it into 4wd then slowly drove down the forty five degree descent into the water. Her hands gripped the wheel tightly and focused on the course everyone else had taken across, as the water rose further up the side of the car, she exclaimed. "Oh Shit, Shit, Shit!" Lilly was laughing with fear and excitement, Elly had her head out the open back window looking around, tongue out and what looked like a smile on her face. It was bumpy, and each time the car lurched over a large rock or into a hole Lilly would gasp. They made it to the other side and Lilly could feel her body relax, she had done it. Paul looked at her and grinned.

"See you can do it, but you know what's funny?" Lilly shook her head. "You have to drive back through that to get back out to the main road." Paul laughed, and Lilly joined in, she had done it once she could do it again. It had been worth it, Fruit Bat Falls was totally amazing with clear emerald water, cascading falls and a rock jump. The broad, steady stream of water over the edge of the falls make for a perfect outdoor shower, which spreads out into a clear pool called The Saucepan. A few kilometres further up they explored the stunning Twin Falls which steps down from Eliot Creek to wash over and split into two distinct flows before settling in a pool at its base. Just upstream was Elliot Falls with a taller drop with parallel ledges of Mesozoic rock that formed the perfect basis for the fall's steady stream, the flow gently churning the waters of Eliot Creek like a never-ending spa bath. Paul also had a drone and put it up into the sky to take some fantastic shots of the falls then it was on to the Jardine River crossing by ferry then onto Punsend Beach caravan park, their campsite for the next two nights.

They set up the tent then drove the five kilometres to The Tip parking the car they walked the final twenty minutes across the beach and then up over jagged molten rocks to the rocky platform jutting out into Torres Strait and the famous sign at the northernmost point of Australia. The Coral Sea was to the east and the Arafura Sea and the beginnings of the Gulf of Carpentaria to the west. There was no one else there, just Paul, Lilly and Elly enjoying the views over the emerald blue ocean and the Eborac and York Islands. They took photos standing with the sign then sat down to enjoy a cold beer they had brought with them as the sun started to set. Elly sat beside her and leaned against her leg, as she patted her faithful companion Lilly felt a sense of accomplishment. She had been to the eastern, southern and now northernmost tip of Australia; she only had to visit the western one now.

For two days they drove around looking at all the historical sights in the area, they did some fishing, sat on the beach at the caravan park and watched the sun go down over both the Pacific and Indian Oceans at the same time, and returned to the tip one last time before leaving. They made a stop at Captain Billy Landing then picked up the caravan and headed for Weipa, a large mining town, with an overnight stop on the way at Moreton Telegraph Station, one of the original telegraph stations that had been built in the 1880s. Lilly sang two nights at The Albatross Bay Resort and during the day they explored around Weipa, Lilly marvelled at the size of the massive mine trucks and wondered what it would be like to drive one.

There was one place Lilly really wanted to stop on her way back, Archer River Roadhouse, she had read the book "Toots: Woman in a Man's World" about Toots Holzheimer, a hard working mother of eight, she drove trucks for a living from the 1960s to 1990s across some of Australia's most inhospitable terrain, Cape York Peninsula. She'd service and load her own trucks, mostly by hand, and would drive for days alone. With her husband Ron they would have to construct their own roads and bridges after each wet season to make it to the Cape. A truly amazing woman with a great attitude "do what you want to do and do it well." There was a memorial to "Toots" at the roadhouse, Lilly had seen her Blue Man prime mover at the National Transport Hall of Fame at Alice Springs. Slim Dusty had even written a song about her "The Lady Is A Truckie." They had a cold drink and a burger here before heading back to Cairns through Lakefield National Park. By the time they arrived in Cairns, they'd had two flat tyres and three cracks in the windscreen as a reminder of the rough road.

Paul and Lilly parted ways in Cairns and Lilly continued on her trip down the Queensland coast with a stop at Paronella Park then Kurrimine Beach where she caught up with Doug and Bev again. Travelling together for the next two weeks, they camped at Rollingstone, Alva Bay and Lake Callide just out from Biloela catching red claw in the dam. It had gotten cold, and they would have a fire at night, sitting around chatting about the places they had been and the places they would like to see. Lilly loved her new lifestyle and friends and could not imagine doing anything else. She was finally becoming the happy, loving, caring woman she used to be.

CHAPTER 37

2015

Lilly had been away for six months, she made a quick stop at Port Macquarie to see her Mum, kids, grandson and friends for a week before continuing south on roads she hadn't travelled before. It was a chance to catch up with old school friends. Calling in at Canberra to see her old Army buddy Linda, they had been friends since they were eighteen, then to Pambula to see Lalicia, her best friend from her high school days at Coonabarabran. Down along the coast road to the bottom of Victoria across to Melbourne, before cutting across to Warrnambool, then a week with Doug and Bev at Nelson. Lilly sang at the pub here as well as a night at Doug's, and he had asked her if she didn't mind singing for them at a BBQ and he would invite a couple of friends too, sixty people showed up. Then back around the Fleurieu Peninsula to Victor Harbour then up to Adelaide where she was meeting up with Linda's daughter Sara, her goddaughter to do the paperwork for their upcoming wedding in January next year.

Lilly loved the suburb of Semaphore in Adelaide, the caravan park was dog-friendly and right on the beach. Today was her fifty-first birthday. She wandered around the quaint shops and stopped and had lunch at a sidewalk cafe, just her and Elly. Tonight she was going to the Fleetwood Mac concert with Sara in the city, the show was amazing, and Lilly hoped she too would still be performing in her seventies just like Stevie Nicks. Linda had organised for her to fly back to Canberra to attend the Centenary of Anzac ball at the War Memorial. It was so surreal, they sat at tables with a Lancaster Bomber G plane above their heads and danced into the night. Then a flight back to Adelaide to pick up Elly from the kennel and onto the next leg of her journey. Lilly had a large Australian map that she would draw lines of all the roads she had travelled, there were still so many to do.

Then it was on to the Eyre Peninsula to Cowell, Port Lincoln, Streaky Bay then back across the Nullarbor free camping in two places before heading down to Esperance and down to Albany to a little caravan park on the bay. Albany was such a beautiful place, and there was lots to see, it just so happened that Prince Charles and Camilla would be coming into town to the War Memorial. Lilly stood at the bottom of the street with other onlookers waiting to catch a glimpse of them as they drove past and waved. Well, I guess that's the only Prince I'll ever get close to in my lifetime, she thought to herself. Then it was on and around to Augusta and Cape Leeuwen, up through Margaret River, Busselton, Bunbury and into Perth for a stop to see her nephew before driving across to the mining town of Kalgoorlie to perform at one of the pubs. Kalgoorlie itself was a great spot to investigate the effects of the large scale mining operations, with the Super-pit which she viewed via the town's lookout and Hannans North Tourist Mine was a great place showing the history of mining in the area and had a wide a variety of machinery and artefacts on display. Then it was onto Lake Ballard where sculptured metal figures of the nearby town's McKenzie inhabitants stood desolately on the Lake's clay pans and made the landscape look alien-like. Lilly had an overnight stop at Leonara, a small town that has most of the original building of its gold-mining days. On her way out the next day she drove out to the abandoned Ghost Town of Gwalia, the corrugated make-shift houses the miners once lived in were open to the public, and many have been refitted to allow a glimpse into their former living conditions.

Lilly was looking forward to driving the Longest Shortcut across Australia, starting at Laverton in Western Australia and finishing at Winton in Queensland. It was over a thousand kilometres of dirt road from Laverton to Ayers Rock with only a few places to stop for fuel along the way. So with her supplies replenished and extra fuel in the spare jerry cans she headed off. Lilly felt a bit apprehensive while driving this stretch alone, but she had food and supplies, and she drove to the conditions so as to not cause damage to the car and the van. The red desert road stretched on into the distance, the road was smooth and better than some of the tarred roads she had been on, along the way every hundred metres were burnt out cars, she passed through the Great Victoria Desert with small sand hills, spinifex, woodlands and the occasional tree to dominate the views. Just before driving into Tjukayirla Roadhouse there was a small section of bitumen which acted as an airstrip for the Royal Flying Doctors Service. Her first stop would be Warburton for the night, she had only seen four other cars in the five hundred and fifty kilometres she had driven that day, the service station had just closed as she pulled in and the gates were shut and locked to the caravan park. Lilly could not go any further, she needed fuel, and it was not safe to drive around alone especially at night, luckily the attendant had seen her drive in and opened the gates for her to enter the safety of the park for the night. The yard was full of peacocks; there must have been at least thirty of them wandering around. Lilly cooked herself some dinner before settling in for an early night. Diesel was two dollars a litre here, but there was no other choice, the pumps were surrounded by thick wire cages and had to be opened by the staff to fill the car, it was then on to Warakurna, if she thought fuel was expensive before it was two dollars forty a litre here. A stop at Giles weather station, a fully functioning meteorological observation station before driving towards the Petermann ranges then across into the Northern Territory near Docker River. The road was rougher on this side of the border with potholes, and there was water laying in puddles on the road. The scenery had begun to change and the flat land started to make way to hills and mountains. Lilly was struck by the beauty of the area, the red soil, vivid blue sky with little puffs of white clouds, then in front of her the Olga's started to appear, they rose up in front of her, the closer she came to them the more impressive they looked, jutting out of the ground, vivid colours of orange. Lilly had been here many years ago, but this time was different, she was doing it on her terms and alone, she felt empowered as she wandered around these ancient monoliths.

Staying a few days in Ayers Rock to look around and walk around the base of the rock, which towered above her, it rose three hundred and fifty metres above the flat desert around her and the rock colour changed as the day progressed. The next stop Lilly was truly looking forward to was outside of Kulgera on the Stuart Highway. The only thing at Kulgera was a pub, service station and caravan park, but that was not her destination, she would leave the van here and drive the one hundred and twenty kilometres of dirt road towards Finke, turning off on a four wheel drive track for fourteen kilometres to Lamberts Centre of Australia. As Lilly bumped along on the rough track only a few kilometres from the centre, she suddenly had a scary thought, what the hell was she doing? She was in the middle of nowhere, alone with only her dog, there was no phone reception, she had left her satellite phone in the caravan, anyone could be in here, what if there was a serial killer in there? She had told the staff at the pub where she was going and what time she expected to be back, a fat lot of good that would do if someone was lurking in the bushes. Too late now there was nowhere to turn around one track led in and another led out. Oh well, she would drive in and look around before hopping out. Lilly hoped she was going the right way. There had been no other signs since turning off the main road, looking at Wiki camps was her only way of getting directions.

The road came out into a clearing and in the centre was a small replica of the top of Parliament house with a flag flying. Lilly looked around as there were no other cars or tracks, she pulled the car up and jumped down letting Elly out to stretch her legs, keeping her close by in case of snakes or lurking serial killers. She checked the visitors' book which was in an old jerry can that had the top cut off and put on with hinges, no one had been in there for over a week. Lilly sat on the square concrete slab underneath the flag, crossed her legs, closed her eyes and listened. It was silent, a gentle breeze caressed her face, she could hear birds chirping and the sound of Elly panting beside her. Lilly settled her mind and gave thanks for all she had in her life and all she had achieved. She felt peaceful and grateful, she meditated for a moment longer before standing up and grabbing her drone, putting it up high in the air to take aerial shots of her below and the surrounding landscape. Checking her watch, she needed to get moving to get back to Kulgera before dark, maybe one day she would come back here and camp, the night sky out here would be truly wondrous.

It was getting close to Christmas, and Lilly wanted to get back to Port Macquarie so with a stop at Coober Pedy to look at the underground houses and the museums then down to Port Augusta cutting across New South Wales through Mildura, Balranald, Hay, Griffith, Temora and back onto the Hume Highway through Sydney to home in Port Macquarie, arriving five days before Christmas.

CHAPTER 38

2016

It was going to be a big year for Lilly, she was to fly to Adelaide to perform her goddaughter Sara's wedding in January then she was going on an overseas trip with her friend Scott in February, they had nineteen days away. They flew into Ho Chi Minh city in Vietnam and had ten days looking around the country with trips to the Cu Chi tunnels, which were fascinating, the small tunnels underneath the jungle, they went down into one they were tiny and claustrophobic, to think that people lived down here hiding from the enemy was astonishing. They cruised through Halong Bay and walked the beautiful towns of Hanoi with its centuries-old architecture and a rich culture. Hoi An is an ancient town with canals with wooden Chinese shophouses and temples and colourful French colonial buildings, ornate Vietnamese tube houses and the beautiful Japanese Covered Bridge with its pagoda. A stop at Hue on the Perfume River and then to the Mekong Delta for a boat ride before flying to Cambodia and Siem Reap and the Angkor Wat and Angkor Thom temples, wandering through the unbelievable temples of where Tomb Raider was filmed. Even though Sara was legally married in Australia, they still had a ceremony and reception in Koh Samui. It was a beautiful wedding with elephants on the beach and fireworks. Lilly sang for them as they danced their first dance together, then she enjoyed a few days in Phuket before flying home.

Lilly now found it hard to stop in one place too long, and after a month, she would get itchy feet wanting to explore more places, she truly was a gypsy now. She could not imagine ever settling in one place. Lilly had booked some shows in Whyalla in South Australia where she would catch up with an old school friend from high school, then on to Venus Bay near Port Kenny to spend Easter with Doug and Bev at the caravan park and perform at the local pub. It was here that she would meet Trevor and Nick Kon, they were of Greek heritage and continuing on the fishing business that their father had started catching prawns out in the Southern Ocean. After a quick phone call to Anna, the CEO of Meraki TV about a possible story she set about filming them fishing and bringing in their catch which was then aired on Foxtel a month later.

After a relaxing week, it was back across the Nullarbor and onto Hyden in Western Australia for a week to perform at the pub and cafe at Wave Rock. Lou and Cathy, whom she'd met at Daly Waters Pub arrived on their trikes and joined her for the week to explore this fabulous area. Lilly also caught up with Phil Emmanuel whom she had had the privilege of being a support act for many years ago. He was an incredibly talented gifted guitarist.

Lilly and Cathy marvelled at the size and shape of Wave Rock it had been eroded by the weather over millions and millions of years to look like a giant wave about to crash down, they climbed to the top and enjoyed the view of the surrounding farmland, shiny salmon gum-forests, and the beautiful salty scrubby bush. They took a drive out to look at some of the sites in the surrounding area and got lost. But that was all part of the adventure. That's when you got to see some of the most amazing things, when you really didn't intend to.

Lilly stayed in Perth for a week to perform the wedding ceremony of her nephew Lucas, Fred's son and catch up with family flying in from around Australia before heading up the coast to Cervantes, a beautiful little seaside town. Lilly had stayed here before and loved the area, she drove around the pinnacles and ate lobster at the local seaside cafe. A monster storm rolled in from the ocean with thunder and lightning. It was so strong that the winds were rocking the van, then it was on to Mount Magnet, one of the Mid-West region's original gold mining towns, and the longest surviving gold mining settlement in Western Australia. Cue eighty kilometres further north on the Great Northern Highway was a lovely town with a lot of history. Thirty kilometres south-west of Cue was the ghost town of Big Bell. The town was established in 1936, and was home to the Big Bell Gold Mine, gold had been discovered in the area in 1904, the mine was still in operation, but now all that stood at Big Bell were the walls of the old pub.

Next stop was Meekathara, originally a gold prospecting town, in the surrounding area, there were a host of old mining pits and relics from the wild Australian gold rush era. Lilly called in to have a coffee at the little gift shop in the main street called "Made in Meeka." It was owned by Anna whom she had met last night at her show at the pub. Anna told her that she had left the city to explore the country just as Lilly was doing now, she had been a successful TV producer in Sydney and had had enough of city life, she had called in here five years ago for a drink and never left. Lilly drove out to the Bureau of Meteorology just outside of town to watch the weather balloon being released, David who was in charge here explained how that all over the world at the same time a hundred balloons were released and that all the information was then put together to give us our weather patterns.

Up the great northern highway to Newman to perform a show then it was a choice to follow the tar road to Port Hedland, or be adventurous and take the dirt road to Marble Bar. Lilly sat at the intersection. Did she want to play it safe or have another adventure, her curiosity got the better of her, she had heard about Marble Bar and how striking the rock formations were, and it was the hottest place in Australia's, so off she went driving carefully on the rocky road. Lilly could feel the caravan swaying a bit behind her, and the car did not feel right, so she pulled over to the side of the road to check her tyres. Sure enough, the back driver's side tyre was flat and had started to shred. She would have to change it. It was only ten o'clock and already thirty-five degrees, she would have to unhitch the caravan to change the tyre, as well as pull everything out of the back of the car to access the spare underneath. Lilly could see dust coming from the south, there was a car coming, thank god she would flag them down to help, she was quite capable of changing the tyre herself but if she could get someone to help even better. John was on his way out to one of the mines to do training and pulled over to help her, not long after

John stopped David pulled up, she had met him at the caravan park that morning at Newman, just before she had left. With the help of the two men Lilly was soon back on her way, travelling slowly, hoping not to get another flat, she had another spare tyre but it had no rim, she needed to find somewhere to fit it and buy another tyre. After thirty kilometres Lilly could feel the car pulling and swaying again, she knew she must have another flat. This time it was on the passenger's side rear tyre, a small arrowhead stone had punctured the tyre, at least she could put a tyre plug in it. Lilly had come well equipped; she had a small compressor and tyre plugs for just such an emergency. It took a bit of effort to get the plug in, and she was just about finished when a white ute pulled up beside her, inside were two aboriginal men, one about thirty years old the other an older grey haired man with a big white beard and smiling eyes.

The young driver hopped out of the car coming around to where she was packing up her tools. "You right love? Do you need some help?" He had a big broad, friendly smile.

"Yes I had a flat, just fixed it, thank you. Is it far to the next town?"

"Nah about thirty kilometres, we've been out here doing some initiations for the young boys at the camp, that's the Elder there," he pointed to the old man in the car. "We will follow you into town to make sure you get there okay."

"Thank you. That would be great." Lilly drove slowly hoping that she would not get another flat, not up here where there was nowhere to get a new tyre, she could be stranded for a week or more waiting. As she came into the town, the ute following blew his horn and with a wave out the window turned off down a dirt track. Pulling up opposite the pub, Lilly got out to inspect the tyre it was still going down, an inch from where she had put the plug was a piece of metal like a nail sticking out, Lilly got out her plug kit and compressor again and was repairing the tyre when David walked up to her.

"Hey what's happening?"

"I've got another flat. I'm just plugging it" she had sweat running down her back and the heat was suffocating.

"Plugging it, I've never seen that done, heard about it though, mind if I watch?"

"Sure no worries, I've had to do this a few times." Lilly repaired the hole and pumped the tyre up, pouring soapy water down the tyre to check that the hole had been fixed. An inch off that was another hole, a split in the tyre, she groaned this was not her day. The three holes were all an inch apart in a triangle, she hoped these plugs worked because she still had a hundred kilometres of dirt gravel road to Marble Bar, then another two hundred to Port Hedland where she may be able to get tyres. It took almost two hours to drive the final leg, Lilly kept pulling up every half hour to check the tyre, finally arriving mid-afternoon. David was already there; he waved and smiled as he saw her pull in. Lilly unhitched and went for a drive out to the colourful marble bar which crosses the Coongan River. The mineral deposit was initially thought to be marble but it was actually made of Jasper. The cryptocrystalline variety of coloured quartz were stunning, there was a watering hole below the bar and Lilly and Elly waded in the shallows cooling their feet. The birds scattered and flew into the trees as they approached, there was an abundance of wildlife around, it was such a beautiful and rugged landscape.

Lilly sat and chatted to David for a few hours before making her way to bed. He was heading the same direction and would keep an eye out for her; they arranged to meet at her next two stops, Sandfire and Barn Hill. He was a nice man, he was from Perth and taking a break from his business to do some travel. Lilly had to be in Broome by Friday in three days as she had shows booked. Barn Hill was nine kilometres off the highway, a stunning campsite. It was on a working cattle farm, and the park was only a hundred metres to the most amazing beach and rock formations. The rock cliffs were vivid red, Lilly and Elly wandered down the beach, there was no one else around just her and Elly, the rocks were entirely alien in appearance and she wandered around them taking photos and just relaxing on the sand. It was so peaceful and beautiful here she wished she had more time, she promised she would return here one day.

Lilly stayed in Broome for eighteen days, performing seven shows at Matso's Brewery and the RSL Club. It was at the RSL Club that she met Merv and

Kaz, they lived a few doors up from the club and offered to let Elly stay in the back yard when she performed instead of the backseat of the car. One of the things Lilly loved the most about travelling was the people she met on the road and would remain friends with for years to come.

It was just over a thousand kilometres from Broome to Kununurra, her next stop to perform four shows at the annual Ord Festival. On the way there she had a car throw up a large rock and put a massive chip in her windscreen. It would be two weeks before they could get another one in and she had to be in Katherine five hundred kilometres away in ten days to perform at the Country Club, then to King Ash Bay to perform, so the wind- screen would have to wait.

Lilly received an email from her solicitor, her divorce had become final, she was finally free of Jeff, she had already changed back to her maiden name when they had separated, and she had no intention of ever changing her name again, let alone getting married. She was on her way out to look at the old river crossing that was now closed to traffic, when she received a phone call from Kay from the Dometic Follow the

Sun competition. She had entered months before and forgotten all about it. It was a three month trip towing your own caravan and raising money for cancer, the prize was a twenty thousand dollar makeover on your van with Dometic products. The van sure could do with some fixing up, for a new off road van it was not holding together too well. Kay told her she had been selected as a finalist and they wanted to know if she was able to start in Cairns in August and make her way to Victoria, she would send her an email with the details and if Lilly could give them an answer by the end of the week. Why was it that everything came at once? She had been asked if she would like to take the kitchen at King Ash Bay from August for three months and also offered a job in Brisbane managing a Transport company starting in the next few weeks. Lilly had already organised shows at Burketown in the Gulf and at Weipa up Cape York, as well as a two-week film shoot back at Hyden, Western Australia in November. Lilly sat and in her usual way worked out all the pros and cons of each thing finally deciding to take the kitchen on.

After having the caravan serviced at Kununurra she made her way to Lake Argyle for two nights to perform, one thing she had wanted to do was cruise the lake taking the three-hour sunset cruise. The sheer size of Lake Argyle was unbelievable, it was five times larger than Sydney Harbour. She saw freshwater crocodiles and loads of wildlife and the reflection of the mountains on the water were astonishing. They stopped just before sunset and everyone jumped in for a swim, floating tables were put in the water so you could have snacks and drinks while floating in the cool water on pool noodles.

CHAPTER 39

KING ASH BAY

Northern Territory

For the next month Lilly did her shows and started to organise for the take over of the kitchen, she would be cooking for up to two hundred people each night to start, and as the season wound down, it would get less. It was the first of July and firecracker night in the Territory a big party was organised at the club with bonfires, music and fireworks. Lilly had met Simon on several occasions. After the fireworks Simon came back to the cottage she had rented, to sit by the fire and enjoy a few drinks to finish off the night. Lilly looked at him across the flickering flames, she liked him, he made her laugh, he was tall, average build with a bit of a belly, but don't we all, his head was shaved, and Lilly found him quite attractive. Did she want to get into a relationship? It had been two and a half years since her break up, she was happy on her own, but she missed the companionship, maybe they could simply have a casual thing. Simon caught her staring at him and smiled. She flushed red, could he know what she was thinking, it had been over a year since she had been with someone.

"Well it's late and I've had a bit to drink, maybe I should head home?" It was more of a question than a statement, and he stared at her over the fire.

"Umm well, I'm going to bed. Would you like to stay?"

Simon stood up and took her hand, and she felt tingles go up her arm, her heart was beating fast. "Yes I would like to stay, but I'm not looking for anything serious, just so you know."

"That's fine by me, neither am I."

When Lilly woke the next morning and looked at the sleeping man beside her, she had enjoyed the lovemaking, and he was such a terrific kisser, when he touched her, her body tingled. Simon opened his eyes and smiled, "Good morning," he stretched and reached for her pulling her into a big bear hug, this is what she missed being cuddled. They had coffee on the verandah before Simon headed off to his shack further down the river. They had come to an agreement they would be friends with benefits, nothing serious and would catch up when their busy schedules allowed. Simon would stay over a couple of nights a week with Lilly, he was a chef by trade but was now working for the government in management. They would go out into the Gulf fishing, play darts at Simon's shack, watch movies cuddled up on the lounge. After two months Lilly knew she was starting to fall for Simon, even though he said he didn't want a serious relationship he was at her place almost every night. Lilly knew she had to ask the question, she needed to protect her heart. She did not want it broken again.

Lilly was enjoying the lifestyle here; she was kept busy with the kitchen but still had time to enjoy the beauty and the serenity. Peak hour traffic was six cars going past at five o'clock for happy hour at the bar.

Lilly loved sitting out on the verandah step at night after work, having a bourbon to unwind, the only sound was the rustling of the grass, the breeze in the trees, and the night birds, sometimes the odd call of a buffalo. The night sky here was striking, so many stars glimmering above, they looked like fairy lights hung in the night sky, the milky way was so clear and brilliant. You didn't get this view back on the coast. Lou and Cathy had arrived two weeks ago and had set up camp outside her cottage. They had caught up several times all around Australia on their own separate adventures. Lilly enjoyed their company and Lou would help out around the cottage fixing things, while Cathy would help her in the kitchen. It was great to have Cathy there to talk to about her concerns with Simon and get some sound advice from someone she could trust.

Simon had arrived late that evening and they lay cuddling in bed. "Simon I need to know how you're feeling about us, I am starting to have feelings for you, and I need to know."

"Don't be so serious, I don't want to talk about it; just go to sleep."

"I'm sorry, but I need to know if you feel the same, can you see this developing into something more or is it just sex?"

"What do you want me to tell you I love you?" He pulled away from her.

"Don't be ridiculous it's too soon for that, I have feelings for you, and I could see myself falling in love with you, but if you don't feel the same way, then I need to know I just don't want to get hurt."

"Oh Fuck! I can't deal with this, I'm going home. Told you I'm not wanting to get serious." Simon was already out of bed getting dressed.

"That's fine, but you're here nearly every night. That's a bit more than casual don't you think? For Christ sake, just go Simon, I have my answer." Lilly was stunned by his reaction, she wasn't asking him to marry her she just wanted to know how he felt about them, she wanted to protect her heart she had been hurt before and did not want to feel that pain ever again. It was three days before she saw Simon again he called into the kitchen while she was doing prep for the evening meal service. He sheepishly stuck his head in through the back door.

"Hi, can we talk for a minute?"

"Sure." Lilly wiped her hands and followed him outside.

"Sorry about the other night, I guess I overreacted a little, I'm not ready for a relationship, my last one ended two years ago, and I really loved her, and I'm afraid of being hurt."

"I understand that I'm also afraid of being hurt Simon that's why I asked the question where we were going with this. It's your choice just friends or friends with benefits, or we make a commitment because I need to have some stability, not this coming and going and in between."

"I do have feelings for you but I'm not sure what I want anymore."

"Ok I'll make the decision then, it's just friends nothing more, so that means no more cuddling, kissing me at the bar and all over me, or turning up at my place every day." She tried to sound firm.

Tears welled up in Simon's eyes, he reached for her and pulled her into his arms and held her not saying anything for a moment. "I don't want to be just friends, can we still try with benefits as well, maybe see where it takes us, I love spending time with you, you make me laugh, and I enjoy your company."

Lilly thought for a moment, could she possibly do that? She knew she was starting to fall in love with him, was it worth the risk of getting hurt. "I'm okay with that, but there will have to be boundaries set if that's all you want. That means only staying over once a week, not every night like you have been. And when we are out at the bar and see each other you can't sit there and cuddle and kiss me, that's not what friends do, that's more a relationship thing. It seems to me it's always when it suits you, so there has to be a bit of give and take."

"Okay, let's try that."

This worked for the next few weeks but gradually one night turned to two, then three, they were sitting on the lounge at Lilly's watching a movie when Simon grabbed her hand. "Hey, I think we should go steady."

Lilly looked at him and laughed "Go steady, like in high school?" She giggled "you mean actually date?" Simon nodded "Are you sure? I've told you that I want my next relationship to be my last, I don't want my heart broken again, so only if you truly want this to be a permanent thing."

"I do Lilly, I love being with you, we get along so well, and when I'm not with you, I miss you, let's give it a try and take it slow." He bent and kissed her and hugged her even tighter.

Lilly worked seven days a week in the kitchen, even though they only opened for dinner each night there was still prep to do each day. Luckily she had a great worker Michelle who would take the pressure off her, and she was even able to have a night off now and then. Simon's contract had finished with the government, and he had got a job working on a road crew down the Tanami Road just out of Alice Springs starting early November, and he would be leaving in three weeks. Lilly's contract finished in four weeks when the kitchen would close for the season, and Simon had managed to get her a job as the camp cook starting when she could get there. They had been together for three months, Lilly had tried to keep her feelings in check but she knew she was in love with him, he had such a great outlook on life, he was kind, funny and he made her laugh every day. They were on the verandah having a few beers after Lilly had finished in the kitchen for the night, Simon had pulled her up to dance to the music, they were slow dancing when he stopped.

"I have to tell you something Lilly, I love you."

"What?" Lilly looked up at him, had she heard him right? "What did you say?"

"I said I love you." Simon was gazing at her smiling. The light flickered in his eyes.

"Simon don't say it unless you mean it, you know how I feel, so unless you want forever, don't say it."

"I love you Lilly and I want to make us work. I mean it."

"I love you too." Lilly was ecstatic she had hoped he would feel the same way she did, she knew this meant staying in the Northern Territory away from her friends and family, but she was in love.

Lilly finished cleaning the kitchen and closed up for the last time. She would be leaving tomorrow to drive the thirteen hundred kilometres to Alice Springs to join Simon at the campsite. They would live in her van and would be working twelve to fifteen hour days, Simon worked on the road crew, and Lilly would do the cooking of three meals a day for the twenty-odd staff. They were only sixty kilometres from Alice Springs up the Tanami Road. They set up a fence around the caravan, so Elly didn't have to be on a lead all day, she spent most of her time inside the van with the air conditioning on as it was usually around thirty- five degrees every day.

Lilly had cleared out one side of the cupboards for Simon to put his clothes in. He had been staying in one of the small bedrooms for the crew . After a week he still hadn't bought his clothes down, when Lilly questioned him about this he snapped at her, he would bring them in his own time he had been busy. Lilly heard an alarm bell ring in her head, had he already changed his mind? She had seen another side to Simon in the last week, one she didn't like. Elly who had always slept on the bed with her was now sleeping on the floor, one night she jumped up on the bed and Simon kicked her off. Elly hit the wall and landed on the floor, the next day he left early without talking to Lilly coming back half an hour later.

"We have to talk about that dog. I can see it's going to cause us problems." Simon stood at the caravan door.

"What? I told you she used to sleep on the bed, it will take her time to realise that she can no longer hop up there. Don't you ever kick my dog again. I will not tolerate it. That's what will cause us problems."

"I'm sorry it was just a reaction. I don't believe dogs should be allowed on the bed, that's just my opinion."

"That's fine we all do things differently, and we need to get used to each other's lifestyles, and it is hard living in such a small space. I have to go. I need to get to the kitchen to start breakfast, we'll talk more tonight." As Lilly did the breakfast dishes she thought about the last month, she knew it was only early in the relationship and there had to be give and take on both sides. The one thing she noticed with Simon, was that he didn't like to be confronted and would rather bury his head in the sand than talk and deal with a situation. He also didn't handle work pressure very well either, it was like he couldn't manage two emotions at once. Lilly knew she had to give it time, it was still early in the relationship. But something inside Lilly did not sit right, and she had a feeling, she pushed it aside she was just being silly.

Lilly's day would start at five am every day, she would prepare breakfast, delivering it out to the crew on the road before coming back and cleaning the crib room and making lunch to then deliver again, sometimes she would be doing a seventy- kilometre round trip to drop off the meals. The kitchen was in a forty-foot container specially set up with a cool room and freezer at one end and a large kitchen and storeroom. Lilly worked alone all day and enjoyed bopping around the kitchen with the music blaring while she prepared each meal. The day would usually end around seven and they would both fall into bed exhausted each night.

They worked through thirty-five days straight before taking a break and driving back to King Ash Bay for a friend's fortieth birthday party. They would stay here a week before driving back to camp where they would stay over Christmas and mind the camp and do a general clean up while the rest of the crew had their break. They also had to get the other kitchen ready for it to be taken another five hundred kilometres up the Tanami to the next campsite in a few weeks.

Two days before Christmas the rains started, and the camp was being flooded, all around the camp was covered in water, the red dirt had turned to slippery mud, they had dug a trench around the van to divert the water away. On Christmas Day the sun came out for a while, they enjoyed a feast at lunch and played darts on the board Simon had set up under the annex of the caravan. Lilly would be flying back to her Mums at Hat Head the next day to surprise her. She had told her she couldn't make it home for Christmas, Angelica and Antonio were flying in as well from Italy to surprise Rose. Simon would be taking care of Elly while she was away, that's if she could get out to the airport the causeways were filling up with water they may be flooded in.

It was Boxing Day, and Lilly was sitting in the Qantas lounge in Sydney waiting for her connecting flight to Port Macquarie when her phone rang, it was Mark.

"Hi Mum, how are you?"

"I'm good darling, just waiting for my flight to Port. I can't wait to see you all tomorrow?" Lilly was excited about seeing her children and grandchildren tomorrow. It was the thing she missed the most when she travelled.

"Umm Mum, we won't be able to make it to Grandma's to surprise her tomorrow. Lori has gone into labour; they are flying her to John Hunter Hospital. We are about to leave."

Lilly's heart started to beat faster; it was too soon for her to have the baby. She was only thirty weeks. "But it's too soon. Is she alright?" A lump formed in her throat and she tried not to cry.

Mark's voice trembled. "So far so good, they may try to stop the labour, but they don't think they can, it will be okay Mum, John Hunter is one of the best in Australia. I've got to go. I'll call you later. Love you Mum."

"I love you too honey, give Lori my love, it will be okay I'm sure." Lilly put her head in her hands and cried softly; she didn't care who saw her in the busy airport lounge. The woman who had been sitting opposite her came over and touched her shoulder.

"I'm sorry. I overheard your conversation. You seem like you need a hug."

The two women embraced, and Lilly let the tears flow, how kind of a stranger to offer her support, it turned out her daughter was pregnant, and she could imagine how it must feel to be alone and receive bad news.

On the twenty-seventh of December, Lori gave birth to a small, beautiful little girl. They called her Ava, she was ten weeks premature, and would spend the next month or so in the hospital until she was well enough to come home.

Lilly spent two days at home with her Mum and a night with Miranda and Jenevieve. Simon called her several times in a few hours to tell her he loved her and missed her. Miranda was ribbing her about the calls, she wanted to meet Simon, so they organised a meeting at Adelaide for Australia Day for the cricket. Simon loved cricket and jumped at the chance, so Lilly booked and paid for the flights and hotel then and there before flying back to Alice Springs with fresh oysters on ice for them to enjoy on New Year's Eve.

New Years Eve 2016

Simon's friends Glen and Helen would be coming to stay with them at the camp as well as Garth, one of their supervisors. Simon was preparing a feast for them all, they arrived at lunchtime and for the next few hours played darts, picked at the nibbles on the table and drank beer. Lilly was enjoying herself but slowed up on the beer, she wouldn't make it to dinner time if she kept up with them. The conversation was light and cheery, and Lilly laughed at Glen's jokes, Helen was easy to get along with, and the conversation was easy.

"I'll go grab the oysters out of the fridge so we can have some, I bought them back fresh from Port Macquarie, they are the best oysters, wait till you try them."

"I put them in the freezer," Simon called after her.

"How come? They were fresh, and they only needed to go in the fridge, they won't taste as good after being frozen will they?"

"Well I didn't know they were fresh. I thought they must have been frozen for you to bring them back on the plane, they will be fine just get them out to thaw."

Simon had a cold, harsh tone in his voice. He had been drinking since nine that morning.

"Will they still taste all right after being frozen?"

"Of course they will, I should know I'm a chef you're just a cook so I think I would know better than you. I know what I'm talking about."

The talk around the table stopped, and there was an awkward silence, his comment cut Lilly deep. She was quite aware he was a chef, he would always tell her what she should add or not add to some of the dishes when she was cooking. Before she took the job, she told him of her concerns that she had to cook after he had been doing it and she was no chef. Lilly stood up and left the table to go to the kitchen to get the oysters. She would not reply, he had been drinking, and it was not worth the trouble. When she returned Helen gave her a sympathetic smile and wink. As it got dark, they made their way up to the crib room to have dinner and watch the celebrations on television. Lilly had retreated into herself a little and sat and listened to the conversations around her, joining in now and then, Simon made a few snide comments to her, and she just let it go, he was more than a little intoxicated, when he bought the food in, Elly followed in behind.

"Elly outside, go on, just sit on the step." Elly stood there sniffing the air and she could smell the chicken. "Go on Elly outside baby." Lilly stood up to take her out.

Simon scoffed "Yea bloody great obedient dog isn't she."

Lilly had had enough; she had taken his crap all afternoon, she did not know what his problem was but he was being a real arsehole, even his friends were uncomfortable with his ramblings. "Well guys I think I've had enough for the night I'm heading for bed. I'll see you all in the morning." Lilly headed out the door and around the side of the crib room, Simon followed her.

"What's your problem?" He shouted at her.

"Me, what's my problem? You have been an arsehole to me with your comments the last few hours, just drop it Simon, we will talk about it tomorrow when you're sober."

"No , what's your problem, can't you take someone saying anything about your dog."

"Well I'm sorry Simon she's not perfect like your dog was, just drop it, I'm going to bed." Lilly took off into the darkness to the sanctuary of her van. She had just crawled into bed when Simon came in.

"We need to talk, what's wrong?" he sat on the edge of the bed.

"Not now Simon let's talk tomorrow, we've been drinking and it's best to wait till morning." Lilly was tired, and she knew if she was pushed now, things would be said and regretted.

"God you're a sook, can't anyone say anything about your precious dog?"

"It's not just the dog Simon it's the comment about you're a chef and I'm a cook, what is up with you, you have been weird ever since I got back."

"You care more about that dog and your bloody kids than you do about me."

"What? Are you kidding me, grow the fuck up Simon, how old are you? At least my kids talk to me. Why won't your daughter talk to you? Just get out and leave me alone, I don't need this shit, Happy bloody New Year." Simon stormed out slamming the door, Lilly laid down emotionally exhausted, who was this person. She was seeing a whole new side to Simon and she didn't like it, they would need to talk tomorrow, now she just wanted to sleep.

CHAPTER 40

ALICE SPRINGS
Tanami Road 2017

Lilly did not see Simon all the next day, and he was probably somewhere sulking with a hangover, that was okay she needed time to think. It was late afternoon, and she was relaxing outside under the annex watching the TV when Simon walked past her and into the van, emerging a minute later carrying a few things, he didn't even speak to her just walked away. Oh my god, how childish was this guy? Well, I'm not chasing you Lilly thought, go sulk somewhere else and when you're ready to have an adult conversation let me know. The next day Lilly was cleaning up the second smaller kitchen unit getting it prepared to be taken to the new camp site, she saw Simon drive his ute down to the caravan, so he was finally coming back. She continued cleaning and had just emerged from the kitchen when she saw Simon putting all his belongings from the van into one of the rooms.

"What are you doing?" she demanded.

"I need some space, time to think" he continued taking his clothes inside.

"Time to think! and you need all your belongings to do that? Weren't you even going to talk to me about it? You sneak down to the van and get your things while I'm working, that's gutless and childish." Lilly was furious. She couldn't believe he was running at their first real fight.

"I just don't think I'm ready for a relationship." Simon would not even meet her gaze as he continued to get his things from the back of the ute.

That was the last straw for Lilly; she lost control. "Are you fucking kidding me? One fight and you run, I told you not to say you loved me unless you meant it and now here we are three months later, and you've changed your mind! You're a fucking arsehole." Lilly stormed off before she could say any more, she was too hurt, she felt numb. How could this be happening? She ran back to the van and threw herself on the bed and cried, how could she have let this happen? She finally let someone in, and he just threw her away.

Simon did not speak to her for two days, and when he finally came down to see her at the caravan he looked nervous. "Can we talk?"

"Sure." Lilly knew what was coming and had tried to prepare herself for it, she loved him and she hoped she was wrong.

"I've done a lot of thinking the last few days, and I realise I'm not ready for a relationship, you deserve better than me, I can't give you what you need, I'm sorry, I do love you, actually I'm falling more in love with you every day and that scares me. I'm afraid of getting hurt, I think it's best we end this now." Lilly was dumbstruck did she just hear him correctly.

"So one fight and you're going to bury your head in the sand and give up?"

"It's more than that I have had doubts for a few weeks now."

"What, are you kidding me it was only a week ago you were telling me how much you loved me and missed me, I booked and paid for our trip to Adelaide in three weeks, how can you go from love to nothing in a matter of days?"

"I'm sorry Lilly, I'm afraid of you hurting me."

"Oh, so you thought you'd get in first and hurt me instead? I told you when you said you loved me not to say it unless you meant it and no matter what happened we would sit and work it out, so was it all just a lie. Just use me when it suits then when you've had enough move on?" Lilly started to cry. Her heart was breaking. She had given him her heart, and he had promised he would never hurt her and here she was only three months into their relationship and he was leaving. Lilly felt totally betrayed and stupid.

"I'm not ready, I thought I was, but I'm not, I need to put number one first, and that's me, I'm sorry. You want forever and I don't believe there is such a thing, you are beautiful and talented, and you deserve so much better than me."

"Yes you're right Simon I do deserve better than you, I deserve someone who will follow through on his promises and not run at the first sign of trouble. You run away and hide when you can't deal with something. I'm scared of being hurt too but at least I was willing to try, you will never know true, real love unless you're willing to put your heart out there. You say you love me, well right now I'm having a hard time believing that, just go please." Simon got up and left, leaving her to think about where her life's journey would take her now. Simon runs from conflict probably because he knows he is wrong and it's easier to walk away than talk about it and admit he was wrong.

Lilly continued to work at the camp, and Simon avoided her as much as he could, they would be packing up this camp and going up towards the Granites mine to do road work. Lilly would be going to the new camp while Simon would stay to finish off a few small jobs. Lilly saw another side to Simon in the next few weeks he could be nasty with his comments and was becoming bossy with the other guys, putting a few of them offside. One of the new grader drivers who was only thirty, propositioned Lilly wanting more than friendship, Lilly put him in his place real quick, this did not sit well with him, and he was rude to her from then on.

Garth and Lilly had left the camp at eight am and had made their way the five hundred kilometres to the new camp, Lilly towing her van and Garth driving the truck pulling a trailer with the generator, a freezer full of food and all the stock they would need for meals until the next truck came through in a week. It was hard going, and the road had been closed to all other traffic except the road crews, it was almost impassable, there were great bog holes they had to try and get around and drive through water two feet deep before finally pulling into the camp at dark. It had taken ten hours to make the trip. They would set up camp tomorrow, Lilly made dinner for everyone in the kitchen in the caravan there were only five of them there so far. More workers would arrive over the next few days once they had the toilets, showers and bedrooms set up.

The generator they had bought with them was not working, so another one had to be brought in, it seemed that most of the gear was old and useless. They still had not put an air conditioner in the container that had been converted to a kitchen so Lilly was cooking three meals a day inside a twenty foot box in forty degrees heat. Plus they wanted her to drive the roller and water truck as well. It was bad enough that her heart was broken, she had to work with the grader driver she had refused, and the other grader driver also made a pass at her. What was it with men? She had just broken up, and they thought she was fair game. After a week of cooking in unbelievable heat and almost passing out from heat exhaustion and putting up with guys with their bruised egos treating her like crap, she'd had enough. Lilly rang the boss and quit. She needed to go home to family and friends to mend her broken heart. She still loved Simon, and it was too hard seeing him every day, and he had made a few comments to her that he just needed more time to sort his feelings out, the timing was not right for them at the moment but who knows what the future holds. He was giving her mixed signals.

It always seemed a one-sided conversation when-ever she tried to tell him how she felt his comment would be "we've already had this conversation" he was rude and dismissive, she would let him say his peace without interruption, even if he had told her the same thing before, it's called consideration. Simon wanted to stay friends and keep in touch telling her if she ever needed him he would be there for her. He was playing with her mind and she needed to get some clarity. Lilly had been willing to change her whole life to be with him. He had to change nothing, why could she not let him go? Lilly packed up the van and headed the four thousand kilometres for home. Relief flooded over her as the sign for Port Macquarie came into sight. She was home.

Lilly had settled in back at home and was comforted by her friends and family, she had started working for Port Demolition driving the tip truck and demolishing things, this part she liked, it helped release some of her frustration, and she was so tired of a night she would fall asleep straight away, she had regular singing gigs in the hotels around the area as well. Lilly missed Simon even though she knew it was probably for the best, but she couldn't get out of her mind that what if they had tried harder was she throwing away a chance of real love? They did have so much fun together, they laughed every day, loved dogs, fishing, so many things were right, but some things were so wrong too. Simon kept in contact with her and would text and tell her that he thought of her often, missed her and loved her this only made it more confusing for Lilly. She could not let him go. Lilly had promised herself that she would finish writing the book she had started twenty years ago about her grandmother Loretta, she would go back to King Ash Bay to the little cottage and take a few months to write it and talk to Simon to see where things stood with them. She needed closure, or something, half of her said to let him go the other half said go get him.

CHAPTER 41

After four months at home, Lilly packed up the van, said goodbye to her family and friends and headed back up the highway making her way to King Ash Bay, three thousand five hundred kilometres away. She settled back into her little cottage and the quiet life of the remote area quickly. It gave her the space she needed to think and start writing her book. After playing darts in the weekly Friday night competition and catching up with old friends with a few too many drinks, she headed home to make a fire. Simon came back with her to have a well needed talk, he apologised for the way he had treated her and told her that he did still love her and thought about her every day but he wasn't sure what he wanted, he was still confused. Simon could cast a spell over Lilly. She still loved him deep down, and she just wanted to be loved. After a few more drinks they ended up back in bed together, Simon stayed over the night leaving the next morning with a kiss and a promise to catch up soon. Lilly did not hear from him for two days, and she was confused about what had happened, did this mean he wanted to get back with her or just a fling? They were still so drawn to each other physically. Lilly sent him a text asking him to call in, they needed to talk about what this meant and where to go from here.

Lilly was sitting on the verandah mid-morning enjoying a cup of coffee when Simon pulled up in his old beat up ute. He smiled as he got out and kissed the top of her head before sitting down.

"Hey beautiful, what's been happening?" he grinned, and that twinkle in his eye made her heart skip a beat.

"I've just been writing and enjoying the serenity of this place. I do love it here."

"Mmmm yes it gets under your skin a bit. Umm about the other night, I well, I don't regret it but I'm still not sure if I want to be in a relationship, I do still love you very much, who knows what the future will bring I just need time, can we just be friends for now?"

Lilly nodded, she was sad that was all he wanted, she wanted more. "Sure that's fine. I just wanted to know where I stood that's all it confused me, but I'm okay with that, friends it is."

They chatted for another ten minutes, and Simon offered for her to go down to his place during the day to write while he was at work. Lilly jumped at the chance, they were building three doors up from the cottage, and the constant banging was making it hard to concentrate.

Lilly sat at the outside table at Simon's; it was only ten metres to the river. It was so peaceful and quiet here she could write to her heart's content, she would pack some food and a thermos of coffee and spend at least six hours a day there. Most of the time she would be gone before Simon returned home but a couple of days he came home early while she was still writing, those days they would end up having a game of darts and a few drinks. Over the next few weeks they went fishing, played darts, had dinner together, and they did end up back in bed together a few times but kept it strictly as friends, part of Lilly still hoped he would change his mind, yet another part was telling her to let go, she deserved better. It seemed that it was always when it suited him; she did realise that he was very self-centred and opinionated. Lilly even met his father who had come to stay for a week, and he asked her to hang in, he had been fishing with Simon that day and he'd questioned him about their relationship. Simon had told him that he still loved her, but was anxious about being in another relationship. He had been so hurt when his last girlfriend left, he didn't want to be hurt like that again. Just give him time he does love you, and I would love to welcome you into our family, you would fit so well.Lilly had finished the first draft of her book in four weeks and was excited how well it was coming together. She spent every day working on the book rewriting and fixing up the mistakes, her sister Ruby acted as her ghostwriter over the internet, she was a tremendous help to her. Simon was going to call in tonight to watch the football with her after he finished work. He was having a bad day at work, she waited but he never arrived, once again he never bothered to message and tell her, she was realising how selfish he really was. Lilly had trouble sleeping that night and around one o'clock she was sitting on the verandah having a cup of tea when she saw his ute drive past going to his house, so apparently he had stayed at the bar, she didn't mind that but he could have of at least let her know, it's just courtesy after all. The next morning as she walked Elly, down the red dusty road, Simon's uncle who lived beside him, pulled up to say hello and told her that Simon didn't come home until really late; he thought he must have been with her. It was eight o'clock the next night when she finally received a message from Simon.

"Sorry I didn't have my phone at work last night. Raced home to catch the end of the game. Very close at the end!! Wouldn't have been much company with me yelling at the TV xxx"

Lilly read the message. She had seen him go past at one in the morning. Why would he say he went home earlier? Why did it take a full twenty-four hours to reply?

"You don't need to explain to me, your uncle saw me this morning and said you were really late getting home last night and still in bed. I was up at one and saw you go past. I just thought you were having a bad day and needed someone to talk to, besides what you do in your personal life is none of my business. We are just friends."

"What tha!!! when you tell someone not to make excuses it insinuates they're lying. Should choose your words more carefully. Disappointed you thought I would lie."

Lilly looked at the message, she never said he lied, how could he get that from you don't need to explain, she didn't bother replying, the one thing she had learned was that Simon was always right even when he was wrong. She would talk to him at darts on Friday. Simon ignored her for the rest of the week, not even waving when he passed her on the road walking her dog. He would drive past flat out, stirring up the dust, sending it into a large cloud engulfing her. Then at darts, he hardly spoke to her, only acknowledging her when they had to play against each other. Lilly had had enough of this childish behaviour and went to talk to him when the game ended, but he had already left, she decided she would follow him to his house and have it out, this would end up being a mistake.

As she pulled up outside, he came out to meet her. "Simon what is your problem?"

"I'm not talking to you. You called me a liar! Get off my property" he shouted at her.

"I did not call you a liar, I said you didn't have to explain yourself to me, for Christ sake this is stupid."

"You called me a liar, and I am not a liar. No-body calls me a liar. We are no longer friends, now leave, I never want you to step foot on my property again." Simon was furious.

"Okay fine, can you get my cd player that you borrowed please. I'll take it now."

"It's back at the kitchen. I'll go get it." Simon went to get back in his car, he'd had far too much to drink. Lilly stopped him and took the keys from the ignition.

"No it's okay, you've had too much to drink. Just drop it on the verandah tomorrow."

"Give me my fucking keys. I'll get it now." Simon tried to grab the keys from her hand; they ended up flinging out onto the ground. "Fuck you, where are they?"

"They fell just there somewhere; just find them in the morning. Go to bed." Lilly turned to get in her car and leave, Simon grabbed her hand, ripping off her bead bracelets from her wrist, they scattered into the darkness and the grass, he took her car keys and threw them away into the dark. "What!!! Well that was bloody stupid wasn't it? How am I supposed to leave now, you idiot, the car is locked." They searched around in the dark, unable to find the keys. "I'll come back tomorrow and look for them. I'll walk home." Lilly didn't wait for a response; she headed off into the dark with the light from her phone guiding her up the dark, dusty road to her cottage. She had a spare set of keys at home if she needed them, but she would not be returning tonight, they both had a few too many drinks to have an adult conversation, and she was starting to wonder what she ever saw in Simon.

When Lilly made it home, she had a shower and was about to go to bed when a car pulled into the driveway. It was Simon in his Uncle's car. "Where are my keys! Do you have them?"

"No I don't, they flew out of my hand when you grabbed me. They won't be far from your car."

"Well I found your keys, come back and get your car. I want it off my property now or it might end up in the river. Come on get in the car."

"I'm not getting in a car with you Simon. You shouldn't even be driving, you've had way too much to drink. I'll get it in the morning." Lilly turned and walked back inside as Simon revved the motor and drove off like a lunatic. She started to make a cup of tea when she thought what if he did something to her car. She decided to take Elly with her and walk back to get the car using the spare key. Lilly and Elly walked back down the dark, dirt road. It was eerie being out in the middle of the night, the only noise was the wind rustling the leaves and the sound of a few night birds, it was two kilometres to Simon's place. Lilly was about to turn down the track to his shack when she saw the lights turn on in her car. The bastard was in her car, he reversed out and started up the road towards her pulling up beside her.

"Get out of my car! Now." Lilly screamed at him.

He left the motor running and opened the car door, almost falling out, Lilly put Elly in the back seat and closed the door, Simon was beside her with the keys in his hand.

"Give me the keys," Simon smirked and lifted his arm and threw her keys into the dark scrub. "You bloody idiot how am I supposed to drive the car without keys." Lilly started to walk over in the direction that the keys had been thrown when Simon hopped back in her car, Lilly turned, and her only thought was he was going to take off with Elly in the car she raced back and pulled open the car door. "Get out of my car you idiot."

Simon gunned the motor, put it in reverse and hit the accelerator. The door hit Lilly full force, knocking her to the ground, hitting her head hard on the dusty, rocky road. The wheel only just missed her head as it sped back, coming to a halt the dust swirled around her. Simon got out and walked away into the darkness towards his house, not even checking to see if she was alright. Her vision blurred, she tried to move but couldn't, her body felt so heavy, she tried to lift her head but it hurt. She rolled onto her side and put her hand up to her head where it was throbbing, as she brought her hand back into the light it was covered in blood, oh god she'd split her head open, Lilly screamed. "You bastard I'm bleeding," Lilly screamed again pulling herself to her feet. She felt dizzy and weak, her head was pounding. Simon reappeared from the darkness.

"What are you screaming about?"

"You just ran me down with my own car you arsehole, and now my head is bleeding. What sort of man are you to run someone down then walk away leaving them laying on the road like a dog to die?"

"You'll be fine, let me have a look, it's not too bad. I'll drive you to the hospital, get in."

"Fuck off. I'm not going anywhere with you, you're a bloody maniac, get out of my way." Lilly pushed him aside and stumbled into the car. Simon just shrugged and walked away, she drove herself home, wrapped her head to stop the bleeding, she climbed into the shower letting the cold water run over her body, she knew she had to stay awake in case she had a concussion. It seemed like history was repeating itself again. What was it about the women in her family that they were attracted to abusive men? Why did she think so little of herself? Lilly had seen the signs in Simon's behaviour earlier on in the relationship, but she chose to ignore it. Did she really want to be loved so badly that she would take this shit? Lilly dressed and sat up in her bed to watch TV staying awake for the next five hours before drifting off to sleep.

The next day Simon arrived, as he walked up to the verandah Lilly met him at the step she would never allow him in her home again. "What do you want?"

"I just thought I would check on you to see if you were okay."

"Really, are you kidding me? What sort of human being are you that you would run someone over then walk away without even checking to see if they were alright?"

"It wasn't my fault! You stood in the way. I've never done anything like this before, I've never hurt a woman."

Lilly laughed, she had seen enough and been with enough abusive men to know a lie when she heard one. "Bullshit Simon you're forty-nine years old, and you're telling me you've never hurt a woman. I don't believe you. I saw you the night you grabbed your cousin by her shirt and was yelling at her remember?

I came out and broke it up. We both had too much to drink last night, and I should know better and should have let it go, but I'm so sick and tired of being treated like shit by a man."

"I'm not a liar! I think it best if we don't see each other again and don't come to darts either."

"You can't tell me where I can and can't go, just because you run darts doesn't give you the right to say who can and can't play. If I want to go I will, and I'm fine if I don't see you, I'll never forgive you for what you did to me last night, now leave." Lilly didn't give him a chance to reply. She walked inside slamming the screen door behind her. What a fool she had been, how did she let this happen? Never again would she allow a man to do this to her; she had to regain control. She didn't need anyone to make her complete; she only needed to love herself and believe in herself. She would be fine. Lilly thought about packing up and leaving to go home, but she refused to allow herself to give in. She would finish her book and leave in the middle of October as planned. It was still six weeks away, it may be a small community, and everyone knew everyone else's business but she would only run into Simon at the club she knew he would not come back to her cottage.

Over the next few weeks Lilly worked hard completing the final draft of what would be her first book, she only saw Simon at darts, she would not allow him to control her life, she was polite to him to a degree. Lilly had some great friends here, and she enjoyed the quiet and would spend days on her own not talking to anyone, she had time to think and reevaluate her life, how she had allowed herself to get back into a destructive relationship. The cut on her head was not too deep and didn't need stitches, but now there was a small bald patch where the wound had healed, a reminder of that night and the real man Simon was.

On her trip back home instead of taking her usual route, she turned south at Mount Isa and headed for Boulia in the heart of the Channel Country of western Queensland and the gateway to the Diamantina National Park and the home of the mysterious Min Min lights, strange shimmering lights that appear at night. It was a three hundred and sixty-two kilometre drive between Boulia and Winton which was also part of Australia's Longest Shortcut. Lilly drove out early, she stopped along the way checking out all the highlighted stops on the map she had picked up at the information centre in town. It was after one of these stops she realised her rear passenger side tyre on the car was going flat so once again she had to plug a tyre and hope she could get it fixed in Winton. The red plains went as far as she could see, far to the horizon, they were covered in small dry clumps of Mitchell grass, occasionally the flat earth was broken by mesas, outcrops left behind by an ancient inland sea. At the Cawnpore Lookout she looked out across the plains trying to imagine how it must have looked when the inland sea kept these plains flooded for millions of years, then it was a stop at Middleton the 4th Cobb and co pillar, which was a changing post for the coaches. There was only a hundred and forty-year-old pub here now, nearby was an old dance hall and a windmill, a phone box, and nothing more. Back on the road past a ramshackle old hut preserved by the outback dust and set on a plain with rocky outcrops in the background, it had been a scene in the movie Goldstone, an Australian film. Finally making it to historical Winton with its wide main street and grand country pubs with wrap-around balconies the birth-place of Qantas and Waltzing Matilda, the soil nearby littered with dinosaur fossils. Lilly was now eager to get home to her family, so there would be no more sightseeing she had travelled this road many times, she turned south at Winton and headed for home.

CHAPTER 42

2018

Lilly stood in front of the small crowd who had gathered for her first book launch in her hometown, she felt nervous, she hoped they would love her first book, she had put her heart and soul into it. She made a short speech about the book and the sequels to come that would follow the three generations of Australian women in her family, the night was a success and she sold quite a few books. Next week her sister Ruby had organised a book launch in Sydney with her friends and work colleagues at Kirribilli, another great success. Ruby did a reading from the book. It was funny to hear someone speaking the words she had put down on paper, Lilly then answered questions after her speech. Lilly was proud of herself; she had finally done what she had set out to do twenty years ago, to write the story of her grandmother's life and publish it. The response from everyone who had bought and read the book was terrific. Everyone wanted to know when the next book would come out, they wanted to know what happened to Rose. Lilly was still working driving tip-trucks and singing as well as writing when she had spare time, and she would be going back to the Northern Territory again in June, she was booked to sing every night at Daly Waters Pub six hundred kilometres from Darwin for eight weeks. Her granddaughter Ava, who was now fourteen months old, had been diagnosed with hearing loss in both ears when she was only two months old, and she had been wearing hearing aids ever since. With regular visits to a speech pathologist in Port Macquarie at the Royal Institute for Deaf and Blind Children, Lori was taught techniques and games that she could play with Ava to help build her language and speech. Ava had a bilateral sensorineural hearing loss in both ears that could deteriorate over time; luckily Ava was eligible for a cochlear implant. The operation on the first of March had been a success, and after twelve days, Ava had her implants switched on at the RIDBC centre in Port Macquarie. There would be nothing stopping this little girl now. Lilly hoped that one day she would be up singing with her on stage.

Lilly was finally feeling great again, she was back to her old self and no longer looked to find a partner in life, she had her family and friends and her beloved loyal dog Elly. She was happy, she didn't want anything else. Then tragedy struck mid-morning in late March. Tom the man she had called Dad for thirty-one years had a massive heart attack, and had died instantly on the front lawn at home. Lilly drove straight to her mothers side, her sister was organising a flight up from Sydney as fast as she could and Fred would wait until Ruby flew in to bring her over. Rose was devastated and cried almost non stop at the loss of her beloved Tom. He had been her rock, the love of her life, how could she go on without him by her side. Everyone rallied around Rose helping her with her grief, the funeral was planned for the next week,

Tom would be cremated and his ashes scattered at the Gap overlooking the sea.

Tom was very loved and respected in the district, and the hall was packed to capacity with mourners. They overflowed outside onto the lawn, everyone had come to pay their respects to this kind, loving man. There was not a dry eye in the room as speeches were made about Tom and as the service concluded and the curtains closed on the casket Lilly sitting beside her mother could feel her heart breaking, her mother seemed so lost, they were still so much in love even after thirty-one years. Tom would tell Lilly every time she came home how much he loved her mother and he had won the lottery the day she had chosen him. Lilly hoped that one day she would find a man just as half as good as Tom. Now she had to be there for her mother.

They all stood at The Gap, Rose, the ten children and their partners, their children and grandchildren to say a final goodbye to the man they all loved and cherished. Tom had been eighty-three when he died and had lived those years well, happy and content, he had left them all with many great memories. Tom always said he wanted to go quickly and at home, he had gotten his wish. Now he would be close enough for Rose to come and visit, she would be able to sit on the headland with him. Tom's ashes were scattered on the wind, they landed on the ground around them, forever close to the ones that loved him.

Lilly looked out at the ocean remembering the man she had called Dad for the last thirty-one years, and she smiled as a tear ran down her face remembering his cheeky grin, silly pranks, but mostly the unconditional love he had shown her, treating her like his own daughter. Tom was always there with a comforting shoulder and a big bear hug when she needed him, he never judged her, he just loved her. He had always wanted daughters and had told her and Ruby that he had gotten his wish the day that they came into his life. Lilly knew it would be hard for her mother now without Tom by her side. They idolised each other. She looked up to the heavens and said a silent thank you to him for loving their mother and told him not to worry about Rose. She would take care of her just like she had promised him.

Ruby stayed for another two weeks, she wished she could stay longer, but she had to return to Sydney and her work commitments. Lilly had nothing to tie her down now, so she moved into the small flat down-stairs and would stay with her mother until she felt she would be okay on her own. For the next three months, Lilly and Rose would potter around in the garden, go shopping or just sit outside on the back verandah and have a coffee watching all the birds in the trees. Hat Head was a lovely seaside town and quiet, it suited Lilly living here with her mother, she enjoyed her company, and after everything her mother had done and sacrificed for them as children, it was the least she could do to be with her now in her grief.

Lilly was grateful to be able to spend this time with her mother, she had been so busy and wrapped up with her own life that she tended to forget the people who were closest to her, the one that gave her life and went through so much and went without, so that her children could have what they needed. Lilly loved bonding with her mother all over again, and now she was older and had been through her own heartaches;

she appreciated her even more. Lilly knew this was going to be one of her most precious memories.

"Are you sure you're going to be okay Mum? I hate leaving you." Lilly was trying hard not to cry. She would be leaving tomorrow to go back to the Northern Territory, she had been booked eight months ago to sing at the Daly Waters Pub every night for eight weeks in August and September. Lilly felt terrible leaving her mother; it had only been three months since Tom had passed.

"I'll be fine, stop worrying, I'll have to do it sometime you know, besides Ruby has already booked flights to come up and stay a few times over the next few months while you're away." Rose hugged Lilly tight trying to reassure her youngest daughter she would be okay. She didn't want to be a burden to her children, she missed Tom every day and still expected him to walk in the door any minute asking for a coffee. "Thank you so much for being here for me over the last few months honey, it's been a great help to me."

"Anything for you Mum, okay if you're sure but I'm only a phone call away, if you need me to come back I will, you're more important than anything else.

I'll call you every day to chat. I love you Mum, you're the most amazing woman I've ever known, and I'm so grateful that you picked me as your daughter." Lilly could no longer hold the tears back and hugged her mother and cried. Ruby, who had arrived a week earlier was also in tears. The three women hugged, it was a bond of love and respect that no one would ever break.

"It's okay Sis. I'll keep a check on her too." Ruby hugged her little sister hard. "Now off you go, you have a long drive ahead of you, make sure you take it easy, love you chicken." Ruby kissed her and gave her a playful smack as she headed for the car.

It was hard to leave, but Lilly knew she had to let her mum find her own feet now, learning to live alone. As she drove Lilly contemplated what she wanted from life now. She still enjoyed her gypsy lifestyle, the fact she could move her home from one place to another, she was happy on her own with just her dog Elly by her side. She no longer craved company, she enjoyed being on her own, no commitments just to see where the wind would take her. Lilly would spend a few weeks in King Ash Bay before starting work.

A PROMISE KEPT

CHAPTER 43

Lilly made her way down the rough dirt steps that had been cut into the side of the river bank leading down to the little wooden jetty. She closed her eyes and took a deep breath in. This place is so beautiful and tranquil. Here in the Gulf of Carpentaria in Australia's remote Northern Territory Gulf, far away from the traffic, the crowds and the hustle and bustle of mainstream life, she felt happy and peaceful. Here she felt at ease. She sat down on the end of the jetty with her legs dangling over the side above the water. Lilly took in the sounds of the river, the small waves gently touching the shore and the birds whistling and calling to each other in the trees, and she was amazed at the feeling of calm that enveloped her. A soft breeze brushed her face and the sunlight filtered through the trees and warmed her skin, she got lost in the moment.

The wind grew stronger pushing the water into small waves making a crashing sound on the shoreline and lifting her hat from her head; she had to catch it from flying away. Looking across the mighty Mcarthur River, she wondered how many people have visited here; this is indeed a beautiful spot. Did they notice the buoys bobbing in the water near the rock bar that was now sticking out of the water in the shallows of low tide, warning boats to go around? The two little islands in the middle with a few trees and shrubs, sandy banks and reeds for the barramundi to hide in which only a few months before in the wet season would have been totally submerged under a torrent of flood water. It's almost unimaginable how these resilient trees and reeds continually survive the forces of nature and yet here they are, reaching for the sky as if nothing had happened. Nature is amazing, after fire and flood it bounces back bright and green and even better than before. Lilly felt a bit like those trees as she reflected on her life, what she had lost, achieved and what she still wished to accomplish. No matter how many times she was knocked down, somehow she always found the strength to pull herself up, dust herself off and try again.

It was at least a hundred metres across the river to the far bank where the brolga's danced their mating dance at the water's edge. These beautiful, majestic creatures mate for life, she wondered would she ever find the "for life" kind of love, would she ever find someone to love her for who she was a strong, funny, intelligent, talented and proud woman. The boats had started to come back in from the Gulf after their day out fishing. The noise of the motors interrupted the peace of the river and her train of thought.

How different her life was now. Emotional pain leaves invisible scars; her scars were the road maps of her life, leading to this new life she was now discovering. A life of freedom and open roads, adventures and new beginnings. It took some work to get here, but right now, she was happy and at peace, loving the life of a travelling gypsy, dancing to her own tune, spreading joy with her music and living with no regrets, knowing that the only person in this world who could truly make her happy was herself. She may not have a lot of money, but what she had now was worth far more. What she had, you can't put a price on, she had her freedom, Lilly would only accept what she deserved and nothing less. She just had to believe. Every relationship good or bad and every failure had taught her something in this life, and she had learned to grow from every experience.

When she had driven out of Port Macquarie five years ago she had felt like a failure because she'd had three failed marriages, but she now realised that everything happens for a reason and people are bought into your life good or bad, they all teach us a lesson in some way as long as we look for it. She'd had days where she would be down and depressed and feel like crap but that's life, she knew that you can't always be happy every moment of the day. Lilly had jumped from one relationship to another thinking that it was what she needed to make her happy; she now knew she needed to be happy within herself before she could make anyone else happy. Here she was five years on, still on her own with just her beautiful dog for company, and it was the happiest and most content she'd ever been.

Whatever she did now was to suit her, nobody else, she had found herself again. She was content with her own company, and she didn't need anyone else in her life to feel fulfilled and happy. It took a lot of strength and courage to embark on this trip on her own not knowing what the future would hold.

All she knew was that she'd let the past go and had forged ahead and found her place in this life, she could wake up each morning knowing that she meant something, she was worthy, she was beautiful inside and out, that had come from her, not from someone else. Not only had she finally finished the novel she had started over twenty years ago, about her grandmother Loretta, but she had also written and published book 2 about her mother Rose and now you're reading book 3, her story. She could do anything she wanted too, Lilly just had to believe in herself.

Lilly had survived fifty-three years of life, and it had been one hell of a ride so far, and sometimes she wondered how she had come through these trials as sane and complete as she was. As the sun started to set, turning the clouds to soft pink and purple, Lilly

made her way back up the steps with Elly at her heels.
Making a promise to herself, one she would keep.

She would NEVER STOP DREAMING.

It was only a dream until she made it a reality.

JUST BELIEVE IN YOURSELF.

THANK YOU

Mum - You are always there for me, no matter where I am in the world. Loving me, encouraging me, keeping me in line and pushing me to be the best version of myself. I am grateful everyday I have with you.

Dad Noel - You may no longer be with us but your presence is felt everyday. Miss you xxx

Rosemary, my big sister. Thank you for your support and being my ghost writer, tweaking and adding to my stories, and helping me on my journey of discovery, even when you are so busy with your own life.

Joanne Everson, my best friend forever. What a journey we've had over the last thirty three years. Lots of misadventures, laughs and love. We will be friends forever because you know where all the bodies are buried!

Linda Mol, my beautiful friend from the Army. Our friendship has endured since 1983. We do not see each other often but it's always just like yesterday when we catch up. Thanks for always being there. (Sadly Linda passed away on the 07/04/2023 it was 40 years to the day that we met.)

Mitch and Jesse, my two amazing sons. Thank you for loving me unconditionally and putting up with your sometimes wild and outrageous mother. You are my two greatest achievements in life. Thank you for my beautiful grandchildren.

Mark Connors - Thank You for answering my many texts and calls when I need help with technology and for all the work you put into my website.

My Grandparents who have all passed away now, you are missed everyday. Thank you for your knowledge and love.

AUTHOR BIO

Marianne Delaforce is an adventurous, brave, take-no-prisoners kind of woman with a big heart. Marianne grew up on a dairy farm at Telegraph Point, NSW. She has raised two sons and has four grandchildren.

Marianne will have a go at anything if it interests her and believes if you're not happy and don't like what you're doing, don't whinge about it, change it! She can drive a road train, ride a motorbike, likes skydiving and bungy jumping.

She has worked as a shop assistant, waitress, axeman on the Forest Commission, sales rep, remote camp cook, furniture removalist and truck driver. She has owned and operated a transport company employing forty staff driving twelve trucks out of two depots, one each in NSW and NT. She has also owned and operated a Mediterranean restaurant on the riverbank of Port Macquarie. Over the past thirty-five years her real passion has been singing and entertaining. She currently works as a marriage celebrant, entertainer and audiobook narrator.

She sold her company and restaurant in 2014, packed up and took off on the adventure of a lifetime to find herself again on the "Free, Fabulous and 50 Tour." Marianne has travelled Australia with her trusty blue heeler dog, Elly, by her side. Towing an off-road caravan with her Land Rover, they have made their way around Australia three times, through the Gulf of Carpentaria, up to Cape York, across the Nullarbor, and have traversed both The Gibb River Road and The Outback Way, Australia's longest shortcut.

"A Promise Kept" is Marianne's third novel in the series "Promises".

Website: mariannedelaforce.com

A PROMISE KEPT

BOOK 1

THE PROMISED LAND

BOOK 1

Loretta was forced into an arranged marriage to a much older man who she did not love, by her strict Italian father. She suffered under his abusive control until World War II intervened and the handsome Italian Prisoner of War arrived on their farm in The Promised Land, NSW, Australia.

Their story of emotional conflict and forbidden love unfolded, and a child was born. When the war ended and he returned to Italy he made her a promise to return for her and the child. But her fairytale did not end the way she had hoped.

This is a story of love, betrayal and courage. Sometimes our destiny has a way of surprising us.

BOOK 2

BROKEN PROMISES

Book 2

At the age of 15, Rose realised her life was going to be very different to the dreams she had once held for her future. She would not live the fairytale life she had imagined. Instead, she would find herself living in a nightmare of broken promises with no apparent way out. But in her deep love for her children she would find the strength, determination and courage to go on, to push forward, if only for them.

Australia is a big, diverse country and Rose experienced many emotions moving around this dynamic landscape more often than she liked. Finding out her mother's secret, and then losing her mother, threw her life into turmoil. To discover more and find answers to the many questions she had, she would have to leave her quiet little village on the mid north coast of New South Wales and travel alone to Italy.

Separated by time and secrets, would strangers finally find each other? And just how long is the road to happiness?

HELP

ORGAN DONATION

By deciding to become an organ and tissue donor, you can transform people's lives.

Around 1,400 people are currently waitlisted for a transplant. A further 11,000 people are on dialysis of whom many would benefit from a kidney transplant.

In 2018, 554 deceased and 238 living organ donors and their families gave 1,782 Australians a new chance at life.

REGISTER NOW @ donatelife.gov.au Phone: 1800 777 203 enquires@donatelife.gov.au

—◦◦◦◦◦—

HELP & SUPPORT

Do not suffer in silence if you or anyone you know is being abused please ask for help.

There are many organisations out there who can help in so many ways, you are not alone.

White Ribbon Australia

Is a domestic violence primary prevention campaign – specifically, they work to change the attitudes and behaviours that lead to violence against women.

Please contact the support hotline 1800 737 732 or visit www.whiteribbon.org.au

Lifeline

Phone: 13 11 14

Relationships Australia

Support groups and counselling on relationships, and for abusive and abused partners.

Phone: 1300 364 277